THE LAST RAINMAKER

A JACK WIDOW THRILLER

SCOTT BLADE

A Black Lion Media Publication.

Available in eBook, paperback, and hardback.

Kindle ASIN: B079QJ5JZK

Paperback ISBN-13: 978-1-955924-17-7

Hardback ISBN-13: 978-1-955924-16-0

(Original KDP ISBN-13: 978-1981076215)

Visit the author's website: ScottBlade.com.

Published by **Black Lion Media**.

AUTHOR'S NOTE

A decade ago, Hong Yeoja, then a young girl of fourteen, fled the clutches of a horrifying reality in North Korea. But her journey only began there. She trekked across miles of frozen river, evaded armed North Korean border patrols, desperately bartered with corrupt Chinese officials, evaded human sex traffickers, and endured through despair and consuming urges of suicide.

It took her, her sister, and her mother two years to escape to the United States.

To freedom.

Currently, she is alive and well with a husband and son.

Hong Yeoja isn't her real name. It means Jane Doe.

I thank her for sharing her story with me and leave her in peace.

CHAPTER 1

The sniper's scope was trained on the target at an incredible range. Impossible for ninety-nine point nine percent of the world's population, with an infinite number of nines after that.

Not for James Lenny. He was a man in the most elite sniper club imaginable.

Lenny was British, mostly. He had some Irish in there and some Scottish on his mother's side. Maybe there was some Welsh, but British was how he identified himself.

He was a little worn around the middle, not much, but a little. He considered himself to be in decent shape for a man his age. His fifty-fifth birthday was only five days away. He wasn't looking forward to it.

He stood six feet tall, only not then, because right then he wasn't standing.

Lenny lay prone on a worn, heavily threaded sniper mat that had seen a lot of action, a lot of wartime, a lot of desert floors, and a lot of other various types of dirt.

His legs were apart, feet apart—an open scissor position—elbows planted in the dirt, feet and toes turned awkwardly so that the arches were flat against the ground. Bright orange earplugs jammed in both ears. He wore a hunter-green camo Castro hat turned around backward to keep it from obstructing his aim. He wore camo pants to match and a black T-shirt under a dark canvas jacket. A pair of sunglasses were folded and stored in a case on the edge of the mat.

The sun beat down from high above him. He didn't worry about it interfering with his target.

Woodland sounds surrounded him, calm, atmospheric, almost hypnotic. Old-world flycatchers cawed in the distance. Their wings fluttered in the wind. Leaves blew and quivered. Clouds were sparse in the sky above. There were no signs of rain—not yet, which was good for a cool, Irish spring day. The green of the land was everywhere, to the point of being all-consuming, nearly overwhelming, enveloping, like being inside of an emerald.

Lenny's body was completely still, his left hand wrapped around his right shoulder, where the stock of an Arctic Warfare Magnum rifle was nestled, a measure of reinforcing the sniper shot.

He was ready to take the shot. Ready to squeeze the trigger. Ready to explode his target into a million wet, red, fleshy pieces.

The AWM, also known by its technical designation as the L115A3 sniper rifle, was Lenny's rifle of choice. Nothing beat military instruments manufactured from the UK, in his opinion. Snipers are notoriously brand-loyal, patriots are country-loyal, and he was both.

The Americans also made pretty good weapons, he thought. *Sometimes.*

For military munitions, the Americans were among the best. Right there with the Germans. Both second to the British.

He would never admit that to any of the American soldiers he knew, of course, or to the Germans. And he certainly would never disclose that opinion to any of the guys from his old sniper unit.

Not that any of them took his phone calls anymore.

He could understand why. His post-traumatic stress disorder made him socially awkward, a little hard to be around. He could see that. It wasn't lost on him.

He tried not to focus on that. It was pointless now. He focused on the thing he loved most in the world, his rifle.

The AWM was a bolt-action sniper rifle, great for extremely long-range shooting, and completely wasted at any other range.

His AWM was chambered with a Magnum round. The Magnum bullets made the weapon system more terrifying to his enemies than regular bullets.

Sure, a regular bullet fired from his rifle would kill a man. But a Magnum would destroy him. It would blow a target apart. It would make identifying the body nearly impossible.

Imagine the destructive force of a Magnum combined with the extreme range of an AWM rifle. The combination of the two made survival after getting hit by one round a miraculous act of God. A man who walked away from such a devastating shot was nothing short of immortal. Plain and simple. No one survived a bullet like that.

No one.

Superman couldn't survive a bullet like that. Man of Steel, meet the bullet that tears through steel.

Lenny and the mates from his old unit used to have a running joke.

Only God survives the bullet from one of their rifles.

Something like that.

The thought made him smile. Made him nostalgic for the good old days.

The AWM was his favorite for those reasons and a few others. But mostly it was because he had used the same gun, the same weapon system, way back in his military days. It was like an old friend.

It got him an impressive kill count—the best in the world once upon a time, a limited time.

It was his favorite possession in the world.

The most important thing in combat was his rifle. The most important thing in his life was his rifle.

The second most important thing?

His boots.

He wore a brand-new pair of combat boots. Unlike the rifle, he liked to update his footwear regularly. Nothing destroys your chances for success in the field like broken-down, worn-out, faulty footwear. He had learned that the hard way ten years ago in Afghanistan. Not personally, but one of his squad mates, his best friend, had been complaining about his boots sticking him in the bottoms of his feet.

The guy was always rubbing the soles of his feet at night before bed.

One morning, at sunrise, he jerked the insoles out to make them more comfortable, more accommodating for their mission.

Later that morning, his unit was clearing out a cluster of abandoned structures, and the guy got himself shot because he turned a corner and inadvertently stumbled down a hidden incline. He had no grip in his shoes, so his feet were slack inside.

The combination of loose gravel and no grip led him to his death. He ended up on his back in a circle of concealed insurgents, five guys in total. All armed with AK-47s abandoned way back in the eighties by fleeing Russian armies.

He found out the hard way that AK-47s were every soldier's worst nightmare in that part of the world.

The AK was a reliable weapon, a very reliable weapon. Lenny had heard stories about Afghan fighters discovering them buried in the sand. They had dug them up after twenty-plus years. Ten times out of ten, they worked the same as the first day off the factory floor, making the Kalashnikov family one of the most powerful weapons manufacturers in the world.

They had no equal.

Before Lenny and the rest of his squad could get down to their teammate, the guy was dead, filled with countless 7.62 millimeter boat tail bullets and countless bullet holes.

It was a massacre.

Lenny could never look at Swiss cheese the same way again.

Of course, his unit took care of the insurgents in a take-no-prisoners kind of way. They killed them all. British ammunition. British weapons. British fingers squeezed triggers and left the enemy lifeless—the British way.

Directly behind Lenny's boots was an unmanned spotter scope set up on a tactical tripod. The tripod's legs were extended all the way out and planted firmly in the dirt between lush green blades of grass.

At the base of the tripod, there was a clipboard and an

expensive pen. The clipboard was covered with technical information about the shot, the target, the direction, and the wind—all nice and neat.

The technical info was in Lenny's handwriting.

The spotter scope was unmanned, and the writing was all his, because Lenny was all alone out there, the way he liked it. This made his shooting take longer than it would if he had a spotter with him. But it also made the range much more challenging. That was what he looked for—a challenge. He wanted to recapture a long-distance shot that he had made once before. Only once. And only back in Afghanistan.

No, he wanted to surpass it. He wanted to beat the new world record. It was rightfully his.

It should've been his. He used to be seen as a hero. The guys in his elite sniper unit used to look up to him. They had worshipped him. He was the guy who shot the world record. He was a king. A god. A man who deserved to be up on the wall.

That had all faded away. That was all crushed.

At first, they acted like they felt sorry for him. At first, some of the new guys still looked up to him.

Now they had forgotten him.

Lenny had no one to spot for him. Besides, part of him wanted to do it without the help of a spotter, unlike the current record holder, who used a military spotter.

And he wanted the world to know it. That was why he also had two Canon XA11 high-definition video cameras on tripods. One was planted to the right of the AWM's barrel, about a meter away. It was on and recording and focused on him. His face, the weapon, and his body from his knees up were visible and in frame.

Then at the end of the range, focused on the target, was an identical camera. This one was angled behind the back of the target so that the muzzle flash from his shot would register with the actual explosion of the organic target.

Everything was set. The only issue Lenny had now was that his mind continued to wander, which was part of his PTSD. Ever since being discharged against his will, he'd had a problem keeping his mind on the task at hand.

He had been married once, but that hadn't worked out either. Now he was alone.

He shook off the regrets of the past and stared through the scope, his safe place. He watched the target. He took long, deep breaths until he slowed his heart rate. He was in no hurry.

The wind blew, lighter than normal. He was positioned in high, lush grass on the apex of a hill, which was the only way to be accurate at the great distance in front of him. He needed the hill, the downward slope, and the curvature of the Earth to make a shot this far away.

Most of the terrain around him and between him and the target was grassy. There were mountains far to the west which started with groups of pebbles that turned into stones that turned into boulders over the course of two thousand–plus yards. There were trees to the west, the south, and the east. Behind him, about two hundred yards, was a cluster of thick trees just beyond the gravel road.

The road was the only way in or out. Lenny's four-by-four truck was parked between him and the road, about fifty yards back.

Lenny watched the target, held his breath. His index finger on his right hand squeezed the trigger back slowly. Then he felt the powerful kick of the gun as the .338 Lapua

Magnum round rocketed out of the muzzle. A devastating long-range bullet, and his favorite.

The AWM bucked and kicked hard, and the bullet was off.

The gunshot *cracked!*—echoing across the landscape like a thunderclap.

Lenny watched through the scope at the target.

The target was a ten-pound overripe watermelon, with a huge bullseye spray-painted on it in red. He had trucked it in the bed of his pickup, trucked it down the range on a dirt motorbike, also in the bed of his truck.

Nine other melons remained stacked in a crate, waiting their turn. He planned to shoot only eight more today; the last one he was going to take home and enjoy—a celebration for accomplishing the unaccomplishable.

To be honest with himself, however, he had attempted to break the current record many, many times before. And each time, he had gone home with a watermelon that he couldn't enjoy. Symbolic. He'd ditched the watermelon out in the street, leading to his house. The neighborhood dogs got plenty of watermelons to eat year-round.

This time, he felt, would be significant. This time he would get the bullet on target.

Lenny breathed out, forgetting that he had been holding his breath for a moment.

The bullet had traveled a distance of more than twenty-seven hundred yards, and it missed. Not surprising. Just disappointing.

He looked once again through the scope and checked the watermelon, checked the red-painted bullseye. He could see the melon stuck on a six-foot stake in the ground. He saw the curved green shell, the red paint, the bullseye. He saw the stake. Nothing had been hit by the bullet. All of it swayed in the wind but remained whole and intact.

He racked the bolt on the rifle back, withdrew the brass, rested it back in an open box of .338 Lapua Magnums beside him. He never left them out in the field, even if it was his personal practice range. He believed in recycling. Besides, he was taught not to leave a trace of where he had been. Not that he was up to no good at the moment. But old habits die hard.

Lenny racked the bolt again. The magazine sprung the next .338 bullet up and into the chamber. Lenny moved his head away from the scope for only a moment and removed his left hand from embracing the stock. He let the AWM rifle slope back; the barrel tilted up on the bipod and faced the sky in a forty-five degree incline. He never let go of the stock. He used his left hand and grabbed an open bottle of water, took a pull from it, and placed it back down on the northwest corner of the mat. Then he returned to his firing position.

He breathed in deep and breathed out slow. He repeated this once again. Then he slowed his heart rate again.

Adjusting the scope's elevation and parallax and focus knobs, he saw something else.

Sudden. Unexpected.

It popped out at him, startled him.

The watermelon and the stake were dug in at the foot of a two-hundred-eighty-yard slope, with a dirt wall more than twenty yards behind them. A standard safety precaution to keep the bullet from traveling beyond the intended target and accidentally hitting a pedestrian, which would've been bad on many levels, primarily because the bullet would kill the person.

Lenny had never heard of anyone surviving a .338 Magnum round before, not once. The best-case scenario was getting an arm or a leg blown off without damaging the center mass. A center mass hit was a kill shot, guaranteed—no walking away from that.

The second worry that Lenny had, just as loud in the back of his brain, was that his rifle was illegal in Ireland. Although, he was way out in the countryside, about fifty miles west and slightly north of Cork, Ireland. He was in a rural area, where the authorities were more likely to overlook the possession of an illegal firearm, being that every family within fifty square miles had firearms on their property. Still, it wasn't a legal weapon. Not for him. Not with his PTSD.

He couldn't help but feel the fear of getting caught with it. War hero or not, he would get jail time. No doubt.

Lenny moved his finger away from the trigger in case the movement he saw was another human being. He didn't want whatever it was to startle him again. He might squeeze the trigger accidentally. And kill someone. He didn't want that. He had enough problems.

Another strange thing was that he was far from the nearest village and at least five miles from the nearest farmhouse. So who the hell would be out here?

He looked through the scope, adjusted it again. He repeated all the same steps to bring it into focus. He veered the rifle up and stared over a ridge into the trees beyond. It must've been almost four thousand yards. Farther than he had ever fired accurately before.

He saw a sparkle of light flash. It was quick, like

someone was signaling to him with a flashlight or a mirror. Then he saw it again. It was not a flashlight. It was a reflection, maybe a mirror.

What the hell? he thought.

He adjusted the sights and the zoom and the focus again. Something came into focus. He saw a figure lying above the lip of the ridge, behind the watermelon, far in front of the tree line. Someone was lying prone on the ground, looking back at him.

How the hell had he not seen him before?

The figure was blurry. He adjusted the scope again until he could see more detail.

He saw the shadow of the figure on the ground, like a heap. It was small and tight. Then he saw the reflecting surface that flashed at him. He saw it clearly. It was the glass end of a rifle scope—the wrong end.

It flashed a reflection at him once again. He breathed in heavily.

He saw one last flash from the rifle; only it didn't come from the scope.

Seconds later, maybe less, he would never know for sure. He would never know, because right then, James Lenny's rifle scope exploded, and a bullet ripped through it and blasted out the back of his head. His skull exploded. Deep red mist sprayed out along with parts of the front of his brain that had mashed into the back of his brain.

From a bird's-eye view, Lenny's clothes and back and a couple of feet past his sniper mat—everything was painted red.

His head had been blown back by the force of the bullet in one quick whiplash, and then his neck muscles had whipped it forward like it was spring-loaded. His empty right eye socket beat against what remained of the scope and stayed there.

The sniper, almost four thousand yards away, stayed down for a long moment, watched through the scope until there was no sign of Lenny getting back up.

The sniper stood up slowly, picked up a pair of field glasses and zoomed in on Lenny's position, saw the damage, saw the red mist wafting in the air like a smoke plume that wouldn't die.

The sniper smiled, then turned back to the rifle and disassembled it in seconds. The rifle fit neatly into a black backpack—the stock, the weapon system, the magazine, the bolts, the barrel, and a box of ammunition, all of it. It all had a place in the backpack because the backpack and the rifle were built and designed together.

After it was all reduced to smaller parts, the sniper zipped up the backpack, rolled up the sniper mat, took off a pair of black shooting gloves, and set off to the kill to take a photograph of the dead body for a keepsake.

CHAPTER 2

Four thousand miles away and twenty-five miles southeast of St. Mark's Memorial Hospital at the center of Minneapolis, Jack Widow rode the Empire Builder, a long, historical passenger train, departing from Seattle first, then easing away from the Emerald City, mostly threading parallel with the Canadian border and winding along only hundreds of miles from it. The train passed through the Cascade Mountains, raged across heavy tracks over the Columbia River Gorge, twisting through Glacier National Park, baking across sandy low and high deserts, barreling through endless grassy fields in Big Sky Country, and traversing the plains of North Dakota.

Remnants of a long, cold winter persisted for half the trip out of Seattle, and finally relinquished a little of their hold on the land at the last leg of Widow's forty-six-hour trip from Seattle to Chicago.

Widow had walked the train several times, eaten in the dining car, slept twice in the sleeping car—two full seven-hour cycles—gone to the bathroom several times, and showered twice—the second time in his clothes, to clean them. After the last shower, he stepped into the sleeping car in the daytime to avoid sharing a car, and hung his clothes over the side of an empty bunk across from him to dry. He lay down on the opposite bunk and closed his eyes.

When he woke, the car was still empty. No one had entered to bother him. Perhaps the sleeping car attendant had checked on him once or twice without him noticing. Normally, Widow wouldn't have believed that anyone could sneak up on him in his sleep, but after meeting the staff, he knew differently. They were professionals. The sleeping car attendants were as quiet as church mice.

They should teach classes in Navy SEAL school, he thought.

Widow had served with top-notch SEALs who made more noise on covert raids.

After his clothes had dried enough, he put them back on and returned to the spot where he'd spent most of his thirty-eight hours so far—the Sightseer Lounge car.

Widow sat in the same chair most of the time. It was in the back corner, south side, which gave him a good view of things coming and cut it off after they passed.

He drank coffee, which wasn't the best in the world, but probably the best he had ever had on a train. It ranked up there with the best he had ever had in his life regarding freshness. It was like they made a fresh pot every time he wanted a refill, which was a lot because the cups were these dainty, white ceramic things, which probably cost fifty bucks apiece. They looked more like fancy British teacups than coffee mugs. Widow seemed to remember a similar design and pattern and trim when he'd visited Buckingham Palace once in another life.

The grip was so incredibly tiny that Widow could barely fit his pinkie finger through it, joint to fingernail, before it got stuck. These were clearly designed for smaller people.

The lounge car attendant served the coffee on little saucers to match. They clinked when the coffee cups contacted the small circular surface. The lounge car was relaxing and quiet, in the way a café can be relaxing and quiet. All he heard were the ambient sounds of clinking coffee cups, the tinkling of stirring spoons, and the low murmur of surrounding conversations.

The car wasn't full, but it wasn't empty either. Widow would guess that it was nearly half full of like-minded passengers who'd rather spend their time staring out the window, sipping coffee, and sharing life stories with fellow passengers over sitting back in coach.

Widow knew little about train design or train engineering or train construction. He considered himself a layman in terms of details of the processes involved in building a train like this one. But he wasn't completely in the dark about the Empire Builder. He liked to learn things. Life is boring without constant new information.

Widow had read a thick booklet about the Empire Builder that the lead attendant had retrieved for him. It was a courtesy gift.

The lead attendant had told him so. He had told him he was free to keep it, but if he wouldn't keep it, then he should return it when completed. It turned out that Amtrak used to hand them out like candy, but most people trashed them or left them behind or used them as coasters, leaving coffee rings on the cover. The booklets were expensive to make, expensive to maintain. So when the publisher hiked up the prices and Amtrak started losing business, maybe ten years ago according to the lead attendant, corporate had no choice but to limit the books to purchase-only. The lead attendant kept a handful of them to loan them out. It was an extra little touch that he added to the experience. He said that occasionally he met a passenger like Widow, who was alone, who took the train more out of tourism than travel, and he would offer the booklet if the passenger showed interest.

Widow set the Empire Builder booklet on the tabletop in front of him. He sat in the Sightseer Lounge, stared out the panoramic windows to the south, watched rolling hills in the distance, saw storm clouds a few miles after that, and swiveled his head to the north, looking past empty seats and empty tables, and out the large windows.

He had noticed that most of the people who were in the lounge car stayed away from him. He wondered about it for a moment, and then he let it pass.

Widow was a tall guy, six foot four, and two hundred twenty pounds, all natural muscle. He had dark features, short dark hair, and a slight beard to match. He had been told that his eyes were both welcoming and terrifying. They were ice blue. To be honest, this was something that he used to his advantage when the situation called for it.

Like back in California when he'd met a woman named Molly DeGorne. With her, he had used his eyes to portray trust, intimacy, and friendliness. But with his enemies, he offered a different look. A look that wasn't friendly. But he wondered if his eyes were a factor in why the other passengers had sat far away from him. Maybe they did.

Maybe they didn't. Maybe it was because he had taken off a black leather bomber jacket and rolled up the sleeves of a blue long-sleeve knit shirt to reveal a pair of sleeve tattoos. Both arms. Both colored in red, white, and blue—American flag designs draping over his forearms and wrists. Tattered, ripped, and torn flags. They represented battle flags from a lifetime ago.

To the onlooker, they were tattoos. To Widow, they were symbols, like scars, in a way. He saw both his tattoos and his scars as symbols. They were reminders, mementos of past lessons and past friends.

It was reasonable that the other passengers avoided sitting near him because of the way he looked, his size, his tattoos, or his eyes—whatever it was. He understood all of it. People judge other people by the way they look, books by their covers and all. It wasn't just an American thing; he had been judged all over the world.

No big deal.

Widow stared down at his watch. The time was eleven past midnight. The wristwatch reminded him of a woman because he had picked it up, secondhand, at a military consignment store back in Seattle, after saying goodbye to Molly DeGorne.

He had stuck around with her for a while after the events at Gray Wolf Mountain National Park, after the cops told her she could return home.

But she had no home to return to. It turned out that it had been burned to the ground before he met her. So they rented an apartment north of the city center, a nice area, overlooking the Puget Sound. DeGorne seemed happy for a time. Widow was happy for a time as well. Before they knew it, a week had gone by, and then two more days, and then the inevitable happened.

The honeymoon was over. Reality slapped them in the face like a crack from a baseball bat. Widow had experienced it several times before, but it took him by surprise every time. It shouldn't have.

He was a nomad. By definition, Navy SEALs are violent nomads. It's one of their common nicknames. They trained to embrace the life of being far out in the field for long stretches of time without support, without communication, without orders. And Widow had been an undercover NCIS agent, embedded with the SEALs, the first of his kind. He had endured very long stretches of being out in the cold.

It was hard at first, but by the time he retired from the SEALs and quit the NCIS, it had become a lifestyle that he couldn't let go of.

DeGorne had to reboot her life after she lost everything. At first, she wanted Widow to be in it. But the reality had caught up to her too.

Her husband had died. Her house was gone. She was reborn, making a fresh new start. She didn't want a man to take up a significant portion of it. She wanted her freedom. She'd told Widow that, the night before he boarded the Empire Builder. He was already thinking about leaving. Her anxiety about starting a new life with him in it had been a blessing for him. It had been a way out. It had been an escape hatch that she opened for him with the red carpet laid out. He could leave her guilt-free.

He took it. He didn't apologize. He stopped her from apologizing. He remembered kissing her one last passionate time. He remembered her latching on to him like she was saying goodbye to an old friend, like she was on the docks, watching her sailor sail away to war, never to return.

Widow hated goodbyes like that, but it was unavoidable. And it was necessary. It helped with closure. He wasn't a robot, after all. He had a heart. He knew he would think about her from time to time, but like relationships he'd had before, he would move on.

Widow brought his coffee up to his lips, recalled DeGorne's lips. Then he took a drink and finished the coffee.

He set it down on the tabletop and stared out the window.

Then suddenly, the train hissed and roared. Time seemed to slow down. He saw flashes of light out the north window. He felt the surrounding air fill with tense sound waves, like violent ripples.

Metallic sounds surrounded him, echoing at first; then, they turned into fierce metal singing and then to brutal screeching. He heard people around him screaming and saw them moving, even running. He heard the horrendous sound of the train brakes squealing in the cars ahead of him. They squawked and wailed.

Widow saw the attendants running up the aisles. He saw the people at the far end of the train fight to stand up. They piled on top of each other to stare out the window to see what was happening farther up the rows of train cars.

One last attendant, the one who had waited on him, started running up the aisle until a sudden ripple of metal and torque and booming that started at the nose of the train undulated back through the tailing cars and impacted theirs.

The train derailed in front of Widow's eyes. He knew it derailed because a second after the booming sounds and the piling of passengers to the front windows, the running attendant had come up off her feet and slammed into the roof of the Sightseer car.

Instinctively, Widow grabbed a safety rail at the base of the nearest windowsill and held on tight with his right hand. His left hand went up into the air, as did the rest of him.

Outside, the train car tore up off the tracks and plowed into the back end of the car in front of it, and the lock bolts ripped off. The front cars had derailed at an overpass and plowed into each other, one after the other.

Cars passing under the overpass below the train tracks were crushed into scrap and shrapnel as the front train cars came piling down. They scattered across the highway below.

Fires exploded out of the front train cars, and two gas tankers were crushed when the train overturned.

The Sightseer Lounge car erupted off its couplers and tore forward and pulled the cars behind it, veering off the tracks, crashing through trees, and leveling empty warehouses.

Widow's left arm crashed into the glass of the window and broke instantly. He heard the bones crack internally and felt the intense pain shoot up to his brain. He curled into himself as best he could to minimize any more damage.

He tried to protect his head the most but was limited because he knew that if he let go of the safety bar, he would go flying and tumbling like everyone else, which happened right then. The Sightseer Lounge car came up again, ramming through a warehouse wall and tumbling over once, twice, twisting free from the cars behind it.

Widow saw the passengers at the front of the car tumble through the air, somersaulting like clothes in a dryer. Tables and chairs banged around. Dishes and saucers and the dainty coffee cups shattered into small pieces. Hot coffee spilled out of the attendant's bar area.

The last thing that Widow saw was the attendant who waited on him, the one who had run forward to help the passengers only seconds ago. She slammed into the roof, banging her head, cracking her forehead open. Now she rolled around, unmoving.

The instincts that protected Widow while everyone else tumbled around inside the rolling train car betrayed him at that moment because they told him to help her. He let go of the safety rail, tried to scramble over to the attendant, and that's when he realized the train car wasn't done rolling.

It rolled one more violent cycle, and he went flying into the air. He held his broken left arm against his stomach, but he kept his eyes forward on the attendant.

The last thing that Widow would remember was that he flew up, headfirst, into the ceiling, not unlike the attendant.

He heard a *crack!* He felt pain in his head that would be described by a medical examiner as blunt force trauma. The last thought that ran through his mind, after wondering if the attendant was still alive or not, contained five words, words that he had heard many times before but never about himself.

Medical examiner. Blunt force trauma.

CHAPTER 3

Widow heard birds chirping. He smelled grits cooking. *Like Mom used to make,* he thought. Until he opened his eyes and remembered that his mother was a terrible cook. She never cooked grits. At least, he never ate them, which was why he learned to cook on his own as a fourth grader. Back then, he only did mac 'n' cheese or simple things like that. He remembered reaching fifth grade and thinking that he could transition to culinary excellence by cooking some kind of complicated Mediterranean thing that he'd never heard of and couldn't identify today in a police lineup if he were asked to do so.

The whole experiment was contingent on two important things. The first was his mom not being present. She never let him cook on the stovetop because of the gas. His mother was working another long night shift, which ticked the first contingency box.

The next thing was that he had to not burn down the

house. That second contingency ended his chef career early.

He remembered the fire. He remembered it getting completely out of control, too much for a ten-year-old boy to handle on his own. He remembered trying to put out the flames with an extinguisher. And he remembered feeling completely stupid when he learned later that you're supposed to pull the pin out of the extinguisher before it will work.

And how could he forget his sheriff mother coming home to see the town's only fire truck parked in front of their house? At ten, Widow burned a hole in their roof, and his mother beat his butt for it. He never started a fire again, not unintentionally, anyway.

Widow lay back in a bed. He knew that much, that he was in a bed.

His vision was fuzzy and bright and filled with blurry images of white light. Tears watered his eyes like he was opening them for the first time, and the exposure of light was too much for them to handle. He closed them again. The light was too bright.

Instead, he listened to the birds. He listened carefully, making a long examination of his surroundings by taking in the sounds, trying to determine where the hell he was.

His first thought was he was outside, but why would he be in a bed?

The birds were chirping. The bright light was like sunlight, but he felt cold. There was no sunlight on his face or his skin. He moved his hands, starting with his fingers. He moved his right hand, index finger first and then middle and ring and pinkie. He made a fist. It felt good. Then he tried his left hand. He started with his index finger, then the middle, then the ring, and then the pinkie. Everything moved. Everything was right. Then he tried to make a fist.

Suddenly, burning pain shot through his palm and his wrist. He jerked his right hand over to grab the left. It was instinct. But the right hand stopped three inches from its horizontal position. He heard a clanging sound, metal on metal. He pulled at his right hand again and got the same results. He heard the same clanging sound.

He opened his eyes, looked down. Everything was still blurry, but he didn't need to see clearly to know what caused that sound. It was handcuffs. Widow was handcuffed to the rail of a bed.

He looked around the room, tried to make out the blurry objects. He let his ears help him. He listened for the birds chirping, craned his head in that direction. It was up about twelve feet above him. He could make out a green blur with a brick texture.

Must be a wall, he thought.

He looked up toward the sound of chirping birds. The sound changed to two people talking. He realized it wasn't birds, not real ones. He was staring at a television, hung up high in the corner of a room with green walls. He looked around the room. He could make out blurry pieces of equipment. Some were lit up. Some were beeping and purring quietly.

He was in a hospital room and a hospital bed.

He squinted and strained his eyes. His eyelids blinked heavily and violently, trying to clear the tears from his eyes, trying to focus his vision.

Another burning spasm of pain shot through his arm. He craned his head up and down, looked over his chest at his left arm. It wasn't handcuffed to the bed like his right arm, but there was something else. Something heavy was on it.

He felt weak. He must've been drugged.

He dug deep and used his left shoulder to pull his arm up higher. The feelings in his arm and fingertips were there, but the arm felt strangely numb, like he had just woken up from sleeping on it.

Widow heaved it up and held it above his chest for five seconds, long enough to see what was so heavy about it. Then he saw it.

From two inches below his elbow, stretching for ten inches to his wrist, stopping where his palm started, was a brand-new white cast.

The pain returned and shot again through his wrist, up into his forearm, and up his bicep. And he had to let the arm drop. It fell and landed on a small pillow that someone had stuffed underneath it.

One or more of the bones in his left forearm were broken.

CHAPTER 4

Widow's vision returned as the first person he had seen all night walked into the room to check on him. It was a nurse.

She was a young black woman. Maybe twenty-seven or twenty-eight. She saw Widow's eyes open, and she walked over to him.

"Where am I?" he asked.

"How are you feeling?"

"Fuzzy. My arm hurts."

She said nothing to that. She just stood near him, out of reach, and looked him up and down.

"The doctor will be in shortly," she said, and she turned, said nothing else. She vanished back through the doorway.

Nearly an hour passed before a doctor came into his room. And she didn't come alone. A man in uniform escorted the doctor. It wasn't hospital security. Widow's vision was still not one hundred percent, but he knew that much. Hospital security guards don't walk the way this guy walked. They don't carry themselves the way this guy carried himself. They don't stand at attention the way this guy stood at attention. He could've been a cop, Widow guessed. Maybe.

The doctor came in close to Widow, stood on the handcuffed side of the bed. She held a metal hospital clipboard with a metal cover to prevent damage to the paper. It was stuffed under her left arm. She stopped and stayed where she was. Then she took out the clipboard and opened it, looked over the first sheet, and flipped it to the second one.

She also held a thick manila envelope. It was sealed. There were markings on the front. Widow couldn't make anything out.

She smelled like maple syrup, which led Widow to believe it must've been in the morning, either that or she'd just eaten her breakfast and was on the graveyard shift. He had been there before. Breakfast, the most important meal of the day, didn't have to be eaten in the morning. Technically, there were two types of mornings: the actual time of day, and whenever you woke up.

Maybe she worked the graveyard shift. Maybe it was one o'clock in the morning.

The doctor got in close enough for Widow to see more details. She had brown, curly hair, the kind that women everywhere would pay to get. Widow didn't think she paid for it because it was pulled haphazardly back in a ponytail away from her shoulders. That kind of hair costs a lot of money for women with straight hair to get. He didn't see someone spending three hundred bucks for curly hair just to yank it back like that.

He squinted his eyes. Still couldn't see, but that didn't stop him from trying to read her name badge, which was clipped to the bottom lapel of a white doctor's coat. She wasn't wearing scrubs underneath, but regular brown khakis and a black top.

Widow noticed a wedding ring, gold, worn. She had been in a long marriage.

He squinted again. Still couldn't make out her name. Or the hospital that he was in.

She spoke with a hoarse voice, as if she had just overcome being sick herself. "Mr. Widow?" she said, looking at him from over the clipboard.

Widow stayed quiet. He felt a draft wash over him. The air conditioner had kicked on and was blowing down from a vent at the top corner of the room near the TV.

"Mr. Widow? Do you know where you are?"

"Aren't you supposed to ask if I know my name first?"

She was quiet for a beat, and then she asked, "Do you know your name?"

"Jack Widow."

"And what about where you are?"

"I'm in a hospital."

"Do you know what city?"

Widow stayed quiet.

"Do you?"

"I'm not sure."

"Do you know why you're in here?"

Widow thought for a long moment. Mostly, he was waiting for his eyes to adjust. He stared at the doctor, who shifted from one foot to the other patiently. Then he tried focusing on the cop behind her, then the TV, which was now playing a show about renovating houses. He realized he could see the people on the screen, the house torn up in the background.

He looked back at the doctor. She was slowly coming into focus. She was younger than he thought. Maybe his age.

"My name's Jack Widow. I was born in Biloxi, Mississippi. I'm thirty-six years old. Birthday is November 9. I was in the NCIS and the Navy for sixteen years."

Till my mom was shot by some asshole back home, Widow thought.

"I returned home one day. My mom died. I took care of what I needed to take care of."

"And?"

"And I never went back to the Navy."

"You went AWOL?"

"If I went AWOL, I'd be in prison. I wasn't military anymore. Technically, I was a civilian."

"Thought you said you were in the Navy?"

"I can't tell you any more than that. Classified."

Widow had been part of an undercover unit with the NCIS while he was in the Navy, which meant that he was ostensibly an officer in the Navy SEALs, but actually a civilian because NCIS is a civilian investigation force.

"I'm not here to ask you about that, anyway. I just need to know if you remember how you got here."

Widow closed his eyes, imagined the scenery he'd spent thirty-five-plus hours watching. He pictured seeing the Empire Builder for the first time. He imagined the two GE Genesis P42 locomotives, half a dozen sleeper cars, a single baggage car, and several passenger cars. He remembered how impressive the machinery was. There was something seductive about it. Then he remembered the moment he was dropped off at the station. He remembered kissing DeGorne goodbye and good luck.

"Train wreck."

"What do you remember about the wreck?"

"All of it."

"All of it?"

"I guess the parts I was conscious for. I remember sitting in the lounge car. I remember flashes of light out the window. I remember loud sounds like metal and screeching. I remember it felt like an eternity. I remember seeing people tumbling around. I figure the train must've derailed and flipped."

"That's right. The train derailed, and your car separated from the car in front of it. And it tumbled through the warehouse district."

"What about the attendant?"

"Attendant?"

"The Sightseer Lounge car? She was blonde, young. She hit her head pretty bad. That was the last thing I remember."

"I'm not sure about her. Not exactly. But there were some casualties."

"How many?"

"Ten. So far."

"What the hell happened?"

"There was a car parked on the train tracks. The engineer didn't see it in time."

"Car?"

"It was a suicide by train."

"The police are sure?"

She said, "Yes. That's what they said in a statement."

Widow looked up at the ceiling for a moment. Then back at her. He said, "Last I remember, we were in Minnesota. This must be Milwaukee?"

"Minneapolis."

"I know. Was joking."

"We're in St. Mark's Memorial Hospital. My name is Karen Green. I'm your doctor."

"Doc, why am I handcuffed to the bed?"

"I can't speak to that. I'm here to talk about your condition."

Condition? Widow thought.

"You mean my arm?"

Green paused a beat and fumbled with the clipboard. She glanced at it quickly and back at Widow. "Your left arm was broken at the ulna bone. It's in the forearm," she said and showed him on her forearm.

"I know where it is."

"Does it hurt?"

"It does when I move it."

"I'd recommend minimal activity until the cast comes off."

"When's that supposed to be?"

"Well, normally I'd say four to six weeks. But in your case, it could be more like ten."

"Ten?"

"Yeah," she said and closed the clipboard and set it down on the blanket over Widow's shins. She took out the manila folder, undid the metal clasps holding it shut, and walked over to a wall-mounted X-ray board. She clicked on a switch, and the board hummed to life. A back light lit up the board's white surface.

She pulled out an X-ray and stuck it up on the board. "Can you see that, Mr. Widow?"

Widow craned his head and stared in her direction. "I can," he lied.

She took out a pencil and pointed at the X-ray. "See, your ulna broke, clean, when you had a sudden traumatic impact. Probably against the window in the train car because you had dozens of shards of broken glass lodged in your arm. We got them all out. Luckily, none of the gashes required stitches. Plenty more glass cut up your face as well. Again, lucky that it's all superficial. No permanent scars."

She paused a long beat. Widow was eager for her to cut to the chase.

"The thing is that after we X-rayed your arm, we found your arm has been broken before."

"I know that."

"Mr. Widow, it's been broken in five places before. See, right here?" She tapped the pencil tip to the screen and traced it along the bones. "You've got rugged healing scars from each place."

"I know. I was there. What's your point?"

"While you were out, the orderlies had to remove your clothes. Put you in a gown."

Widow looked down, realized that's why he'd felt the draft earlier. He wasn't in his clothes. He was in a green hospital gown. Then he saw the ID bracelet on his right arm, just above the handcuff.

She continued, "They saw your back."

Widow was dumbfounded for only a moment. Then he remembered what was on his back.

"They saw the bullet wounds."

Widow stayed quiet.

"You've got three wicked scars on your back. The only discernible thing is that someone shot you three times. So we did X-rays. There're no signs of bullet fragments or even massive penetration from a bullet in your organs. Most of the damage back there was surface level, some major nerve damage, and it looks like four badly fractured ribs, all of which healed a long time ago."

She stared at Widow like she was waiting for a response that would answer the bubbling questions she had in the back of her mind.

Widow stayed quiet.

"So, naturally, we became concerned about who you are. We ordered more X-rays and found a lot of healed bone scars."

"What about it?"

"Have you ever heard of Evel Knievel?"

"Of course."

"It's like him."

"No way. Knievel was a crazy daredevil who had four hundred broken bones over a long career of doing stupid things."

"Four hundred thirty-three broken bones."

"I don't have that many."

"No. Maybe not. We don't know because we stopped counting at two hundred fifty. And some of those we couldn't rule out aren't double infractions."

"Infractions?"

"Some of your bone scars overlap."

Widow said, "I was in the military. Been around. I told you that."

"I wasn't in the military, but I called around. First, to

the Marine Corps here in the city. They transferred me around a while, until I got patched over to McCoy, spoke to a surgeon there. He's never encountered a soldier with half as many broken bones as you."

McCoy, Widow thought. That's in Wisconsin, not Minnesota. Then again, he really was fuzzy on details that normally he knew well. "So?"

"So, I'm concerned. I looked on the internet, and there are people who've had a lot of broken bones."

"So?"

"The most I could find were with Knievel and several champion karate fighters."

"Karate?"

"MMA or whatever."

"And?"

"And you rank somewhere in the middle. My initial thoughts were that you were involved in dangerous criminal activity. The bullet scars. All the broken bones. So I told the MPs over at McCoy."

Widow said, "The guy standing behind you. He's not police, is he?"

Green looked back over her shoulder at him and said, "No. Well, yes. He's military police."

"He from McCoy?"

"The Lakes. I think. I don't know. He'll tell you that in a moment. First, I need to explain something to you."

Widow waited.

Green took down the X-rays of his broken arm. She tucked them neatly back into the manila folder like they were precious records that couldn't be damaged under any circumstances. She took a breath and seemed to calm down a bit, like she had been on pins and needles before.

Perhaps she was a little afraid of who Widow was exactly.

She took a new X-ray out of the folder. She whipped it gently to straighten it out, and then she slid it into the frame of the white X-ray box. She repeated the whole process with a second X-ray. This one was a profile shot of the same part of the body—Widow's skull.

He stared at it. He stared at both of them. He realized that the good news was his vision was syncing up properly. The bad news was that he was staring at two X-rays. One was his skull from the top. The second was the side of his skull. It showed the starboard point of view.

Widow's vision was almost back to normal, which was to say it was still not perfect, but he could see details again. His far vision was worse. The X-ray box was within twelve feet of his bed, which was close enough to see discoloration on the starboard side of the skull, like the outer shell of his skull was hit so hard that it almost cracked.

Green pointed the pencil back at the X-ray. She pointed at exactly the spots he was staring at.

"Do you know the difference between a mild concussion and a severe one?"

"One is worse than the other?"

"Yes. Of course. But do you know what that means exactly?"

Widow shook his head, noticed that some bruises he had seen on the skull moved with his vision. Those weren't bruises at all. They were vision spots. But the major bruising didn't move.

Now, he was a little afraid. Brain injuries were no joking matter.

Green said, "Because there are only two classifications of concussions, there is no classification for a moderate concussion. But that's what you have. Technically, you have a severe concussion. But I've seen much worse."

Widow stayed quiet.

"I tell you this so that you know not to worry. But you have a severe concussion toward the lower end of the spectrum."

"I've seen concussions before. What can I expect?"

"It all depends on each individual case. You've experienced a blackout. Very common with this type of injury. You said you remember the events of the train wreck, but you seem to have forgotten some things. You weren't out the whole time. When the paramedics brought you in, you were conscious and speaking."

"I was?"

"Yes. So you don't remember that, which is normal. You may never remember it. That's okay. The rest of your memory doesn't seem to be affected. What about vision?"

"It's spotty."

"You can see the X-ray?"

Widow nodded.

"How was your vision before?"

"Twenty-twenty."

"Then it will return. No worries there. How does your head feel?"

Widow stopped and intuitively tried to reach his forehead with his right hand, clinking the metal of the handcuff again and feeling frustrated by it.

He said, "It's not that bad. I've got a headache."

Green nodded. She added, "You may not experience many of the symptoms till later on. It is my understanding that this officer is going to explain things to you and take you into custody. So you'll be active. I'd rather you stay in bed, but I don't think that's an option."

She craned her head, reversed her position, and stared back at the guy standing at the opposite side of the room. Widow followed her gaze and saw the guy was coming more into focus.

The guy looked to be about forty years old, probably closer to forty-five. He was one of a thousand guys Widow had seen before. The kind of elite sailor or soldier or Marine who took extra steps in his fitness and diet regimen to make sure that his body was as young as it could be for as long as it could be.

The guy stayed where he was. He didn't give a nod or say a word. He wouldn't give out any information, not in front of Green. She was a civilian. Whatever he was there for was for Widow's ears only. That was obvious.

Green said, "Okay, Mr. Widow. I'm giving you this bottle of Extra Strength Tylenol. I want you to take them as needed throughout the day. Don't exceed six in twenty-four hours. Only two at a time. Try to drink plenty of water."

"How long will I have the concussion?"

Green shrugged and said, "Could be a few days. It could be several. It depends on you. Try to get plenty of rest. And don't get into any more train wrecks."

Green smiled, took up the X-rays, and inserted them back into the folder. She tapped Widow once on the leg, picked up the metal clipboard.

"Take care, Mr. Widow," she said, and she walked out of the room.

The officer who came in with her waited a full second after she left, until the door sucked shut behind her, and then he stepped forward.

He looked to be six feet flat. He wore a navy-blue blazer over street clothes, a pair of green chinos, a black leather belt exposed only over the buckle, a white polo shirt, untucked, and black oxford shoes. Everything neat. Everything polished, even the leather of the belt.

Widow could make out a very slight bump on the guy's right hip. A gun, no doubt. It was probably a Beretta M9 or a SIG Sauer P228 M11 pistol. Widow figured that because of what the guy's official department was, only because Green had said that he came from the "Lakes," which meant the Great Lakes. Had to be NAVSTA Great Lakes. NAVSTA just meant Naval Station. He was from the Naval Station Great Lakes, which meant that he was Naval Police, which was officially called master-at-arms. The Navy loves to be different.

The guy said, "Commander Widow. My name is Crews. I'm here to transport you."

He reached down and raised his shirt, which revealed an M9 Beretta holstered in a paddle holster, nicely concealed. He snatched a badge off his belt, fast like a draw. It clipped off, and he approached, put it directly in Widow's face.

It was a gold badge with an eagle at the top and wings draped around the outer top edges, connecting with two olive branches on opposite sides of the bottom of the badge. There was a single bold black star stamped into the bottom center. An anchor with a rope looped and hooped around it occupied the middle. Widow knew it was a master-at-arms badge because it said so right there on the badge's surface. It had four letters, spaced slightly apart: *C M A A*, which meant, "Chief Master-At-Arms."

Widow asked, "You a chief warrant officer?"

Crews nodded but didn't give his exact rank.

"Wanna tell me why I'm in handcuffs, Chief?"

Crews rubbed the stubble on a two-day-old shaved head and said, "Mister, not Chief, okay? And you're only in the cuffs as part of the story."

Widow had called him Chief, knowing full well that it would irritate him, at the very least. Not as a sign of disrespect, but more like making himself feel better for being handcuffed. Since he had done nothing wrong, nothing that the Navy knew about.

Petty, he knew, but being handcuffed for doing nothing, for a cover that hid some mysterious reason the Navy wanted him back wasn't good enough a reason to be handcuffed.

"Part of the story? What story?"

"We need you back, Commander. I wasn't told why. I was only told what the cover was to prevent the doc and hospital staff or reporters from asking questions."

"There are reporters here?"

"Yes. There was a major train accident. They love train accidents. Two major networks are outside. All the local boys and CNN and MSNBC."

"What? Nothing coming out of the White House to cover today?"

Crews smirked a little. Widow figured he had jabbed at the guy enough. Better to have him on his side. Apparently, he was going somewhere, and he had no say in the matter.

Crews added, "Plenty coming out of the White House. Plenty of scandals. You know how it goes."

Widow nodded and asked, "Wanna tell me what this is all about?"

"My orders are to escort you back to the airbase in Minneapolis–Saint Paul and put your butt on a plane."

"A plane? What the hell is this?"

"I honestly couldn't tell you, sir. I'm only a messenger."

"A messenger without a message."

"You're the message, Commander."

Widow said nothing to that. He pulled his head up and adjusted his elbows so that he could rest on them.

"I got a choice in this?"

"Sure. You could resist."

"I doubt that'll come out in my favor."

"Doubt it will too, sir."

"Guess I'm coming with you then."

"Guess you are."

"Does the concussion make a difference?"

Crews shook his head, said, "I was told if you were walking and talking, then your butt's flying."

Widow took a deep breath and asked, "Wanna get me some pants, then?"

CHAPTER 5

It turned out that Crews was deadly serious about keeping the cover intact because he rolled Widow out of the hospital in a basic metal wheelchair with Widow's right hand cuffed to the arm of the chair and his left in a cast in a sling around his neck. The handcuff clinked and clanged all the way down the corridors and to the elevator, and back through more corridors because one wheel wobbled all the way. Widow figured it was a backup chair because the hospital seemed almost overrun with patients from the train wreck.

The halls echoed the sounds of chattering voices, both from conversations one-on-one and from radio chatter because there were a lot of police around, probably to keep order.

Crews took Widow down back halls, through a kitchen, and through a laundry. White steam rose from heavy washing machines against the back wall.

"Can you tell me who exactly sent for me?"

"Can't tell you that. I don't even know who. I know it came from Washington."

"Is that where I'm going?"

"Could be."

Crews rolled Widow down a ramp and out the service entrance of the hospital. Bright sunlight bathed over Widow's face, and his vision went from getting better to blinding whiteness, which lasted for several moments and then passed.

Crews rolled him out to a navy-blue sedan parked in the alley behind a delivery truck.

Widow said, "You can let me out of this chair now. I think the cover is maintained."

Crews stopped the chair just in front of the driver's side back door. He took out a handcuff key and undid Widow's cuffs, opened the door for him. Then Crews paused for a moment like he was considering putting the cuffs back on Widow. He didn't seem to know what the right call was in this situation. Widow wasn't a prisoner.

Widow saw him working it out in his head. He didn't let Crews get the chance to put the cuffs back on. He hopped into the back seat and buckled up.

Crews shrugged, returned the cuffs to a holster on his belt and shoved the wheelchair away from the car. He closed Widow's door and slid into the driver's seat.

The engine fired up, and they were off.

Crews took Widow to exactly where he'd said he was going to take him. They pulled up at the guard gate to Minneapolis–Saint Paul Air Reserve Station. They traversed through the gate with no problems. Then Crews wound through the streets and buildings and Widow realized Crews was no longer driving on roads. He was weaving between airplane hangars.

They came to a stop in front of a parked C-20B. It was mostly white, with blue trim along the bottom. It had a designated tail number and two twin engines mounted above and between the wings and the tail.

The plane looked like Air Force One, only one-third the length. That's when Widow knew he was in deep because the Air Force C-20B is basically a civilian Gulfstream jet that's been converted, reinforced, and armored to shuttle government officials from place to place. The problem with that was most government officials flew commercial. The ones who needed an Air Force jet weren't ordinary government officials. They were DOD people—important DOD people—like the Secretary of Defense, for example. This meant that whoever was racking up taxpayer dimes to pay for the flight was someone important, someone with clout, someone with a much higher pay grade than Widow was when he discharged.

Crews accompanied Widow to the staircase leading up to the plane's entrance and stopped. He put his hand out for Widow to shake.

Widow turned back and stared at him.

"You're not coming?"

"No, Commander. You're on your own from here."

Widow took Crews's hand and shook it.

Before he boarded the plane, Crews saluted Widow and said, "Try to keep yourself from getting any more broken bones, Commander."

Widow said nothing to that, just climbed the stairs and boarded the plane.

Onboard, he was greeted by a steward, or possibly the pilot. He wasn't sure. Not until he stepped into the aisle and the guy said, "Have a seat anywhere, sir."

Steward.

Widow picked a spot in front of the wing window seat. The interior was all butterscotch leather and walnut veneer and pristine white carpets and white walls. There were no overhead bins or other clutter. There was a nice-looking kitchenette area in the front, stocked with bourbons and expensive vodkas.

This was a private jet for the rich and famous—only the rich and famous were members of the DOD, the Pentagon, maybe, and whoever else.

The steward said, "Sir, buckle in. We're taking off right away."

"Where are we heading?"

"We're going into the sky, of course."

"Of course," Widow said, and sat back. The steward stood around for another long second, waiting for Widow to buckle his seat belt, which he did.

The steward returned to the front of the cabin and sat in a jump seat near the cockpit hatch and strapped himself in. When the steward had said they were taking off right away, he wasn't exaggerating. Thirty seconds later, they were on the runway. A minute after that, they were climbing into the clouds.

CHAPTER 6

It was halfway into the flight that the steward informed Widow he was Air Force, along with both pilots, whom Widow never saw, not once. They never came out of the cockpit.

The steward brought Widow a coffee in a foam cup with one sugar packet and one creamer and one stirrer. Widow hadn't asked for any of it, but was grateful for one part of it. He drank the coffee, black, which was better than nothing, far worse than the coffee on the Sightseer Lounge car of the Empire Builder, which made his mind wander back to the near two-day trip and back to the blonde train attendant who he'd tried to help. He wondered if she was going to be all right. Within a moment, he forgot whether he had asked Green about her. He also realized that he had asked no one how much time had gone by since the train wreck.

How long had he been out?

Admittedly, he'd find out, eventually. Then he thought

about DeGorne for a moment. She'd be in her apartment, thinking, planning her future.

Another thought occurred to him: he'd better call her when he got the chance. Crews had said that there had been a lot of news coverage about the accident. Good chance DeGorne might've seen it. She dropped him off at the train station. She knew of his plans to get on a train. She might've known about his plans to head east. Then again, he might not have even had plans. He couldn't remember.

His vision was getting much better by this point. He had stared out the window for one hour and forty minutes, and seen everything below with no problems. He watched a couple of Great Lakes and lots of blue-collar states pass under the plane.

It was clear where they were going. He'd known it way back when they headed over Lake Michigan. They were going to Andrews, which is a joint base for the branches of the military. It's a major base.

The C-20B adjusted and started decelerating before the pilot came over the intercom and informed the steward that they were landing. Fifteen minutes later, they were on the ground for a total flight time of five minutes less than two hours, twenty-five minutes faster than Widow had calculated in his head, which was both good and bad. Meant that his calculations were off, although they were usually right on; it also meant that he was calculating things.

Better than losing that part of my brain, he thought.

As they landed, Widow stuffed his empty coffee cup into a cup holder near the arm of the chair and left it. The plane taxied off the runway, and the steward got up off the jump seat.

Widow took this as a sign to get up. He tried to stand, but felt light-headed. Not a severe thing, but annoying enough. He remembered the doctor had given him a bottle of Extra Strength Tylenol before he left the hospital. He reached into his front pocket, pulled out the bottle, popped the top, pitched a pill down his throat, and swallowed it.

Widow hated taking pills, but it was better than forcing an Air Force crew to have to half-carry him to wherever he was headed.

He stepped out into the aisle and walked to the front of the plane. He stood next to the steward, who said nothing, until the aircraft stopped and the hatch opened to blinding sunlight.

Widow stepped out onto a portable staircase on wheels and climbed down, using the rail the whole way. He couldn't cover his eyes from the sun and use the rail, not with only one hand available, so it took him several seconds longer than it should've to reach the bottom step.

Another CMAA warrant officer met him with a navy-blue sedan, only this WO was in uniform blues, and the sedan was a military police car. The WO had the light bar going off. Blue lights circled around and around.

No siren.

Widow walked up to him, didn't bother checking his name patch, partly because he couldn't make it out just yet and partly because he didn't care. Truthfully, he was over meeting new military people, learning their names, and having them keep him in handcuffs.

Luckily, this guy didn't even offer, and better yet, he didn't refer to him by his last known rank.

The guy said, "Jack Widow?"

"That's me."

"Glad you're not too beat up."

Widow stayed quiet.

"Come on. I'm driving you."

Widow nodded and stepped to the passenger door, but the WO cleared his throat and signaled to the back door.

Widow wasn't surprised. Warrant officers were usually boy scouts. They followed the rules to an insane amount of loyalty. Andrews Base's official policy for civilians riding in police vehicles was that civilians always ride in the back seat.

Widow didn't argue, and slung himself down onto the rear bench. Twenty seconds later, they were off.

Widow stared out the window. His eyes adjusted to the sun, and he watched the buildings. Long-forgotten memories of countless meetings, conversations, and undercover investigations that involved or took place at Andrews came flooding back into his mind. Some occurred at the very buildings he passed, which promptly triggered the replay of the memories. Then he wondered how many of those actually happened at Andrews. He wondered if any of them were memories misplaced by his concussion.

Minutes and several turns later, they were parked in front of a low building that Widow didn't recognize.

"This is your stop," the WO said.

Widow waited for the WO to get out and open his door because, like civilian police cars, military cars don't open from the inside of the rear bench. Like civilian police cars, that's where criminals and suspects go.

Widow climbed out and walked forward, and stopped.

"Here. Clip this on. Outside your jacket. Make sure it's always visible."

The WO handed him a name badge that had the word VISITOR in all caps, boldly across the front of a photograph. The photo was one that Widow hadn't seen in years. It was the last photo on his official Navy ID. Black and white. His head shaved to the stubble. No smile.

He took it with his right hand, fumbled with the clasp, and clipped it onto the outside of his bomber jacket. He had to readjust his coat because it nearly fell off his left shoulder. His cast was in a sling, tucked underneath the jacket. The left sleeve hung empty.

"You coming?" Widow asked.

"No, sir. Just you. My rank stops me here."

Stops you here? Widow thought.

"Just head through those doors. Stare into the camera. They'll buzz for you. Someone will tell you where to go."

The WO saluted Widow after all and turned and drove off in his car. He didn't wait to make sure Widow didn't get cold feet and take off in another direction. Then again, where the hell else would he go?

CHAPTER 7

The whole process seemed like overkill. By the time Widow arrived at what he had guessed was his destination, he had gone through two electronic checkpoints, without armed guards, until he finally arrived outside a door that led up a bland staircase. At that point, there was one sentry—a military MP. Army, not Navy.

The MP asked him to stay still for a pat-down. Which surprised Widow. They were on a major military base, and he had been escorted by a warrant officer, straight from the hospital, straight to a plane, and then straight here.

The MP patted him down, checked his cast, all his pockets, and even the inside of his empty jacket sleeve for any weapons. Afterward, the MP asked him to take his shoes off.

Widow said, "You serious?"

"'Fraid so, sir."

Another "sir." What the hell was he getting himself into?

Widow sighed and pushed his boots off with one foot and then the other. He didn't want to use his one good hand because that would've meant that he would sit on the floor. He stepped back out of the boots and stood there. The MP bent down, picked them up. Widow wondered how important security was to them. The MP bent over right in front of Widow. If he had wanted to, a fast knee to the guy's head, and Widow could've taken him out cold.

There was no need for any of that.

The MP finished checking his boots and then picked them up. He handed them over to Widow.

Widow took them with his good hand and switched them over to his left. Just kept them in his left. He stayed in his socks.

"Go on up, sir."

Widow stayed quiet and walked through the open door, stepped onto the bottom step. He felt the cold metal through his socks.

The top of the stairs opened straight up into an unused set of military surveillance equipment, counterterrorism stuff. There were dozens of TV screens lit up. Some were playing American news channels; others played foreign ones. They were all muted and had English captions turned on.

The whole floor was dark except for the light from the monitors. He checked them out as he passed.

Other monitors showed surveillance video from around the world. There was some CCTV stuff. As Widow stepped out past a set of unmanned cubicles, he saw multiple rows and aisles of the same thing. This was some kind of counterterrorist unit or plain old counterintelligence, he guessed.

There was no one in sight, but Widow heard voices at the other end of the floor. He looked and saw an open door. A bright artificial light beckoned him to it.

He threaded the aisles and rows of cubicles and electronic equipment and stepped into the room.

It was an Army conference room, which meant that the walls were painted green. The carpet was green. And the long oval table at the center was plain wood.

Huddled at the table were three people—two men and one woman.

One man and the woman were in dress uniforms. They were Army.

They both turned and faced him as he walked in. The man was an older guy. Probably close to sixty. He was tall and had a sense of refinement about him, like a man who came from poverty, got paid, and discovered the better side of life.

He was a one-star general. Widow saw that from his patches.

The woman was a sergeant. She held a notepad in her hand, clamped shut, with a ball-point pen in the other. She had a pair of black-framed glasses on and was thirty years younger than the general, easily. Widow assumed she was his assistant or desk sergeant or whatever.

The other guy was the only one, besides Widow, to wear street clothes. He faced the other direction. He sat on the edge of the table, one leg waving under him, slowly.

All Widow could make out about him was that he was of average height, medium build, and had thick, curly hair, which looked more like wool than human hair. The light reflected countless curls of gray mixed in with jet-black hair.

In front of the room, a large TV monitor and a camera on a tripod faced them.

The general said, "Ah, Mr. Widow."

The man with the wooly hair stayed where he was, but Widow sensed he became suddenly uneasy. His shoulders tensed under a sleeveless zip vest, black. The guy didn't turn around.

"My name is Sutherland. Tom Sutherland. This is my assistant, Sergeant Andy Swan. We're both US Army."

Widow stayed where he was.

"Come on in, Commander." Sutherland summoned him with one hand. But the other, his left, rested on his belt, near a holstered M9 Beretta.

The firearm was loose in its holster. It was pulled up higher than it should have been, which meant that either Sutherland was a poor excuse for a man who had access to an Army-issued weapon, or he had just slipped it back into the holster, not pushing it in all the way.

Widow guessed it was the latter, because the holster's safety snap was undone.

Widow's vision must have cleared up because he could see the red indicator dot on the side of the M9. The safety was off. The hammer was pulled back. The gun had a chambered round. It was set to single-action fire mode and ready to roll.

Brigadier generals rarely carry firearms, not walking around their own office.

The M9 was there because of Widow. Had to be. The sentry from below had radioed up, told them that Widow was on his way. Sutherland drew his weapon and disengaged the safety. Then he readied a bullet to fire.

"Come in," Sutherland repeated.

Widow stepped in, kept one eye on the M9, an old habit with or without the knowledge that it was there because of him.

He walked in about five feet, smelled hints of cigar smoke. Probably from the general's uniform.

"Commander, I hate to be direct, but I need to ask you if you're going to be civil."

"What the hell is this about?"

"Just answer the question."

Widow said nothing.

"Please."

"I've been dragged out of a hospital bed, flown all the way out here. Not to mention, I was in a train wreck. I've got a broken arm. I'm concussed. And a little irritated that I'm even here. I'm as civil as you're going to get, General."

Sutherland nodded and said, "Fair enough. I guess."

"So just cut to the chase?"

Sutherland glanced over at the face of the man with his back to Widow. He nodded.

The wooly-haired man stood up from the edge of the table, slipped both his hands into the pockets of his vest, taking them out of sight, and turned around slowly.

Widow stood still, questioning his eyes for a long moment because he was staring at a man that he'd once warned.

Never let me see you again, he had said to him.

"Hello, Widow," the wooly-haired man said with a hint of a Spanish accent.

Widow said nothing. He glanced at the M9 Beretta in its holster, safety off, ready to fire. Ready to kill. But was Sutherland ready to use it?

They had gone through a lot of taxpayer-expense and

trouble and manpower to get him out here, not to mention jet fuel.

Would Sutherland really pull that gun? Probably. But would he shoot an unarmed man for doing what Widow was about to do?

Only one way to find out.

With his boots in his left hand, Widow's face gave nothing away. Not that it would've mattered, because it would all be over in a second and a half.

Widow stepped forward, left foot, his socks sliding a bit, but not enough to kill his momentum. He twisted at the waist like a pitcher gearing up to throw a fastball. His right hand bunched up into a massive fist. Doctor Green had mentioned all his broken bones and scars and doubled bone scars. She never mentioned the ones on his hand and under the skin on his knuckles. He had calluses bunched up like a set of natural-formed knuckle-dusters.

He lunged with devastating force and whipped forward from his shoulders and plowed a thunderous right hook straight at the wooly-haired guy's face.

It wasn't enough force to take out an eye or push a nasal bone up into the guy's brain, but it was enough to break bones—no doubt about that.

The wooly-haired guy was expecting it. He anticipated it like he knew from the second Widow walked into the building that Widow was going to break bones in his face.

He expected the attack, but he had underestimated the speed. Maybe he assumed Widow was older now. Maybe he assumed Widow was out of practice. Maybe he assumed Widow was weakened from the crash, from the drugs. He was wrong on all accounts.

There was no time to dodge. No way. He was getting punched in the face—no question about that.

The next best thing was to moderate the power from the blow, to alleviate the damage. His training was all he had to rely on.

The wooly-haired guy moved as fast as he could. He tucked his chin down and threw his arms up to absorb the impact of the punch.

It half worked—sort of.

Widow's fist punched straight through, but it impacted the wooly-haired guy's left forearm first. Then the jumbled mass folded back into the wooly-haired guy's face. He went tumbling back over the table.

Widow wound back, fast, ready to step forward and stomp on the wooly-haired guy's throat while he lay on the ground.

But that was all put to bed instantly, because Sutherland had drawn the M9 Beretta after all. He shoved it in Widow's face.

"Hold it, son! I'll shoot you where you stand!"

Widow looked up in the general's eyes. He saw two things. First, there was terror. Not the kind of terror that a non-soldier experienced when confronted with an assaulter. That was the kind of fear only untrained citizens experienced.

This was the kind of fear that a seasoned one-star general experienced only one or two times in his career. It was the kind of thing he got when facing down a madman.

At that moment, Widow was that madman.

The second thing that Widow saw was that the general wasn't bluffing. He would shoot him.

For the first time in a long time, Widow had to ask himself a serious question.

How far would he go to kill a man he should've killed twelve years ago?

CHAPTER 8

Widow stood over the wooly-haired man, ready to stomp down on his head and break his nose, or stand on his throat and break his voice box. Whichever he could get away with first. The throat would've killed him. Instantly. If Widow wanted.

The head wouldn't kill him. Not when Widow was still in socks. But it would hurt like hell. He could break the wooly-haired guy's nose. He could shatter the guy's cheekbones. Maybe he could dislocate one of his eyes from the socket. Maybe even crush it.

But Widow had to ask himself: *Do I want to kill the guy?* The simple answer was that he didn't know. Not for sure. He was thinking.

Another question: *Am I willing to die just to kill him?* The answer to this question was not complicated. No, he didn't want to die. Not here in a conference room on an Army base. That was a newspaper headline that he didn't want to be written. Not about him.

"Widow! Hold it!"

Widow put his foot down, consciously, just now realizing that he had it hiked up, ready to stomp down violently. His body had already made half the choice for him.

Andy Swan had stepped way back, making plenty of room between her and the madman. Some might say she was overly cautious. But that's because they didn't know about Widow. They hadn't read parts of his file. She had. To her, it was not cautious enough.

She pushed her back against the wall. She had dropped the notepad and the pen during the commotion. They lay on the floor.

Widow took a deep breath, held it. Waited a long second and let it out. His brain relayed signals to the rest of his body, telling him to stand down, which was repeated at that moment by an Army general. Verbally.

"Stand down, sailor!" Sutherland said.

Widow stepped back away from the wooly-haired guy and repeated the deep breathing. Once. Twice. And a third time.

He said, "You're not in the Navy, General."

"Technically, neither are you."

"There's no reason to call me sailor. I haven't been a sailor in years."

Sutherland retreated from a shooting stance, slowly, and lowered the M9 down to his hip. He didn't holster it.

The muzzle, the barrel, and the front sights were all targeted on Widow. Staying where they were. He had no intention of changing that.

Accuracy from the hip was harder. Widow knew that. But not at a range of two yards—less even. Widow knew that, too.

"Are you okay?" Sutherland asked the wooly-haired guy without glancing at him.

"Yeah. I'm fine. Goddamn it, Widow! Was that necessary?"

The wooly-haired guy stood up and picked carpet fibers out of his mouth and off the stubble on his face. He had the beginnings of a cylinder-shaped black ring around his eye. It formed at the base of his left eye socket. Widow watched it in real time.

The wooly-haired guy's cheek was already swollen and mottled and bruised. The blood gathered and painted half his face the color red, like the flag itself.

"I warned you. I told you what would happen if I ever saw you again."

The wooly-haired man stood up. He was trying to act like he was not afraid of Widow. An act that everyone saw right through. And he twisted at the waist like he was stretching after a judo match.

No big deal, guys. His body posture was attempting to say.

Sutherland ignored the wooly-haired guy and said, "Andy, come back over. It's okay."

Swan walked back into the room, picked up her notepad and pen. Stopped at the edge of their circle and stared at Widow like he was some kind of mountain man come out of the woods, a look he had seen so many times. He expected it when he met new people.

Sutherland said, "Commander, you're right. Neither of us is Navy. But we both wear a uniform. I expect you to act accordingly."

Widow stayed quiet.

"Can I holster my sidearm?"

No answer.

"Will you play nice?"

"Can't make any promises."

"Widow, I need an affirmative acknowledgment of the order given."

Widow turned his gaze and stared at him, said, "You're not in my chain of command. You don't give orders. No one gives me orders. Not anymore."

"Commander?"

"I'll be good. Put that gun away."

Sutherland paused a quick beat, thinking it over. Then he clicked the safety switch. The hammer was uncocked. He slid the M9 back into the holster by degrees, like a shuttle using rockets to slow its landing.

Sutherland didn't button the safety latch on the holster.

"It's apparent that you know Benico. So let's skip all that. Have a seat."

Widow stared back at Benico Tiller, who was cupping the left side of his face.

"Andy, can you grab me a pack of ice?"

Swan nodded and set her stuff down on the table. She took off through an open door, into an office break room, Widow figured.

He stepped back, set his boots down on the edge of the table, and dumped himself down in the closest empty chair. He kept Tiller and Sutherland in his line of sight.

"Will you just get to it?" he asked.

Sutherland said, "Widow, you're here against my better judgment."

Tiller said, "I asked for you."

"You? What the hell for?"

"For this," Sutherland said, and walked over to a table

below the TV monitor. It was hooked up to a MacBook, some kind of connector cable plugged right into the back of the TV from the front corner of the laptop. Sutherland clicked and patted the trackpad with his index and middle finger.

The TV monitor burst to life. First, the screen was black, then it blipped, and then it displayed the MacBook's screen.

On the screen, Widow saw a topographical map, satellite view. Google Earth, he figured. It was over a two-mile patch of land that he recognized immediately, like no time had passed since Tiller had shown it to him once before, twelve years in the past. And he was reminded of what had happened right there. It was a mission gone terribly wrong. The reason he hated Tiller. The blame that he placed on himself. All of it. Right there.

"I can tell by the look on your face—you know where that is?"

Widow nodded.

"He knows it," Tiller said.

Swan returned with a bag of frozen peas in one hand and a plain white mug of hot coffee in the other. She handed the cold bag to Tiller. Desperate to keep the swelling down, he immediately crammed it against his cheek and under his left eye. He was brazenly superficial, just like every CIA operator that Widow had ever known, minus a few exceptions. The first thing he cared about was how he appeared. These guys were all about taking credit when things were good and obfuscating when they were bad.

Swan handed the coffee mug to Widow, who didn't offer to take it with his hand. He just waited.

Swan set it down on the table in front of him. She said, "I read in your file that you like coffee. Hope that's right."

"That shouldn't be in my file."

"It is."

Widow didn't know what to say to that. Apparently, his file extended beyond his years in the Navy. Someone's been keeping tabs on him. Apparently, it covered much, much more. He wondered what exactly was in there. But he didn't ask.

He smiled and nodded a thank-you for the coffee. He pulled it close and studied it.

"It's not poisoned," Sutherland said.

Widow took a fake sip, just in case. "So, what do you want me to do in North Korea?"

"China."

Widow stared over at Tiller.

"Technically, that's China. Not North Korea."

Widow pointed at the side of the map and said, "That part's North Korea."

"True."

"I'm not going back there. If that's why you brought me all the way out here, you're wasting your time. You could fly me first-class all the way there. Private jet and all. Even if it was on Air Force One, I'm not going."

"It's not why you're here."

Widow listened.

"Not precisely. It's more like, proximate to why we brought you here."

Sutherland clicked the trackpad on the Mac again. He stayed standing near the TV. A new photo came up on the screen like a slideshow, only on a TV monitor instead of from a slide projector.

The photo was of a sniper in field gear. His face was weather-beaten and sandblasted. He had a serious tan going on. A combat helmet covered his head from the sun. He had shades on. But the rest of his face was visible. He was posing for the camera.

There was an L115A3 sniper rifle, a serious weapon, cradled across his chest, pinned there by one of his gloved hands. The folding stock and the handguard matched the desert-brown bulletproof vest he wore underneath. Everything was desert camo; only it wasn't American camo. The patterns were slightly different. He was British Army.

Widow guessed he was a corporal of horse in the cavalry by his uniform and patches. The COH was the basic equivalent to a sergeant in the army in any other part of the world.

The guy was a sniper, obviously. Take out the big sniper rifle, and you were still left with a sniper stance, a sniper way of carrying himself, that translated through the photographs.

Widow had seen his kind before. Many times. Take a trained soldier, throw him into intense sniper school training, and this was what you'd get—a guy who stood like him and posed like him. Snipers held their rifles like an extension of themselves, like a lover and a child all wrapped into one. They held their rifle like it was one of their severed limbs off a battlefield, and they clinched it close, desperate to reattach it.

Widow was also sure about the terrain in the background. The guy was in Afghanistan. Widow knew the desertlike mountains in the background. He had been there. Not that exact location, but close enough.

"Do you know who this is?"

"A British sniper."

Tiller asked, "How did you know that?"

"He's holding an L115A3 rifle."

Sutherland asked, "How do you know he's British? His flag is covered."

"His teeth."

"Be serious, Widow."

"Those aren't US Army fatigues. He's a sniper in Afghanistan. That's obvious. Must be a ten-year-old photo. So I'd guess Brit."

"You're right."

"His name is James Lenny," Tiller added, pushing the frozen peas harder into his cheek. He turned and stood up from the table and stepped away from Widow.

"Is that supposed to mean something to me?"

"Does it?" Sutherland asked.

"Never heard of him."

"He used to hold the record for longest confirmed sniper kill in the world."

"Used to?"

"He got that record back in 2009."

Sutherland added, "About eight years later, his record was completely shattered."

"What was it? His record?"

"Twenty-five hundred meters."

Which was about twenty-seven hundred yards, or a hair over a mile and a half. Widow stayed quiet, but his face registered his shock at the number.

"That's a hell of a lot of yards," Sutherland said.

Widow nodded. "What's the new record?"

Sutherland and Tiller looked at each other.

Sutherland said, "Thirty-five hundred forty meters."

"Bullshit."

"It's true. Someone came along and shattered his record. Literally. A record that never existed before, and it was destroyed eight years later."

Widow stayed quiet. He converted the meters in his head and then calculated the miles for a grand total of three thousand, eight hundred seventy-one yards, or two and a quarter miles, almost.

He caught himself after the fact, but he still muttered it. "Two miles."

Tiller nodded, said, "Over two miles."

"Who broke it?"

"That's part of the mystery. We don't know."

Silence.

Sutherland continued, "It was a Canadian. Canadian forces have a great sniper team. They hold five out of the top ten longest confirmed kills."

Tiller added, "They're really one of a kind."

"Why is there no name?"

"They claim their sniper is still enlisted. Still in. They don't want his name out there."

"Protecting his safety?"

Sutherland nodded.

"That's part of it. They're worried about enemy forces taking steps to find him and eliminate him. Beating that record at a thousand more yards is like putting a target on his back for enemy snipers all across the world. Some people would see him as a trophy kill. Like a challenge. They'd love to take him out."

Widow took a drink from his coffee, letting go of his fears of poisoning. Realizing it was stupid. The Army doesn't poison. They use bullets and bombs. The CIA, however, that's a different story. But they wouldn't do it like this. He hoped.

He took his time, swallowed. He said, "This is all fascinating, but why am I here?"

Sutherland clicked the trackpad again. Another photograph came up. This one was of a sniper, dead in the dirt. His head was blown apart. Blood was everywhere, covering everything. The soil. The long, overgrown blades of grass. The dead man's clothes. Everything.

"Who is it?"

"It's James Lenny."

"He was killed in combat? So what? Part of the risk."

"This isn't combat, Widow. Lenny was discharged from the Army back in 2014. His file cites he had PTSD. Badly."

"Where's this?"

"This is from three days ago."

Widow stayed quiet.

"This photo is from a patch of land in Ireland. Where Lenny is from. Apparently, he still shoots. This is a makeshift range out in the middle of nowhere. He's been shooting out there for years."

"Someone shot him?"

"That's the thing, Widow. Someone shot him from the other side of the range."

Tiller added, "While he was target practicing."

Widow stood up slowly. He kept the coffee in his hand and walked over to the screen. He stared at it. He stared at the gaping hole in the back of Lenny's head. Noticed that it was empty of blood. Noticed the huge exit wound, could tell that the entrance was Lenny's right eye.

Widow looked closer.

"He was shot through the scope?"

"That's right."

Tiller said, "Straight through the scope."

Sutherland said, "No damage was done to the windage, parallax, illumination, or magnification knobs. Only the focus was scratched up."

Tiller added, "A bit."

Widow stared back at the bloody mess on the screen.

Sutherland said, "The bullet traveled straight through the scope and barely touched anything until it exploded out the back of Lenny's head."

"You said it was fired from the end of the range?"

"It was fired from over Lenny's target."

Tiller said, "He had it all set up to match his record. Twenty-seven hundred yards."

Sutherland said, "He was trying to beat it. The sniper who murdered him shot from far behind it. Making him a much better shot than the second-best shot that ever lived."

Widow's jaw dropped. He turned, faced Sutherland, Swan, and Tiller, mouth opened wide.

Sutherland said, "We're working with the Brits on this."

"And the Koreans," Tiller said.

"Technically, it's a case for the Irish, but they're hitting some walls. And they don't want to implicate anyone outside their own jurisdiction. Not yet. Plus, there's the obvious thing that the killer is very good. And that's a terrifying prospect."

Widow remained silent.

Sutherland continued, "Imagine a sniper out there with this capability. Imagine what he could do. Imagine how easy it would be for him to kill a head of state. He could simply wait for the US president to give a stump speech in a field in Iowa or on the back of a corn truck in Nebraska or on an outdoor stage at the state fair in Indiana. Hell, he could take out the president while the president was giving a speech to the troops on the runway onboard a docked battleship. And he could do any of it from two miles away. No one could stop him."

Widow pictured it.

"This sniper just made the US Secret Service completely obsolete."

Tiller squeezed the bag of peas harder again, took a deep breath, and just stared at Widow like he was waiting for something to click.

Widow said, "Who did it? The Canadian?"

"That was everyone's first thought."

"But?"

"There are some obvious implications to that since the Canadians claim he still works for them."

"Has Ireland reached out to them?"

"No. But MI6 has. They didn't tell the Irish. Assorted feelings of jurisdiction and all. Plus, their priorities aren't to solve a murder but to spy for their government. They've reached out to us."

"Is MI6 working with Ireland at all?"

"It's gray."

"But a joint effort with the CIA? That's not likely."

Tiller said, "We're playing nice these days. You've been out a while."

Widow nodded, didn't believe it. In his experience, you can always tell when a government spy is lying, because his lips are moving.

"What do you need me for?"

"There's another possibility," Tiller said.

"What's that?"

"It wasn't the Canadian. It was someone else."

Widow paused, stared at Tiller with cold eyes.

Tiller had seen that look before. He nodded and said, "That's right."

"No one believed me twelve years ago. Now, you believe me?"

"Don't be angry with Tiller. He told us about your ghost sniper. Back then. Back in China. And he's the one who suggested we find you now."

Widow closed his eyes. He saw the nightmarish faces of ghosts, but not one of them was a ghost sniper. He saw something else. Nine faces. All in a row, standing one by one over each other's shoulder. They were aligned like they were posed by some unseen photographer who had one goal in mind—to haunt Widow for the rest of his life.

CHAPTER 9

Ignoring the faces of the dead as best he could under the circumstances, concussion and all, Widow didn't acknowledge them. He looked ahead like they weren't there. He closed his eyes tight but faced the direction of Sutherland and Tiller. He was reminded of the mathematician John Nash, a guy who made significant contributions to game theory and modern economics but was more famous because he saw imaginary people.

They talked to him every day like real people, almost pushing him to the brink of insanity.

Widow opened his eyes and said, "So what? Now you believe me?"

No one spoke.

"I told the truth all those years ago. I always did. Now someone else is dead. It's on you!"

Tiller said, "It was the Pentagon who didn't believe you. Not me."

Widow paused, took a breath, and looked at Sutherland. "Is that true?"

Sutherland said, "It's true, Widow." He paused a beat, walked over to Tiller, placed his hand on the CIA agent's right shoulder like he was defending a nephew. He said, "Tiller fought for your side of the truth. He went to bat for you. Don't put the blame on him. I'm sad to say that it was my office that let you down. It was my call to ignore your story."

"You?"

"Yes. I oversaw the op. I gave the okay. I approved it. Not Tiller. The CIA can't conduct military actions without the military part. You know that."

Widow asked, "Why was a government desk jockey giving orders involving Navy SEALs in the first place?"

Silence.

"General? You guys got your own snake eaters for that."

Widow threw out SEAL slang that he hadn't meant to. *Snake eater* is a generic term for USSF operators such as SEALs, Green Berets, Rangers, and others.

Sutherland didn't seem to notice. He ignored the quip and said, "I was leading a committee overseeing ops on the Korean Peninsula. We had an admiral in the loop, and the Air Force and the Marines. My authority over you was tethered to the admiral."

"Why isn't he here instead of you?"

"Back then, that would've been Admiral Holland. He's long retired by now. I believe."

"No, he's not. He's dead," Widow said.

Tiller said, "Dead?"

Sutherland asked, "You knew him?"

"Yeah, I knew him. He died. Natural causes. Years ago, now."

"Sorry to hear that."

"Don't be. He was a tool."

Sutherland said, "You show little respect for the military, don't you, Widow?"

"Is that a joke? I respect the military more than you'll ever know. But with the politicians, not so much."

"Holland wasn't a politician."

"Course he was. He wore a uniform, sure, but he began his career as the son of a politician. He went to college on the Navy's dime. Started playing politics with the lives of his men. Found how easy it was for him to move up. He was no sailor. He was a bureaucrat."

"Why did he stay in the Navy? It takes decades to reach the rank of admiral."

"Guess he got so good at playing the game with the higher-ups that he saw a better future for himself inside over the one he'd have in the private sector. Why give up the huge paychecks the higher-ups make? He would never see an actual battle."

"You were an officer. Are you lumping us all in together?"

Widow shook his head.

"I'm not like Holland. The only time that man ever fired a service weapon was in boot camp. Far as I know. I'm just calling it like I saw it, General."

Sutherland nodded and said, "That's pretty much how I remember him. That's why he didn't say no to sending in a SEAL team instead of my guys. Not to defend him, but we really thought that six would be enough."

Silence.

Swan cleared her throat quietly. Tiller lowered his hand, and the frozen peas with it. He reached up with his free hand and touched his cheek. It hurt. He winced, returned the frozen peas slowly.

Widow said, "Tiller made the call to leave the others behind. He was the one there. Not you. Or Holland."

No one spoke.

"Five of them were our guys. Since when does the US military leave men behind?"

"They were dead," Tiller said.

Widow didn't respond to that.

Sutherland said, "Take deep breaths, Widow."

Widow did as instructed. He breathed in and breathed out.

Tiller said, "Don't you think I regret that?"

Widow stayed quiet.

"I see a lot of dead faces, Widow. Just like you, I'm sure. More than my fair share. That's counterintelligence life. Right there. That's life in the field. Soldiers die."

"They weren't soldiers."

"Sailor then. Whatever. I am still haunted by their faces. Plus, a half dozen others. I've had a long career."

Silence.

"Ops go bad."

Sutherland said, "You ever heard the saying, 'What's done is done?'"

"Of course."

"It applies here. I'm a soldier and a commanding officer in the US Army. I've sent a lot of people to their deaths. Mostly young boys. I can't linger on it. It's already done."

Widow said nothing.

"Instead of being pissed off at me or at Tiller, why

don't you redirect that anger at the men responsible? The Rainmakers."

Widow stared at Sutherland, said, "The Rainmakers?"

"That's what they're called."

"Who?"

"They're snipers," Tiller added.

Widow looked at Tiller and back at Sutherland. Apparently, they believed him after it was all too late.

Tiller said, "After what happened twelve years ago, the DOD noted the possibility of your ghost sniper being real. They buried it. But they didn't ignore it. Not completely."

Sutherland said, "There's a file in Fort Bragg."

Fort Bragg meant that the file on the Rainmakers, or whatever they were, was deeply classified.

Tiller said, "The Rainmakers is a name they got from locals. There's a Korean word for it. Basically, it translates as 'men who make rain of fire fall from the sky.' Catchy, right?"

"Who are they?" Widow asked.

"As you know, we don't know a lot about North Korea."

Sutherland added, "All we know is what we get from the South. And their intel isn't the best."

Widow said, "And what you see on satellite and drones."

Sutherland nodded, said, "For decades, the North's had ambitions of nuclear proliferation."

"That's why we were there twelve years ago."

Sutherland nodded, said, "But building nuclear weapons is only one aspect of their military ambitions."

Widow stayed quiet.

"They also formed a sniper team. Very elite, Widow.

Apparently, they spent a fortune to build it up. And the intel that we've gathered was that the applicants were only given so many chances before things got bloody."

"Bloody?"

"First, the government would threaten members of the sniper's family. They cut off the fingers and limbs of their children. Things like that. If that didn't work, then they just killed the sniper."

Widow nodded.

"That made quite the incentive to be the best of the best."

"Why would anyone join this group?"

"They weren't volunteers. They were volunteered. The military tested soldiers for aptitude and..."

Widow said, "If you could shoot, then you were automatically a volunteer?"

"Right. North Korea's whole goal for getting nukes is to be taken seriously and to instill fear among the rest of us. The fear that they could strike."

Tiller said, "Anywhere."

"That's why they formed the Rainmakers. Possibly the world's most elite snipers. Imagine it. The Rainmakers were meant for covert assassinations."

Sutherland paused for a moment, took a breath. Then he said, "Did you see on the news, last year, the assassination of one of the North Korean dictator's brothers?"

Widow nodded and said, "I remember. He was poisoned. Some kind of nerve agent or something very high-grade."

"That's right."

"They caught the assassin."

Sutherland nodded, said, "They did. But what you

didn't see on the news was she killed herself. Right in the police jail. Cyanide pill in her tooth. After she was caught. She had been trained to kill and then trained to kill herself when caught."

"Cyanide tooth? That's a real thing?"

Tiller said, "It's real."

Sutherland said, "Imagine it. The Rainmakers are sent abroad and trained to kill from ungodly distances. They'd never even be caught if they played their cards right. Imagine the terror around the world."

Widow nodded. It sounded like a terrifying scenario.

"Anyway, they never deployed the Rainmakers. Not before now. They've been stationing them along the borders. Often, they wait for defectors to cross over a mile of frozen river and terrain, and then they shoot them. Each time trying to get better. Each time trying to shoot farther."

Tiller said, "There's only been one encounter—that we know of—that they've ever shot over two miles and killed with deadly accuracy."

Sutherland said, "It was your op."

Widow said, "That sniper killed nine people in that encounter. I'd say he's proven he can shoot ridiculous distances."

Sutherland and Tiller both nodded at the same time.

"Now you want me to catch him?"

Everyone paused a beat.

Sutherland spoke first. He said, "You're not in the Navy anymore, Commander. But we'd sure like your help."

"With what, exactly?"

Sutherland said, "Twelve years ago, you went on a

mission. An op that was so covert only a small SEAL team was spared to take it."

Sutherland didn't have to say their names. Widow knew it. Concussion or not.

Sutherland clicked the trackpad again, and the photo changed. It was an aerial view photo of Lenny's corpse, taken by a small drone, Widow figured.

Sutherland clicked it again, and the photo changed again. The next one was of the target area that Lenny was aiming at. There was a tall, wooden stake stabbing into a green watermelon.

"Interesting target," Widow said.

Sutherland nodded, clicked the trackpad again, and another photo from the drone came up. This one was farther back and above where the target had been. It was a higher elevation, which made sense. Lenny would've been firing in a downward slope. Partly because of the range. And partly because he didn't want to shoot someone on the other side of the target accidentally.

Sutherland stopped on the photo.

Widow studied it. There wasn't much to see. There was heavy grass, collapsed and bent over.

He said, "That's where the sniper who killed him was."

Sutherland said, "The Rainmaker. We believe."

"What is it I'm supposed to see here?" Widow asked.

Tiller said, "Widow, we know you were really an undercover investigator with NCIS."

Widow shrugged, said, "You're CIA. And you're Pentagon. I know you know. So what?"

"We need you to investigate."

"Secretly," Sutherland added.

Widow took another pull from the coffee, stood up,

kept it in hand, and walked over to the screen. He looked hard.

"Nothing to see here that's not obvious."

"Indulge us."

Widow looked again. He switched the coffee over to his left hand, set it down, bottom in his palm like a space shuttle landing, and held it there. His left hand hurt from the effort, but he knew that broken limbs fell under the principle of "use it or lose it."

He pointed at the screen with his right hand, traced over the outline of the crushed grass. "This is where the sniper lay prone and killed Lenny. He used a sniper mat. That's why it's shaped like a rectangle."

Sutherland and Tiller nodded. Of course, they knew that part.

Widow said, "Can you zoom? Make this section bigger?"

He pointed at the top corner of where the mat would've been laid.

"Yep," Sutherland said, and pinched and clicked his fingers on the trackpad. The whole process took a long second.

The screen was filled with grass.

Widow looked hard. He saw broken and crushed and destroyed blades of grass. It started at the center, where it was destroyed, then moved up in a direction that Widow guessed to be east because of shadows on the ground.

Widow traced the variations of grass with his index and middle fingers. He said, "Yeah."

"Yeah, what?"

"Nothing."

"What is it?"

Tiller said, "Anything is better than what we got."

Widow said, "I'd guess you got two killers here."

"What makes you say that?"

"The grass. It's not just pushed down. It's crushed. It's destroyed here and here," he said and pointed.

Swan interjected for the first time. A natural, involuntary act, like being sucked into a story by a stranger involving a monkey and saying, "What happened to the monkey?"

She said, "And there too." She pointed at the third section of grass destroyed. Not pushed down. Destroyed.

Widow looked at it and nodded.

Tiller said, "A single person could've done that."

"Not likely."

"Why not?"

"First, the guy would have to be more than two hundred pounds. Probably two-twenty or more."

"Plenty of guys are two hundred twenty pounds."

"Sure, but not snipers."

Sutherland said, "I've seen guys out at the range that heavy."

"Maybe at a civilian range. Maybe retired snipers. But not an elite sniper. Not a North Korean."

"'Cause Koreans are smaller?"

Widow said, "On a general level, sure, they are smaller than us. But that's not what I mean. They are underfed. North Korea doesn't provide for its people. I'd be surprised if the military gets three squares a day. Elite snipers or not."

"What's the second thing?"

"The second thing is that this guy would've had to

have been rocking around to make three different destroyed grass patterns."

Tiller said, "So?"

"Snipers don't move. Not a sniper who got this good. He'd be silent and still. Very. This guy would have to be like a Shaolin monk. I'd be shocked if his breath would even register in freezing temperatures. To be that good."

They all nodded, staring at Widow.

Sutherland asked, "Two snipers? You're sure?"

Widow said, "There's another thing."

They waited. No one spoke.

Widow said, "I don't think it's two snipers. I think it's one sniper and one spotter. Snipers in the military use spotters. I'm impressed that Lenny could shoot that far on his own. Must've taken him a long time to set up the shot and zero his aim that close to target."

"Then we're looking for two Koreans. Both light. Both well trained."

"That'd be my guess. If they really are Rainmakers."

Sutherland nodded. He stared at Tiller, who nodded back. "Widow, before we go any further, we'd like for you to work with us on this."

Widow stayed quiet.

"We need you. We have to stop these guys before they do irreparable damage in the world."

Tiller said, "Next, they might shoot someone who matters. You know? On the world stage."

Widow stared down at his coffee.

"What do you say?"

"What exactly are my parameters?"

"You'll answer to Tiller, who will report to me."

Tiller added, "Our goal is to find and capture—if possible."

"And if not?"

"Then we dispatch the targets."

Widow took a deep breath. He said, "If this is the sniper team from twelve years ago, I'm not interested in capture."

They said nothing to that.

"I'll do it. But know that for me, it's not about putting to bed any fears that some politicians might have. For me, it's about a thirteen-year-old girl."

Tiller nodded. He knew exactly what Widow was talking about. Sutherland nodded eventually. He caught on. Swan didn't know what he meant by that.

CHAPTER 10

The steward from the C-20B—who had flown with an unlogged, unmanifested, unkempt giant of a passenger from Minneapolis–Saint Paul Air Reserve Station all the way to Andrews Air Force Base just ninety-eight minutes ago—finished up his daily checks on the interior of the plane. Then he gathered his paperwork and flight check-ins and collected the little trash that had been produced from the two flights—one empty paper coffee cup from the recent one—and he stowed everything away and rechecked that it was all in its place. A place for everything. Everything in its place. One of the Air Force credos.

After he finished, he stepped off the plane and out of the hangar. He pulled his carry-on suitcase along the pavement as the hard plastic tires jerked across the tarmac.

He looked at his watch. The time was fifteen minutes past four in the afternoon.

He walked past flight crews readying to board a nearby C-130 and stepped into the crew center. He walked past more crew members. Only one recognized him. He nodded at her and moved on.

He passed one officer who outranked him, and he stopped and saluted. Then he continued until he was in front of the crew center. He waited at the sidewalk for a base shuttle to take him to his car.

He stared at his watch again and looked at a posted sign with shuttle times and routes. According to the posted schedule, he was going to be waiting for ten more minutes before the shuttle arrived. He figured this probably meant twenty minutes. It was the later part of the afternoon, which meant that the military day shift would be looking at the clock, waiting for five o'clock so they could scramble to their cars and fight Maryland traffic for thirty-plus minutes before they could get to their homes and kick off their shoes.

He had just flown from Minneapolis to Andrews, not a long flight, but before that, he had already been on a six-hour, twenty-five-minute flight from Andrews out to Davis-Monthan Air Force Base in Tucson. Right at landing, they were ordered to fly to Minneapolis–Saint Paul to pick up some VIP, another three-hour, fifteen-minute flight.

All things considered, he was in a pretty good mood but dog tired. He was ready to go home and get some sleep.

To kill time and to earn a couple of bucks, he decided it was time to call a journalist friend he had at the *Washington Post*. No one special, just a low-level researcher. Which was her official title, but it didn't mean that all she did was write briefs and summaries by reading articles on Wikipedia or by interviewing willing witnesses. Some people she interviewed, called sources, were people she had to pay to buy information.

The more valuable the information, the greater the risk. The greater the risk, the higher the price tag.

The steward pulled out his cell phone and dialed her number.

It rang once, twice, and on the third ring, she answered.

She said his name and a hello. He said her name and hello back. Then he asked her how much she wanted a tip about a top secret VIP transport package.

She said, "Depends. What are we talking about here?"

"Something very valuable."

"How valuable?"

"Plenty."

"Specifics?"

He said, "I want to get paid first."

"I'll send money by PayPal. Per usual. Tell me the info first."

"No way. You send the money. And if it's high enough. I'll tell you the intel."

Silence.

The researcher said, "Give me a minute."

She put him on hold. No warning.

A minute and ten seconds later, she came back on the line.

"Check your account."

The steward said, "Okay."

He took the phone out of his ear, clicked the screen and swiped, and opened an app to his PayPal account. *You received a payment.*

He smiled, saw the number, and smiled bigger.

"Is that enough?" he heard her ask, even with the phone away from his ear.

"It is. That works."

"Give me the intel."

He told her all he knew. He told her about the urgent turnaround from Davis-Monthan to Minneapolis–Saint Paul Air Force Reserve Station and waiting, and how the pilots told him they weren't logging the flight in with the tower nor reporting the secret passenger who had gotten on the jet.

She said, "Is that all?"

"We took him to Andrews. Some kind of top secret thing."

"What else?"

The steward was quiet.

"Who was he?"

"I don't have a name."

"This isn't enough. What's so strange about this guy? The unlogged flight is unusual, but no one here is going to be interested in a phantom flight."

"I can tell you what he looked like."

She was quiet.

"He was a big guy. Like *Terminator*. And he wasn't military."

"What was he?"

"I don't know. But important. They sent a Navy MP to escort him, and we dropped him off at Andrews. An MP picked him up. My guess is he's some kind of secret agent or a CIA assassin. Maybe. He wasn't a normal guy we pick up."

"Is that all?"

"That's what I got."

"Okay. Thanks. If you think of anything else, call me."

And they disconnected.

Secret agent, she thought.

The researcher at the *Washington Post* was good at her job. She had worked there for three years, right out of college. A lot of competition went into securing a job there. Once she had gotten a foot in the door, she taught herself the ropes. The thing about the ropes was learning that the news business was cutthroat. In order to maintain her position in the ranks, she had to be cutthroat. When she couldn't dig up a story, sometimes she had to take extreme measures. She had to stir the pot and see what came to the surface.

And sometimes, she just liked to make a little money on the side herself.

She couldn't do much with the intel she had paid for. But she could make a little money off it herself. She could always use it if more to the story ever developed.

She ignored the landline on her desk, pulled out her cell phone and dialed a number that she had written in her notes, not logged as a contact.

She waited and listened to the number dial.

A voice with a Chinese accent answered the phone. It was a man. He said, "Chinese Consulate. This is Lu Er."

The man on the line wasn't a secretary or even a desk jockey at the Chinese Consulate, but he was there. Probably. He was a midlevel official. She didn't know his job title but knew that it was just a generic title like "agent." It could mean many things.

His real name wasn't Lu Er, as no one in China was really named that.

In America, John Doe was the standard name for a man unidentified. The Chinese put a common name together with a number, like John Four or Joe Two.

The man on the phone's name was Lu Er, which just meant Lu Two. Nothing too clever, but Americans never caught on. Neither did almost any other person from any other continent.

She said, "It's me."

Lu said, "Hello."

"I've got a story for you."

And she told all the parts she knew. She told him about the man flown in top secret. The jet. The covert nature of it all. She told him about all she had so far. She didn't know what it meant or if it even applied to the Chinese government. Random chance it was.

Technically, what the Air Force steward had done wasn't illegal, not in the civilian world. It may be a court-martial offense in the military world. She had no idea. Not her problem.

But what she was doing, selling military secrets to a foreign government, might be a breach of federal law, but only if she was selling privileged knowledge to a foreign government, like spying. Theoretically, she wasn't telling him anything that she was privileged to. She didn't work for the US government. She wasn't in the military. She wasn't the Air Force steward. If he had sold the information directly to Lu, that would constitute a felony.

To her, right then, it didn't differ from her selling information to a newspaper, like the *New York Times*. That would have been a fireable offense since they were a competitor to her organization. But it wasn't illegal.

Lu listened and took it all down.

She asked about payment, which, normally, she would've done up front, but that's not how the Chinese government does business. They want to know the information first, know if it's valuable, and they decide the amount of payment based on that.

They were good for it. She knew that. She had sold information to them in the past. It was just a way to make some extra money. Living in DC was very expensive.

They used none of her information anyway, she figured.

Lu told her the payment was being sent. Then he paused a long, long beat. It was so long she had to ask if he was still there.

He answered he was, and then he did something out of the ordinary. He said, "Never call me again. Good luck to you." And he hung up the phone.

She took the cell phone away from her ear and stared at it. *That was odd*, she thought.

CHAPTER 11

An hour later, the local time was fifteen past midnight when the woman got off a plane at Dublin International. She had flown China Southern Airlines from Beijing with a layover in Amsterdam, which pissed her off because it was only two hours, and she had never been to Amsterdam. She'd caught her connecting flight with KLM and had just landed without delays.

She walked softly across the linoleum floors in the terminal like it was carpet and she was gliding on bare feet. She stepped lightly because she was light. Her hair was pulled back, a no-nonsense ponytail, and she wore no makeup. Not on a flight. She flew a lot for her occupation and had learned long ago not to wear makeup when she didn't have to. To the men in her profession, it sounded like a meaningless topic. But among the few women who worked at the high level she worked, it was a topic of heated debate.

Wear makeup; get noticed by men for being attractive.

Don't wear makeup; get noticed by women for not following the rules of engagement deemed by social norms.

Ultimately, it was a case-by-case kind of decision to make. Here, she chose not to. Mostly, she chose not to because she had to endure a thirteen-hour, fifty-minute flight over eight countries with commercial carriers. At least she flew first class. That made things a little easier. A little more bearable. At least she could sleep since they had reclining seats with one hundred percent horizontal tilt capabilities, which was good.

She got to sleep on a portion of the flight. Enough to make her appear to be awake enough when she met with her Irish counterparts.

The only thing about flying first class was that even though she could skip putting on the makeup, she had to dress the part. She couldn't wear comfortable workout clothes. She had to look like she belonged. Official policy from China was to not draw attention to herself needlessly.

She stepped off the plane wearing a dark-green pantsuit with a Chinese collar, notched. She believed the fabric was part bamboo and part cotton. It was comfortable. The single-breasted jacket had sleeves hastily pushed up over her elbows. It was part of the Western style. She had been told it'd be fashionable in Ireland.

She hauled a carry-on behind her. It was a small thing with an extended arm for pulling across the ground. Unlike the Air Force steward's, her wheels weren't jerking.

She walked out through the local customs area, where she had shown her passport and been given a stern look-over, partially because she was a foreigner with a Chinese passport. Not a lot of Chinese people in Dublin, she figured.

She stopped at the last point of international land before she was officially on Irish soil. And she glanced down at the official line at the airport. It was one of those "you're crossing over into a new country" lines.

A frown came over her face because she had expected it to be green. But it was a red line. She stepped over it and out into the general population, into Ireland.

After following the signs to arrivals and taxis and passing the baggage claim area, she walked out the front doors, where normally there would be a line of limo and taxi drivers waiting to pick up arriving passengers. But this time of night meant that only one guy was standing there.

He was one of the other people in Dublin with a Chinese passport.

The only difference between them was that she was not Chinese. Not by birth. Only by citizenship. She was Asian by birth from one of China's neighbors. Most people couldn't tell. She looked Chinese enough.

No one in her adopted country ever guessed that she wasn't. Why should anyone in Ireland be any different?

The man wore an all-black suit. Black jacket. Black pants. That was the first thing she noticed, naturally. The second was that he was armed. He had a Glock 17 in a pancake holster at his right hip. It was well concealed, but not to her. She had been trained. She knew what to look for.

The last thing she noticed was that he held up a sign with her name on it. It was her real name. No need to use aliases. Not here. Not when the name was written in Chinese.

Who the hell here was going to read that?

She stopped out in front of him. He smiled at her, gave a nod, and spoke Chinese.

They made introductions. They shook hands. And then he told her she was going to her hotel first. Nothing they could do tonight. They'd have to take another flight first thing in the morning to a city called Cork.

She didn't know why she was there. Not yet. In Beijing, they hadn't told her anything. She just knew that she was going to Dublin first because there was a Chinese embassy there. That's where they would update her.

That's where she'd learn that her assignment wasn't a regular assignment. That's where she'd learn that it was personal.

CHAPTER 12

Sutherland and Tiller finished their sales pitch with Widow and wrapped everything up. Tiller took the bag of peas, handed it back to Swan, who must've thought to return it to the freezer right then because she got up and walked out of the room.

Sutherland scratched his belly over his uniform shirt, moving his gun hand out of drawing distance for the first time.

Widow noticed but said nothing—did nothing.

"I want to remind you of a couple things. First, you report to Tiller. Second, we don't need any collateral damage. Got that?"

Widow nodded.

"Third, remember you were granted top security clearance once upon a time."

Widow nodded again. He remembered.

"Remember the paperwork that you had to sign to get that security clearance?"

"That was like a hundred years ago."

"But do you remember?"

"I remember it. How could I forget? Two lawyers came to see me. Made me sign a book worth of documents."

"In that book, some clauses grant us the right to have you locked up until you turn old and gray if you violate any of the stipulations in that agreement."

"What's that got to do with anything?"

"It means you can't tell anyone about what we have told you here or what happens in this investigation."

Widow said, "That agreement still holds water?"

"It does."

Widow nodded.

"Last, don't get caught. If you get arrested in a foreign country, we can't help you."

"Am I going to another country?"

"Of course."

Tiller said, "Lenny was a Brit. Shot in Ireland. As far as we know, the Rainmaker is still there."

"I won't get caught."

"Good," Sutherland said and closed the MacBook. "Tiller will take it from here."

Widow nodded and watched the general walk to the door, heading off in the opposite direction that Widow had come from. He paused in the doorway, turned, and looked back. He was contemplating whether to leave Widow alone with Tiller. That was obvious.

In the end, he did.

"What now?"

Tiller said, "We get started. Let's get out of here."

They went down the same elevator that Widow had come up in. The whole time Widow couldn't help but have thoughts of doing more damage to Tiller. But he held back.

They went down the same corridor, passed the same guard station, and passed under the same security cameras on the way out.

This time, there was a black Escalade parked on the street. Engine running. Two men inside. A driver and another guy in the back seat.

The guy in the back seat got out and waited for Tiller to step up. He opened the front passenger door for him like a chauffeur. Only the guy looked more like a Secret Service agent. He was not.

He didn't open the door for Widow. Widow got in the back seat on his own, one-handed, all the way. He could feel the warmth.

Tiller introduced the two guys as part of his team. Widow forgot their names two seconds after learning them. His impression of them was that they were the muscle and nothing else.

After everyone was in and buckled up, the driver took off, and the Escalade was on the road. Five minutes later, they were back at the runways. Thirty seconds after that, they were parking at a jet hangar. Not the same one that Widow had come in to.

"What are we doing here?"

Tiller turned around from the front seat and looked at him. "We're going to Ireland. You got your passport, right?"

Widow dug in his pocket, pulled it out.

Tiller looked at it, shrugged. "You won't need it."

"I will in a foreign country."

Tiller said nothing to that. Instead, he swung back around and got out of the Escalade. The muscle got out after him. Widow followed.

He followed them out onto the tarmac. There was a Lockheed C-5 Galaxy parked around the corner on the edge of the tarmac in what used to be grass and was later covered with gravel and then repurposed with filled-in concrete.

The engines were on.

Widow followed as Tiller and the two muscle guys boarded the plane. They climbed up wobbly portable jet steps and entered.

They fumbled in past the cockpit and into the belly. They stopped just before the cargo area. There were four seats stacked and plain and all metal. No cushions. They folded out of the wall like the jump seat Widow had seen the Air Force steward sit on.

In the cockpit, Widow saw two pilots and an airman, who was set to fly with the plane to watch over the cargo.

In the back of the plane, there were stacked crates and boxes and various packages. There was one military Humvee locked in place by tire boots, jacked into the floor on a track. The Humvee was empty.

Tiller sat in a jump seat, followed by both muscle guys. They were just like Rosencrantz and Guildenstern, two characters from Shakespeare's *Hamlet* who were so indistinguishable from each other that Hamlet was always confusing them. Only these guys were worse because they were like puppets who followed Tiller around with no original thought between them.

In *Hamlet*, the prince ended up leading Rosencrantz and Guildenstern to their deaths, but only because they were supposed to trick him and betray him and lead him to his execution. He outsmarted them.

The thought of tricking them into stepping into their executions crossed Widow's mind.

Widow looked at the last seat with disdain. He didn't want to sit next to Tiller, and he didn't want to sit on a metal seat, taking off in an overstuffed metal box. The days that he had to fly bare-bones were long in his past. He had hoped.

In that instant, Tiller saw him eyeballing the jump seat. He put a hand up and spoke. "Not here. This is for the crewman."

Widow looked over at the third airman and back at Tiller. "You serious?"

"Sorry."

The airman walked out of the cockpit toward the jump seat.

"Am I supposed to sit on the floor?"

The airman reached out to touch Widow's arm but decided not to.

He said, "Sir, you can sit in the Humvee."

Widow looked over at the Humvee. "Are you serious?" He looked at Tiller. "Is that legal?"

Tiller said, "This isn't LAX, Widow."

The engines echoed throughout the hull and the fuselage and the nose, loud and brassy. The vibrations and the noise rattled through the metal and through Widow's legs and his bones and his broken arm and his skull.

He remembered being in Humvees. Hundreds. Maybe thousands of different ones in his past. Not one specific memory came to mind. It was more of a military blur.

Widow shrugged and walked back past more metal and cargo nets and stacked boxes and various Air Force equipment. All of it boxed up or stowed away in containers. And all of it strapped into countless pockets and netting.

The airman was right behind him, offering a hand getting into the Humvee. Widow shoved it off and maneuvered around strapped-down cargo and the hood and two of the big tires, and opened the passenger door to the vehicle. He pulled himself up and dumped himself down on the seat.

He decided not to get behind the steering wheel. The passenger seat offered more legroom.

"Buckle your seat belt."

Widow wasn't used to doing that in a Humvee. The Navy didn't require it. The Army did. The Marines, he was pretty sure, didn't. He didn't know the policy of the Air Force regarding wearing a seat belt in a Humvee.

He buckled in and nodded at the airman. The guy nodded back and walked away.

At least Widow didn't have to sit next to Tiller on the flight over the pond. And at least he was in a cushioned chair instead of a crappy jump seat. So he smiled.

A few moments later, the C-5 Galaxy was up and off the ground and airborne. About five minutes into the flight, the captain came over the intercom, which was blasted out of back speakers behind the cockpit.

The crew wore crash helmets with headphones in their ears. The speakers were only for non–Air Force members' benefit.

The captain introduced himself, announced the flight time of five hours and some change, and said they were flying to an American Air Force base in the UK called Lakenheath.

Widow never heard of it and had never been there. He

wasn't sure how it worked. Was it a British installation with an American unit? Did the US Air Force have a continuing contract with the government? Or was it US soil, kept after World War II?

He wasn't sure.

He had no window view, only military ordnance, and the inside of the cargo plane, and Tiller's group, which he really didn't want to look at or think about.

Widow took a moment to fumble with his pill bottle and pop the top. It took him a long moment to get it open. It reminded him of a pressurized hatch on a submarine that won't open. He suspected the bottle lid was his mortal enemy. Finally, he popped it open and downed another pill. He returned the lid to the bottle, the bottle to his pocket.

Widow stared at the lifeless dash on the Humvee for the first twenty minutes. His gaze never moved. He did this until he closed his eyes and drifted away into a nightmarish sleep. A memory that he had locked away had been rattled loose by a train crash and a concussion. Like he had it all squared away in a lockbox in his mind, but now someone had broken the lock.

He thought back to a pair of volcanic eyes he would never forget.

CHAPTER 13

Her volcanic eyes stared up at him. She held his hand tight. He could feel her grip through the Navy-issued tactical glove, which was white and thin and tough and durable. The best material. It protected against harsh weather, and overheating from firing rounds from any assault rifle or submachine gun systems.

Widow had needed them. They did their job—protection against anything.

Only there were some things in the world that they couldn't protect him from.

One was those volcanic eyes.

He held her hand.

She was the last one alive. The last man standing. Minus himself.

He stared into those volcanic eyes. He watched the life slip away. She was out in the snow. The mist hung around her like dust settling. Only it never did.

The surrounding snow had been white only seconds

before. Now it had turned to a deep, deep red. The way he imagined a giant vat of ruby-red lipstick would look at first in a huge metal container on the factory floor of a lipstick company.

The red was blood. She was bleeding out. Shot. She wouldn't make it. No way.

He moved his eyes to her lips. They faded to pink and then to gray.

He stared into those volcanic eyes.

He watched her die.

CHAPTER 14

The Navy spared no expense training the men who crossed through BUD/S, or Basic Underwater Demolition/SEAL training, and Widow had delivered more than twenty-five missions by that point.

Twenty-five covert missions were in one of Widow's files, locked away in Virginia at the Department of the Navy. But another dozen or more were locked away offsite in Quantico, in the secret basement offices of Unit Ten.

His double life.

The border between China and North Korea was primarily composed of two rivers fused together as one. Plus, there was the rugged mountain terrain to deal with.

From west to east, the waters of the Yalu River swallowed the violent torrents that flowed south out of the Paektu Mountains and the Tumen River. The rivers divided the two countries.

To the north, there was one main bridge connecting nation to nation over the Tumen.

In the summer months, it helped to expedite importing

and exporting between a city in China and a main village in North Korea.

But in the winter months, it was frozen completely over.

Widow and the other SEALs on his team were there in the dead of winter. A snowstorm had blown through only a day before.

They had used the day after the passing storm to achieve their mission.

This winter, the river waters rose to near flood levels, and the drawbridge was raised, and the ice froze over the road top, leaving both sides of the drawbridge gaping open. They stood up out of the ice at thirty meters apiece, like they were the saber teeth of some unspeakable horror that lived below the ice.

A dense and heavy mist rose from the top of the ice and plumed up into wafts of thick white fog. The skies were gray in the early morning hours. The sun must've been up somewhere because the far-off recesses of the sky were white, but nothing was blue. No blue in sight. Only the grayish blue of dreary gloom.

Widow's boots sank into the drifting snow, as did those of the five SEALs that brought up his rear. Widow was leading a SEAL team on a secret mission.

Widow was nearly out of breath when he reached the middle of the distance between North Korea's last steppe, just before the rocky ice on the frozen river and the edge of the highway in China.

Before crossing the river, Widow had to wait and look in all directions. He had to make sure that no one was around, watching him and his guys. The last thing they needed was to be seen by Chinese natives who might call the cops. The local police doubled as soldiers. They'd send a guy out in a patrol truck with snow tires to check out the foreigners who didn't belong. Maybe they'd send cops.

Once the cops saw that Widow and his team weren't Chinese, they would bring out the sirens and spotlights and guns. They would cuff them, throw them in the back of the truck, and haul them back to headquarters. If this happened, it wouldn't be good. It would be bad for Widow and his team, and bad for the US. And that was the best-case scenario.

They would know Widow and his guys were special operators just by the weapons they carried. Widow was armed with a SIG Sauer P226 Legion RX edition, which was the same as the standard, only better. His SIG Sauer had a red-dot sight and other features he didn't care about. He liked the Romeo sight. It was great for nearly guaranteed accuracy.

Besides the SIG, he and his guys were armed with Heckler & Koch MP5SD submachine guns. The MP5SD came suppressed. This was an SMG made for covert ops, and they were engaged in a covert op. No question.

This was a CIA black op. Widow knew that because he had met the guy in charge—a shady agent named Benico Tiller.

When one of the other guys in his op, a lieutenant named Lyn, asked Tiller in a five-minute briefing if this op was against regulations, Tiller responded, "Regulations are regarded more like guidelines when it comes to special ops."

Widow shrugged. He didn't respond to that.

The snowfall had stopped an hour earlier, which was

good because he, Lyn, and the others were getting worried.

The mission was to rescue and extract a North Korean civilian—a scientist. The man knew something about the regime's nuclear program. Which the pointy-heads at the Pentagon were still hoping to curtail.

Widow never knew exactly what the guy's function or knowledge was. It wasn't mission-critical. Widow was on a need-to-know basis. And the details didn't need to be known.

The scientist's name was Kweon. Widow didn't know Kweon's first name. Not important. Not for identification, because the guy would defect from North Korea by crossing over the frozen river at the coordinates that Tiller gave Widow.

They were given the place. They were given the time. And they were given the number of defectors.

The defector was taking his family out with him. They were getting asylum in America. A good deal for them. They'd get relocation money. They'd get new names. They'd get new passports and new identities.

Widow imagined they'd be put up somewhere in Indiana or Oklahoma or Kentucky or Kansas or whatever state was deep in the middle of the country. They would relocate to a small town and given monthly allowances and education, and probably a small business. They'd have a good life, a real change from the horrors of living in North Korea. Especially for a guy like Kweon.

Widow could only imagine that Kweon, being some kind of prominent scientist, was under a big-brother type of surveillance. From what he knew of important people in North Korea, of guys critical to the success of the nuclear program. If they weren't cooperative, then they were forced to take part.

Widow could only imagine what Kweon must've gone through on the other side of the border to get all the way to the edge and cross the barbed wires and the fences and the armed patrols.

It must've taken a lot of CIA funding to get known North Korean diplomats and maybe border guards to look the other way for a small window of time, while Kweon and his family hiked across miles of rugged, snow-covered terrain to make the final leg of the journey to cross a dangerous, frozen river.

Widow had been briefed on countless failed attempts by previous non-agency important defectors.

But it wasn't until that moment when he saw dead bodies frozen in the ice below that he realized how often people died trying to escape.

Widow stepped slowly through the snow and over the ice. He paused a beat about two hundred feet from the edge of China's highway. He had seen movement and small figures on the horizon through his field glasses back at the checkpoint.

The checkpoint was two klicks behind him.

That's where Lyn and Reyes waited. They were posted on the roof of the only structure within ten square miles. It was part of the remains of a hardware store. It had been closed, abandoned, and looted a decade in the past, like the rest of a small enclave on the side of the highway. Initially, it was a lived-in small town on the route to the next city. Now it was abandoned and long forgotten. Perfect for Widow's SEAL Team to set up camp the night before.

Reyes acted as backup for Lyn, who was in Widow's ear on a tiny wire receiver. The wire was tucked away behind Widow down his back, down to a small radio rig strapped to the side of his rucksack.

Widow and his team were decked out in all-white-and-blacks to camouflage them with the terrain and the snow.

Their faces were painted in camo blacks.

Lyn watched him from the checkpoint through a rifle scope. Reyes knelt over Lyn's shoulder.

Lyn took his fingers away from the trigger housing and squeezed the talk button on his laryngophone—a mic rig that's circular and fits around an operator's throat—also known as a throat microphone. It's ideal for covert work in harsh weather.

Lyn said, "Scorpio, do you see them?"

They were using zodiac animals as call signs for the mission. Widow had been born in November. Therefore, he was Scorpio.

Widow pulled down a bandana that was covering his mouth and nose so he could breathe in the icy winds. He glanced from one side to the other. On his left, there was a SEAL he'd worked with before named Clery. On his right, there was a SEAL he'd only just met named Hollander. Pulling up the rear was another SEAL called Slabin. Widow made eye contact with Clery, who nodded and then at Hollander, who also nodded. He didn't look back at Slabin.

Widow took a breath and pressed the talk button on his laryngophone. The transducers kicked to life and picked up his voice, crisp and bright against the harsh, icy wind.

Widow said, "No. I can't see a damn thing out here. Just lots and lots of white."

Silence.

Widow asked, "You got them still?"

Lyn said, "Affirmative. I see them. About sixty, maybe fifty yards ahead."

Widow let go of the MP5SD and let it fall back on a sling over his back, out of the way. He held one hand up over his eyes and scrunched it into the shape of a makeshift visor. He stared off into the gloom.

Widow waited.

He clicked his throat mic and said, "I see nothing."

Static fired over the receiver in his ear. And then a long pause. He heard Lyn breathing like someone about to say something but holding onto the last breath.

Lyn said, "About twenty-five yards now. To the north-east. Over the snowbank."

Widow turned and looked in the direction Lyn indicated and paused. Then he heard noises. Frantic. Like heavy breathing. And whimpering.

Widow clutched his talk button and spoke.

"How many?"

"Four. Yeah. Four. Two are small, like children. That's gotta be them."

"Okay. I'm going to meet them at the bottom of the hill."

Widow clicked off, and Lyn said nothing.

Widow glanced at his team again. He gave them hand signals, informing them what positions to take. The other men took their positions, guns at the ready. Then, Widow stepped forward, leaving the bandana loose on his neck. The wind batted against his face. Gusts slapped hard several times. He felt his breath ripped out of him.

After seven minutes of carefully stepping and sliding

through snow and ice, the Team made it to the bottom of the hill. They set up there, awaiting an ambush. A necessary precaution.

Widow planted one boot in the snow and went down on one knee. The Team followed suit. Widow held his MP5SD up and out. Kept the muzzle pointed down at the four o'clock position. He didn't want to accidentally shoot whoever was walking over the snowbank. Or scare away the family he was there to rescue. He didn't know if they knew who they were meeting. He didn't even know if they spoke English.

A mistake just hit him. He clutched at his throat mic.

"Chicken. Come in."

"Rooster" was Lyn's technical zodiac animal, but not his assigned code name for this op. His code name was the American calendar year's counterpart.

Since he was Chinese and born in the right month and right year for it to apply, January 1982, Widow was just having fun with him.

Widow heard static. And a puff of air, like exhaling. And Lyn's voice. "It's not Chicken. It's Capricorn. We're using American astrology signs."

Widow said, "I didn't know we'd decided on that yet."

Lyn ignored that and asked, "What is it? You see them?"

"Not yet. But I just realized, why am I down here, leading the extraction and not you? I don't speak Korean."

Lyn was Chinese, but he was a polyglot. He spoke Chinese, Korean, English, and Japanese, which made him a damn valuable member of the SEALs.

"That's because you studied no other language."

"So why am I out here instead of you?" Widow repeated.

"Two reasons. First, you're expendable and I'm not. And second cause you can't shoot a sniper rifle for shit."

The other Team members chuckled around Widow. He shot them a stern glance, one for each of them. They all went back to being quiet.

Widow said, "Seriously?"

"Ten seconds. You'll see them."

Widow stared up at the top of the hill. He slipped a quick hand into his coat pocket and slid out a device that looked like a cell phone. Only this one cost about ten grand. It was a military device. Like a cell phone, it was also a multifunctional device.

He clicked on the home screen and thumbed to a photograph of what Dr. Kweon looked like. The photograph was dated. It was taken in the eighties—a close-up of a class photo. In order to learn the trade of nuclear weapons and technology, Kweon had to go outside of North Korea. He attended school in China.

The image was black and white. Widow had to tack on decades in his mind. But he had a clear picture of what Kweon should look like today.

Widow reversed the device and held it up and showed the photograph to Clery and Hollander and then to Slabin. They all took a look and memorized the face and nodded back to him when they each had it.

Widow took one last look at it, memorized it for himself, and slipped the device back into his pocket and returned his hand back to the MP5SD.

Lyn said, "Just repeat to them what I tell you. It'll be fine."

Widow stayed quiet.

Just then, he saw them.

Four figures climbed up over the snowbank. Panting and sweating and breathing hard, like they had been running for their lives, which they had.

First, Widow saw a tall figure. He checked his mind's photograph of Kweon and waited. After a moment, the tall figure came closer and into view. It was the father, Kweon.

He wasn't tall by nature. He looked tall because he was holding a young girl. A teenager. Thirteen. Maybe.

She was latched on to his back like she was playing a normal game of piggyback. Like they were a normal family at the lake. Minus the ice and snow and a six-million-man paramilitary stretched over the country behind them.

Widow studied the other members of Kweon's party.

He saw a woman, about five years younger than Kweon. She was his wife, the children's mother. He also saw a teenage boy, about fifteen—maybe. The boy was helping his mother. They were holding hands. He helped her climb the hill.

Widow saw them. He made eye contact with the father, who then glanced over the other SEALs. They ignored him and scanned the terrain around them for hostiles.

Widow called out the guy's name.

"Kweon bagsa?"

Kweon was the guy's name. And *bagsa* was the word for *doctor*. Widow knew that much Korean. Or he thought that was right. And Lyn heard him say it and didn't correct him. So he assumed he pronounced it all well enough.

Silence.

Widow repeated it. *"Kweon bagsa?"*

There was no answer. No response.

Widow raised the MP5SD, a precaution. He hoped. Clery, Hollander, and Slabin did the same.

Finally, Kweon called out to them. He asked, "American?"

Widow answered, "Yes."

"I am Kweon. This family," the Korean man said.

Widow nodded and lowered the MP5SD but didn't release it altogether. The other SEALs kept their guns up, not pointed at the Korean family walking towards them, but not pointed far away either.

Lyn said over the radio, "Sounds like he speaks some English."

Widow clicked the throat mic and said, "Affirmative, Chicken."

The Kweon family got close, within earshot. Kweon let the teenage girl slip off his back, then he asked, "What is chicken?"

He panted, but seeing Widow seemed to boost his spirits. And then the other three followed suit.

Their eyes opened like they had been wakened by shots of adrenaline right to the heart.

Their postures changed. They stood erect. And their shoulders straightened. The mother seemed ten times stronger.

She was the second one to speak. She spoke to the doctor in Korean.

Lyn came on over the radio. He said, "Get in closer. Press your mic button. I'll translate."

Clery, Hollander, and Slabin moved outward around them and guarded the perimeter. They kept their heads on a swivel, scanning the horizon and peering through the thick white fog.

Widow stepped closer to the Kweon family. He got about three feet away from the doctor and clicked his throat mic.

The mother continued speaking, and the doctor listened.

Widow studied them. The teenage girl moved closer to her brother. She squeezed his hand and stared at Widow with huge volcanic eyes. They were brown. And deep. There was a fiery quality to them. Like they were blazing right in front of him. Right inside of her eye sockets. Like swirling brown lava. Like the center of a hurricane at night. Circular and unrelenting and completely hypnotic.

Growing older, she'd have to deal with the local boys of wherever she ended up. They'd bust down her door trying to get her to go out to the creek or the fields or the abandoned railroad or the school after closing hours or the dying shopping mall or wherever kids hung out these days.

Her father was going to have a hell of a time keeping them in check.

Maybe Widow could give him pointers if he had to sit on them for several more hours until they could get the chopper to extract them.

He'd have to play it by ear. Not because of the North Koreans. But because of the Chinese. The Chinese had the technology and the know-how to catch the SEALs' Black Hawk on radar. Caution was required and would be taken.

The Pentagon would play it like they were running exercises out of South Korea. Apologize for inadvertently popping up on Chinese military monitoring devices.

Believable enough unless they were spotted on the ground.

Kweon said, "We all here. We ready to go."

Widow said, "I'm Lieutenant Commander Widow."

Then, Widow introduced the others quickly. Kweon glanced at them, but looked confused. He wasn't a military man. The designations meant nothing to him.

Widow said, "Just call me Widow."

Kweon offered a shivering hand, and they shook. Before he shook any of the other SEAL Team members' hands, he said, "We go now. They might be behind us."

Widow looked up and back—a long-held, innate instinct. Clery and Hollander reacted the same. Slabin kept his gaze on the rear, at the road.

Widow waited and stared at the horizon, behind the Kweons, past the frozen lake, and into North Korea. He paused in case there were troops rushing behind them. But he saw no one. No enemy troops. He saw nothing but white mist and snow.

"I don't see anyone," Lyn said in his ear.

Widow said, "Affirmative. Follow me. Stay close."

They turned and trekked back through the snow and over hills and across the ice. Widow led the way. Clery and Hollander took up the flanks and Slabin stayed at the rear.

Kweon said little about himself, but he did try to speak to Widow along their trek back to the road. Kweon had a lot of questions about where they were going and if they would be protected from their *Supreme Leader*. This was exactly how he said the man's title every time he mentioned it. Like a mustered-out Catholic making the sign of the cross every time he passed by a church, even though he had long since converted to atheism. Old habits die hard.

You can take the servant out of servitude, but not the servitude out of the servant, Widow thought.

They continued for another twenty minutes, but they were slow-moving, hiking only a mile across the snow and ice.

Halfway forward, Lyn came on over Widow's earpiece and said, "Scorpio."

"What is it?"

"The mother is limping."

Widow looked over at her. She was limping. The son was half-carrying her. And he seemed exhausted. Clery reacted first, but Widow put up a hand and stopped him. Widow gave him a signal to continue taking up the right flank. Then Widow slung his MP5SD across his back and offered to take over, helping her walk. The son was happy to let him.

Widow helped her walk for another half mile. The mother thanked him in broken English.

He smiled at her, and they continued.

"We go there?" Kweon asked. He pointed in the direction of the road up ahead.

"Yes. We go there," Widow said.

Kweon seemed half-scared of the road and half accepting that it was their destination.

He feared Chinese patrols. That was Widow's guess. They were almost as bad as North Korean patrols. At least the Koreans would've just shot them on sight. The Chinese had clear shoot-to-kill orders for illegals crossing the border, but they were more famous for trying to make a buck, which made the fates of any defectors worse.

Widow had been briefed on the corruption and illegal activity that occurred for most defectors who had been caught by the Chinese. They weren't known for their compassion for prisoners. Especially in that region.

Underpaid border guards had to make a buck. They were notorious for selling off the women to Mongolian sex traders. If they couldn't bribe the defectors to pay them to look the other way, and no sex traders were interested in who they had captured, then they'd just shoot them.

What if they caught a group of Navy SEALs extracting illegal aliens through their territory?

Widow didn't want to think about what would happen then.

The SEALs and the Kweons pressed on. They crossed around a frozen and overturned boat left abandoned in the river. The ice had twisted it and overturned it and captured it, where it would stay until the spring.

They followed a path beyond it. It led them the rest of the way. It wound and twisted until they stepped over the last patch of ice.

Widow saw Kweon breathe out. The breath came out cold and frosted. Widow said, "We're almost there."

Kweon nodded and smiled.

They approached the road, which was half-covered in snow and ice. Plenty of areas were shoved away by car traffic over the course of the day.

Widow looked both ways, a habit and a precaution.

He saw nothing in the gloom. No traffic. No headlights. Nothing but drifting fog and yellow vapor lights. He could see them for a long distance in both directions. They were above the low mist.

The lights shone hazy and bleak and high in the air.

Most of them were on. Many of them flickered and gleamed like extinguishing firebugs in the dark. Some spots where he expected lights to be were black.

The air was growing wet, like rain might come at any moment, or more snow.

He motioned for the SEALs and Kweon and his family to follow. He led them across the dark highway. Everything was still. Clery stopped on the road, faced the south, and watched for oncoming traffic. Hollander did the same to the north. And Slabin maintained the rear.

Widow saw the girl with the volcanic eyes look around. Not with fear in her eyes, but a kind of bravery. He recognized it. He had seen it countless times in the eyes of sailors and marines. Common among the military. Rare for a little girl.

The highway was like a road out of a post-apocalyptic future—the last road made by man to survive the inevitable nuclear war.

Vast sections of concrete exposed in the snow and ice were cracked and broken.

The trees on the other side were white and dead. They climbed up over rugged hills and down into valleys.

Widow looked in Lyn's direction, toward the highest of a cluster of abandoned structures. He couldn't see Lyn or Reyes in the dark. But he knew they were there. Lyn was behind the sniper rifle. And Reyes was his lookout.

Widow looked back at Kweon's face, which was frozen. His body was frozen. The boy had stopped. The girl with the volcanic eyes had stopped.

Lyn came back on Widow's ear receiver. "Truck! Truck!"

"Where?"

"From the north!"

Widow froze in place, looked north, and saw Hollander staring ahead. He had already seen it. Widow focused and tried to see it too. Then, he saw it. Faint headlights appeared in the mist. They were coming on. Fast.

"Got eyes on the driver?" Widow asked.

Lyn said, "Affirmative."

Widow asked, "A passerby?" But he already knew the answer. Lyn didn't need to tell him.

Widow knew because after he saw the headlights, he saw blue and red lights rotating from a police light bar.

CHAPTER 15

"Military," Lyn said.

Widow hand-signaled to the SEALS and the Kweon family to stop in their tracks. The SEALs responded first. Everyone froze. Clery kept an eye on the south. Hollander aimed his weapon in the direction of the oncoming headlamps.

Widow stayed quiet. The other SEALs stayed quiet. The Kweon family stayed quiet.

No one moved. They were frozen in place, like the countless dead people in the frozen waters behind them.

Widow waited.

The vehicle was headed right for them. Maybe it was two or three klicks away.

Widow asked, "Headcount?"

Lyn said, "Can't tell. More than one."

"Okay."

Lyn said, "Back! Get back!"

Widow waved the other SEALs and the family back off the road and into the snow and ice, back toward the river.

The Kweons may or may not have understood the words, but they understood the urgency.

The son took the mother and helped move her away. The father and the daughter followed close behind. Widow stayed in the back. He waited until they were out in the darkness, then he waited behind, five meters out of earshot.

Lyn said, "We can't get compromised here."

Widow said, "I know."

"I should take them out. If they stop."

"No. Sit on it. I repeat, observe only."

Silence for a moment, and then Lyn said, "Affirmative, Lieutenant."

Widow looked back at the family. They were behind a snowbank. Slabin stood back to their rear and Clery guarded them from the south. Hollander was further to the north, watching the moving vehicle, awaiting Widow's orders.

Widow remained on the road, watching, waiting. Then, he turned and ran toward the family and the SEALs. He blazed through the snow and dipped down behind a dead tree stump. It was frozen over, like everything else.

Widow sat back against the icy, lifeless wood and called out to the SEALs over his throat mic. He said, "Guys, stay back and down, but stay frosty. We have to protect the Kweons at all costs."

Each SEAL responded by clicking their throat mics as acknowledgement of the order.

Widow was the closest to the road. He kept himself between the Kweons, his guys, and the headlamps. He watched the oncoming vehicle's lights. The blue and red lights strobed and grew larger in the mist. The beams vapored and washed over the road.

The vehicle was coming on fast. The slipstream echoed and cracked in the wind. The tires rolled and crunched on the pavement. The engine thrummed in the silence.

Lyn said, "Ten seconds."

Widow clicked the MP5SD to full auto. He pulled the bandana up over his mouth and nose, in case he was spotted. A white man in northern China on a guarded border would be more easily identifiable than the abominable snowman, despite having painted black camo on his face.

He waited and breathed slowly.

The vehicle approached.

Lyn said, "Five seconds."

Silence.

Lyn said, "They're slowing."

Widow whispered, "Shit."

Lyn said, "They're stopping. Side of the road. One on the dial."

Widow stayed quiet. He pushed off the stump and faced the direction of the headlights. He peeked around the stump.

The vehicle was a Chinese police SUV. It was ancient but well maintained. Some kind of Mitsubishi, Widow figured.

The vehicle brakes hissed and the tires skidded slightly in the snow. The police vehicle came to a complete stop. The engine idled. Widow didn't hear the driver slip the gear into park. But he heard the passenger door open. He heard voices. They spoke Chinese. It was too far from his throat mic for Lyn to pick up what they were saying.

It didn't matter anyway.

Widow understood the context. They suspected something in that vicinity.

There were maybe thirty miles of abandoned highway along the frozen river.

Did the North Koreans call them? Widow wondered, but he had no idea.

Lyn said, "Two. Three. Four guys. All armed."

Widow stayed quiet.

Lyn said, "Three on foot. The fourth is still in the cab. Behind the wheel."

Widow glanced at Clery, who was the closest SEAL to him. He raised his MP5SD and aimed down the sights at the vehicle ahead of Widow. But stayed hidden. Widow glanced at Slabin and Hollander. They nodded at him. They were ready for anything. Widow looked at the Kweons. He saw the girl with the volcanic eyes peering from over the snowbank. She looked right at him. Pleading. Afraid.

Then her father appeared behind her. Low down. He put a hand on her shoulder and whispered to her—a comforting word from a concerned father.

Widow was struck with wonderment about what it must've been like to live under North Korean conditions.

He imagined it was horrifying.

Widow returned his gaze to the parked police vehicle. He pulled the MP5SD up, slipped his finger into the trigger housing, and readied himself.

Widow called to the others over his throat mic. He said, "Clery, Slabin, and Hollander, you guys stay down. Keep the Kweons safe. The mission is to get them out."

Clery said, "Sir, we can take them out together."

Widow said, “Negative. Stay on mission. The mission is the Kweons. Not me.”

Hollander came on the mic. He said, “But, sir…”

Widow interrupted him. “That’s a direct order. Keep them back. Don’t engage unless absolutely necessary.”

The SEALs went quiet.

Lyn said, "Lieutenant, they're drawing weapons."

Widow heard it. Right then. All sidearms.

Lyn said, “Wait. One of them just took out a rifle."

"What kind?" Widow asked.

The Chinese police are good, but they have old military ordnance, especially way out in the rural areas of the huge country, like this stretch of road. Some of their rifles and weapons were the same ones they had carried for five decades or more, unless these guys were special units, which was why Widow had asked about the rifle.

Lyn said, "It looks like a QBZ-95."

Not the ideal answer, but better than something else. The QBZ-95 was a bullpup-styled assault rifle. It was effective in the right hands. Widow assumed that if only one guy had it, then he was the right guy for it.

Widow asked, "What else?"

Lyn said, "The sidearms are all revolvers."

Widow breathed a sigh of relief. Not intentional. Just by instinct. Chinese police with revolvers meant they were front men or beat cops. Basically. Although, these guys might've been a little higher up the food chain than ordinary foot patrolman. They were still assigned to the border, which meant they were a little better than the average rural cop. They also could've been some kind of highway patrol equivalent.

Either way, it was better than going toe-to-toe with special units.

Widow said, "Lyn, keep your scope trained on them."

Lyn said, "Roger."

How did they see the Kweons? All the way out here? Widow wondered.

They had crossed the frozen river. In the dark. In the thick mist.

Widow glanced back out over the river. He saw faint light. Maybe two miles away. Nothing was coming their way. Not a truck or a helicopter or a snowmobile. There were no North Korean patrols or vehicles of any kind. There was nothing back across the frozen river.

All Widow saw were the same rural lights that had been on for most of the night.

He assumed they were border security lights.

Lyn said, "Widow?"

Widow said, "Yeah?"

"The SUV is backing up without the three guys."

Widow waited. He scooted up to the stump and peered an eye through a crack in the top. He saw the SUV and saw the three men. They stood out in front of the SUV in a triangle formation. The front man had the QBZ-95. They looked in all directions. They were definitely searching for something.

The men were thirty-five yards away. The SUV was ten yards behind them.

Suddenly, the point man called back to the driver. An order. Clearly.

He was the leader, which could've been good or could've been bad. Chinese military and police were notoriously corrupted. If he was the group leader, Widow could conclude two reasons for him to have the assault rifle. One, he was the best with it. And the best in combat, which was why he was designated with the better weapon.

Second, he possessed a superior weapon because he was the guy in charge. A simple case of outranking the other three. And therefore, he got to pick the deadliest weapon.

Widow took a peek at the revolvers. They were basic nine millimeter weapons. Small. Almost dainty. He couldn't recall their designation. A fact he wouldn't want to admit to Lyn or the others.

He knew Norinco manufactured them. They were Chinese-made and cheap. It wasn't an opinion. It was a fact. They were terrible firearms.

But they fired bullets effectively enough. That was all that mattered.

Widow couldn't help but wonder if they would work in the extreme cold.

He wasn't planning to find out. But he was ready to find out, if necessary.

Just then, the orders that the leader barked at the driver became clear.

The SUV had a standard door-mounted spotlight on it.

The light came on. A bright beam coned and spotlighted a big area. It was a small light. But in the vast flatness of the frozen river's surface and emptiness, the spotlight might as well have been mounted on a Black Hawk helicopter and been ten times the size. It was quite effective.

The beam was everywhere. Even in the early morning hours, it did the job that the sun couldn't against the mist.

The point man called out into the gloom in Chinese. Widow pressed his throat mic. Let Lyn listen in.

Widow listened for a long minute until he realized the guy was repeating words. Widow picked up that the guy was repeating the same commands over and over.

Widow asked, "What's he saying?"

Lyn came on over his ear mic and said, "He's calling out to them. He wants them to come out, slow, and to turn themselves in. Then he promises they will be safe."

Widow said, "That's what we didn't want to hear."

Lyn said, "It gets worse."

"How?"

"He used their full names."

Widow was quiet for a long second. He listened to the repeated Chinese commands. Then he heard it. Right at the end. The commander said, "Kweon."

Right there.

Widow muttered, "Shit."

Lyn heard it over the throat mic and said, "Yeah. Shit. Lieutenant, they know who the Kweons are."

Widow stayed quiet.

Lyn asked, "Think they know about us?"

"No way. We'd be surrounded by Chinese paramilitary by now."

"They could be on their way. Maybe they got a warning about the escape from the North Koreans."

Widow took another look back. The frozen river. The snow. The gloom. The far-off lights.

Maybe, he thought.

Lyn said, "What do you want to do?"

Widow didn't know. The second to last thing he wanted to do was engage with members of the Chinese military. But the last thing he wanted to do was get captured by them. Undoubtedly, they'd be imprisoned for espionage and never seen ever again.

Giving up wasn't an option. SEALs don't give up. And they wouldn't outrun them. Not out here on the ice.

"Widow, they're moving in."

Shit, he thought.

Kweon looked up over the bank at Widow. And the girl with the volcanic eyes did as well.

Widow signaled for them to get down.

Lyn said, "I can take them. Should we engage?"

Widow said, "Not yet." And he backed onto his feet and stayed low. He looked back. He looked right and looked left.

No choice. They'd have to take the Chinese police down. The only other option was to make them give up, which was not likely.

If he and the SEALs engaged, maybe they could wound them. Leave them alive. But even that seemed unlikely. In the special operators' world, one dead foreign adversary was as good as ten or twenty or five or four. If they killed one, they already crossed the line of engagement. It didn't matter to the Chinese government how many they shot. One dead was as good as a hundred dead.

The thing that mattered at that point was leaving witnesses.

"Lieutenant?" Lyn asked.

Widow asked, "You got clean kills?"

Lyn paused a short beat and said, "Affirmative."

Widow said, "Take out the point man first. Then light up the others. I'll go for the driver."

"I've got them."

"Go."

There was a loud *crack!* It was the gunshot from Lyn's sniper rifle. The sound was muffled by the suppressor. Even without the muzzle flash and the full sound, the muzzled shot echoed over the trees and the snow and the ice. It must've carried on to the edge of North Korea and beyond.

Widow leaped out from the side of the stump just in time to see the point man's head explode into a red cloud of brain and skull and bone. An eyeball burst forward and blew out of the guy's head, like it had been flung out of a slingshot.

The body collapsed forward and slid down the snow. Blood sprayed everywhere.

The two standing soldiers looked stunned.

Shock and awe.

They looked at each other. Fast.

Widow had expected them to turn around toward the gunshot and stare at the trees or the abandoned structure. He expected them to pinpoint the origin of the sniper that killed their leader. A natural thing to do for any person—soldier or otherwise.

But they didn't look. They didn't search for the sniper. Not in the first and last seconds of their lives.

They didn't look at Widow either. They must've sensed he was there. The spotlight from the vehicle was bright. It shone in his direction like it was waiting for him to leap out.

But they still didn't look in Widow's direction. Instead, they stared at each other.

Widow knew what they were doing. Each was looking at the other to see if they were in agreement on what to do next. They were thinking about giving up. Their leader was the head of the snake and he was dead.

Against their training. Against their SOP. They were already considering giving up. Obviously.

Widow hated to shoot unarmed men. Taking prisoners was out of the question. And he couldn't leave witnesses behind. *No witnesses* was SOP for covert engagement. That was clear. These guys had to go.

Better to do that now rather than give them false hope of survival.

Widow aimed the MP5SD at the SUV. He squeezed the trigger, took out the spotlight. It exploded. Glass shattered and sprayed in tiny fragments across the Mitsubishi's hood.

Widow saw the driver react. He raised his hands to cover his face. He knew what came next.

Widow shot him in the face.

A look down the iron sights. A brace of his feet. A held breath. And a squeeze of the trigger. Three rounds sprayed out. One after the other. Fast.

The windshield exploded and shattered, leaving behind three gaping holes. Glass spider-webbed in cracks around all three. And red mist and blood filled the space in the vehicle where the guy's head used to be. He was dead. Instantly. No question.

The two remaining men turned fast, towards Widow. They raised their revolvers, but not to give up. They raised them to fire back.

They realized they wouldn't get the chance to surrender. They realized it was a take-no-prisoners kind of situation.

They aimed at Widow.

They had no time to squeeze the triggers because right then, the head of the guy standing on the north side exploded. Less than a second later, maybe a half a second later, the next guy's neck exploded. Both were thrown forward off their feet.

One.

Two.

The same muffled *crack!* echoed and rattled, and rang out over the trees, over the snow and over the ice. The echo tapered off somewhere behind Widow.

The north guy's head was gone. But the revolver was still gripped tightly in his lifeless hand. Index finger on the trigger. A fraction of a second away from squeezing it.

Widow had a split-second fear that he still might fire it.

The south guy had let go of his revolver. It slid down the snow and stopped on a patch of ice.

The guy gripped his neck.

Widow walked over to him and stared down at him.

Terror hadn't filled his eyes yet. Mostly he still looked like he was in the shock-and-awe phase, just before he realized he was a dead man.

Widow readied his weapon for a mercy shot to the head. There was no reason to leave him to suffer. But it was unnecessary because the guy stopped staring at Widow. He stopped clutching the huge bloody hole in his neck.

He was dead. Blood seeped out and blanketed the snow. It left a macabre image of crimson red over paper white snow.

Lyn spoke into Widow's ear.

He said, "Better check the driver."

Widow looked up. The driver's side door was still closed. The red mist was still settling over the headrest.

He looked back at the SEALs and the Kweon family. They stayed hidden. Clery stood up and started to edge out of hiding like he wanted to join Widow before he went any further. Clery wanted to back Widow up, but Widow threw up a hand and gestured him to stay where he was. Clery nodded and stayed put.

Widow turned to the SUV. He walked back up the river bank and up the hill and onto the highway. He looked both ways: north and south. There were no new headlights, no sirens, and no flashing light bars.

Widow checked the misty horizon. Both north and south. No signs of helicopter beacons or drones. He looked east and west. Same thing. No sign of any kind of backup. Not yet.

He stared into the SUV driver seat. Then he gripped the throat mic. Widow said, "The driver's dead."

Lyn came back on and said, "We're all clear from up here. I see nothing."

For the first time, Reyes joined the conversation. He said, "There's no enemy radio chatter, boss."

Widow said, "Come on down. Both of you, and meet us. Bring the gear. We gotta get out of here."

Lyn said, "Affirmative."

Reyes repeated the same response.

Widow dropped the MP5SD to let it rest in the sling behind his back. He opened the SUV's door and reached in and grabbed two handfuls of the dead driver's police uniform. He hauled him out—all the way. The legs came out last.

Most of the guy was still in one piece.

Widow turned the dead guy over and grabbed him from behind. He dragged him, shoulders first, off the road, down to the river. He dumped him down the bank and watched the dead guy roll down the hill like a bag of rocks.

Then he called out to the other SEALs and got Clery and Slabin to help him. He ordered Hollander to stay with the Kweons and keep them from coming out. He didn't want the children to see what he'd done. No need to give them nightmares.

Widow, Clery, and Slabin made their way to the three sniper kills and did the same to them as Widow had to the driver.

Widow wasn't concerned with burying them or hiding them in a hole. Leaving them just off the highway out of view was good enough. He and the SEALs and the Kweons would be up in the air and out of there in twenty-five minutes, Widow figured.

By the time Widow and the other two were done disposing of the bodies, Lyn and Reyes had shown up on the road. Lyn's rifle was in his hand. He held it down in a safe trail-carry position. Reyes carried his MP5SD in the safe trail-carry position also.

Lyn walked past the SUV, up to Widow, and patted him on the bicep, congratulating him. A gesture used by SEALs all over the world. Reyes did the same to Widow's other bicep.

Widow said nothing.

Lyn said, "Nice work, Scorpio."

"Back at you, Chicken."

Reyes moved on to join the others in the snow, off the highway. He introduced himself to the Kweons.

Lyn remained on the road with Widow a beat longer. And then he nodded and walked over to the edge of the highway, leaving Widow standing there to stare to the north in the direction the Chinese police had come from. The road was dark and quiet.

Lyn kept his rifle in one hand and used the other to wave out into the gloom. He shouted something in Korean to the Kweon family.

A moment later, Clery, Hollander, and Slabin emerged with the Kweons in tow from out of the mist. They came up out and around the dumping ground for the four dead soldiers. The Kweon parents kept their hands over the children's eyes while they passed the dead.

The SEALs went first, then the father led his family. He climbed up the edge of the highway first. Lyn helped them. He held his free hand out to help bring Kweon up. Lyn repeated the same gesture with the daughter and then the boy. He had to step down a little farther to help the mother up onto the highway. Reyes helped. Clery, Hollander, and Slabin scattered around Widow and around the police vehicle. They checked out the vehicle and the surroundings.

Lyn spoke to the mother in Korean.

He said something about medical attention, Widow figured, because he started inspecting her like a combat medic doing a quick once-over as he would for a wounded soldier.

Afterwards, Lyn said something else to her in Korean. Then he offered her help, and he helped to guide her up the edge of the highway. They all gathered in front of the lights of the SUV.

Widow joined them.

Lyn made introductions in Korean. He introduced each of the SEALs, and himself and Widow last.

The girl with the volcanic eyes glared at Widow, a bit of terror in her eyes. He could only imagine how he appeared to a child. She was maybe five feet tall and weighed less than a hundred pounds, maybe ninety pounds soaking wet.

Widow was six foot four. But he weighed more back then. He was in the Navy, on the SEALs team, and had to lift regularly. And he had to eat a lot. He had a lot of gym-muscle mixed with real-world muscle. He might've been pushing two-forty to two-fifty, all muscle, all heavy muscle.

The girl moved back out of the light. She hid behind her father, who joined his wife to speak with Lyn and the others.

Lyn noticed the girl's uneasiness when looking at Widow. He spoke to her in Korean as well. She stared at Widow and whispered something to Lyn. Using context alone, Widow was certain she had a compared him to some kind of Korean bogeyman, like the American Bigfoot.

Lyn laughed out loud and pointed at Widow. The other SEALs joined in on the laughter, even though they had no idea what she was saying. Lyn bent down and whispered to the girl with the volcanic eyes.

She giggled and stepped half out from behind her father. She looked at Widow and said a word, but she said it in English.

The girl with the volcanic eyes said, "Chicken."

CHAPTER 16

Twelve years later, Widow woke up in the passenger seat of the Air Force Humvee secured to the bed of a Lockheed C-5 Galaxy.

He squinted. His vision was still iffy.

The Humvee and the plane and the surrounding cargo rattled as the plane changed its flight pattern to a descent. He heard the landing gear crank and lower. It resonated throughout the plane until he was sure the plane was coming in for a landing. He braced himself.

The engines were louder just before the plane's wheels hit the concrete. The Lockheed C-5 Galaxy was on the ground seconds later.

It landed on the edge of an airstrip at the Royal Air Force base of Lakenheath. Which he had guessed was where they were landing.

Tiller unbuckled, and his two guys followed him. He moved to the cargo space and told Widow to come out.

Widow unbuckled, stepped out of the Humvee.

They left the C-5.

The jet wash from the slowing engines breezed through Widow's hair. No big deal. His hair was short, but Tiller was a different story. His hair was thicker than the brush he must've used in it. Widow was amazed at how much it blew around and, yet, whipped right back where it was after he distanced himself from the C-5.

They walked twenty-five yards away from the landing spot and met a local airman in another Humvee. This one blue, like the last. But this one seemed smaller, lighter, thinner. Widow figured it wasn't armored as heavily, which made him wonder where the other one was headed. He figured it must've been slated for Iraq to continue the fight with ISIS or to Syria to help the rebels, all while pretending not to be fighting the Russians when actually they were basically fighting the Russians there.

The airman was a staff sergeant. His nametape said Meter, which made Widow think of the British measure close to a yard. But the staff sergeant introduced himself, pronouncing it *met*-er. Not *meet*-er.

Tiller introduced himself and Widow, and no one else. Not his guys. They didn't complain.

They piled into the Humvee, Tiller in the front passenger seat, Rosencrantz and Guildenstern on the window seats in the rear bench, Widow squeezed in the middle, crammed like a sardine in a can. He didn't complain. His arm hurt. His head hurt from the air pressure. He was feeling jet-lagged, even though he'd slept on the plane. And he felt double jet-lagged because he had part of the nightmare of the memory of twelve years ago, and he had been ripped out of it.

He stayed quiet.

Meter drove them out to the front of the base, where

they stopped in at the main office. Tiller got out alone and met an Air Force officer who stayed too far away for Widow to see his rank or name. But he was sure the guy was an officer in charge of something. Maybe the base. He knew that because the guy walked like an officer, stood like an officer, nodded like an officer, and shook hands with Tiller like an officer. All of which was a bureaucratic nature and demeanor. Widow had seen it a million times before. Perhaps he was a guy who had started out with ideas in his head and love of country in his heart, but over years, he had gotten swallowed up and beaten up and molded and transformed into the system's version of a good military citizen, someone who goes along to get along. Not a boat rocker. A simple yes-man.

Widow didn't care what they were saying, but he could imagine it was something about their being there. And a lie about their goals and another lie about where they were going.

After words were exchanged, Tiller walked back to the Humvee and dumped himself down into the front passenger seat. Meter drove off, took them to the main gates. He drove through and nodded to the guards, who were already expecting to see them come through—a prearranged phone call from the bureaucratic officer, no doubt.

They drove out of the gates and onto the main streets. They drove for thirteen more silent, uncomfortable, sardine-squeezed minutes before Widow spoke.

He asked, "Where are we going now?"

Tiller spoke, didn't look back. "We're going to the airport."

"We just left the airport."

"That's a military airport. We need to fly commercial."

Widow didn't ask where they were headed. He already knew. He dreaded another flight, even if this one was a shorter trip than the last two.

After fifty-nine minutes of driving the English countryside, partially suburbs and partially cityscapes, they arrived at Norwich International, where Tiller had everything already prearranged, as a CIA agent often does—part of why Widow never trusted him. Constant preparation at his level of operations equaled a man who planned, schemed.

They got through ticketing and local security. Tiller gave Widow a boarding pass, which read, "Cork, Ireland," as the destination. He was in economy class with one guy. Either Rosencrantz or Guildenstern, he still didn't know which, and he still didn't care.

He got a window seat this time and got comfortable and stared out the window, hoping to see one of his favorite views out of all the flight paths he had seen, the greens of Ireland. He knew he wouldn't be able to because it was night outside. He wondered what time it was. He had lost track of time from the flight from Minneapolis to Andrews, the international flight from Andrews to Lakenheath, and now another flight from Cork.

Plus, he had lost his wristwatch. He pictured an orderly back at St. Mark's Memorial Hospital finding it and keeping it. It's an occupational hazard.

The last captain he had flown with had mentioned the time in an announcement. He was an Air Force pilot. No need to mention it.

Widow shrugged to himself in his seat. Rosencrantz or Guildenstern, whoever, looked over at him as he did it.

Widow moved the fingers on his left hand, felt pain in his broken arm under the cast from the movement. Then he turned, stared out the window at the night stars, not the green views he had hoped for, but he was satisfied with them.

CHAPTER 17

The woman from Beijing told Lu what to do, and he did it. Why wouldn't he?

She waited in the car in the back alley behind Cathery's Pub.

Everything was as green as Ireland was famous for. All the clichés of the local dialects were there. All the clichés about the men and the drink were also apparently something they took literally.

Lu went into the pub alone. No backup. She was his backup, but he wouldn't need it, she figured.

She heard a crackle of thunder in the sky. She leaned forward from the passenger seat of a rented black two-door Lexus, made by Toyota. Not the official choice for a person in her position in her line of work. Not something that she'd advertise back home in Beijing.

Her coworkers wouldn't approve. After all, they were Chinese, and it would embarrass them to have one of their employees renting a Japanese car. They weren't fans.

She figured they wouldn't care because there was no other option on the lot that was Asian. And Lu wouldn't say a word about it, not to her.

Just then, lightning flashed. She saw it. High to the west. A jagged flash cracked and spider-webbed across the sky, lighting up the gray from copious cloud cover. Then came a thunderclap, echoed by rumbling.

The rain came next. It started as a drizzle for about ten seconds, and then it was a full-on downpour. The drops bounced off the windshield. She looked over at the keys hanging in the ignition where Lu had left them. He had left the engine running. He had left the headlights on. She sat in the passenger seat. She leaned across the seat and the console, reached around the steering column, and clicked the switch for the wipers. They fired on and wiped at a medium pace. The water cleared for fractions of a second and then returned and cleared and returned. It repeated in a predictable pattern. Soothing. In a way.

She sat back up and heard gunshots—two of them.

Cathery's Pub was not open yet, naturally. The time was too early in the day. It wasn't an all-night establishment. Although she figured it could've been. All the other clichés about the Irish had been proven in her mind.

She looked back and around. Saw no one coming. No one heard the gunshots. And if they had, they'd ruled them out, chalking them up to thunder.

The back door to the pub, right there at the top of a flight of stone steps, one o'clock from the hood of the Lexus, came slamming open in a single violent arc, like someone had kicked it open from the other side, which was almost true.

What actually happened was that Cathery himself came flying out the door.

He rolled and bounced off the bottom step. He rolled again on the dirt and cobblestone in front of the car. He stopped right in front of the car, about a yard in front of the grille.

He got up slowly on one knee. Then on both.

The woman from Beijing saw blood on his face. He had taken a beating. Nothing too serious. Nothing fatal. Nothing hospital-worthy. Not so far. Outpatient maybe. That's all. His nose was broken. That was obvious. It was black and blue and gushing blood. One of his eyes swelled.

Lu appeared behind him, standing in the doorway, top of the steps. He looked both ways up and down the side street. He saw no one watching. No one was coming.

He had a Glock 17 in his hand, held down low. Smoke exhausted out of the muzzle.

She decided it was time to get out, play her role, play good cop, only without the cop part, which would've made both of them dangerous, deadly, not to be trusted.

Hopefully, Cathery wouldn't figure that part out.

She looked up at the pouring rain and looked to the side of the pub near the stone steps. There was an awning, but it was too high and far from Cathery to be an effective interrogation point. She was going to have to get wet. She looked around the car's interior and checked the footwells in the front. She checked the back seat and smiled. Lu had brought an umbrella. She grabbed it and got out.

She popped the umbrella and stood under it.

Rain drops sounded over the top and echoed underneath the umbrella's dome. She walked out in front of the headlights.

Cathery was up on both knees. Face bloody but not serious. He could talk. He could answer questions.

"Who are you?" he asked and spit blood, far. The projectile hit her shoes.

She looked down and sighed. Guess good cop was out.

She raised her boot, like she was inspecting it, and in a swift, vicious blow, she kicked him right in the same broken nose.

If it hadn't been all the way broken before, it was now.

The remaining unbroken bones in it snapped and cracked and split. The sound was loud, like a habitual knuckle-crack in a dead-silent church. It was so loud that the woman from Beijing looked around instinctively for more thunder.

Cathery grabbed at his face and howled in pain. "What the hell do ye want?" he shouted.

Lu walked down the steps into the rain. He circled around Cathery like a predator.

"I dun told ye that I don't work for the Chinks anymore."

Lu tapped the guy on the top of the head with the Glock's barrel. A hard tap. The sound was audible, not the metal-on-skull sound one would expect to hear, because the Glock 17 was constructed mostly out of a hardened polymer, but it was loud enough.

"Mr. Cathery, that kind of talk isn't necessary."

Lu brushed the barrel of the Glock against the guy's ear. A reminder, in case he forgot the last one, that there was a gun present. A reminder that he had already fired it into the guy's ceiling—twice.

The woman from Beijing said, "I'm not here for the matter of unearned wages that you took from my government, and that you, so far, haven't held up your end of the deal. In fact, I don't even know exactly what they would want with a flatfoot like you."

He stared up at her.

"What I want to know, which I'm sure that Lu has asked you already, is about a stranger."

"The only strangers here, lass, are you!"

He spat more blood in defiance. But not on her boots. He had learned that lesson, which meant that he could learn. That was good. That was going to keep him alive.

She said, "Mr. Cathery, if you don't cooperate, I'm going to have my associate shoot you."

"You won't do that. This is Ireland. You can't get away with that here."

The woman from Beijing laughed. "Of course I can."

"No way, lass. If you shoot me here, you better kill me here."

She smiled at him, bent down, stayed out of grabbing distance. The umbrella came with her. The whole move was a dramatic thing. She knew that, but these things were about shock and awe. He had gotten the shock part. Now it was time for some awe. Theatrics.

She said, "What do you think I meant when I said he was going to shoot you?"

Cathery said nothing.

"He'll shoot to kill. We don't waste time. We don't have time to waste. You don't tell me what I need to know, we'll just shoot you dead. No problem. You think the Gardaí will give a shit? They'll find your dead body out here in the trash. And when they do, they'll search your pub and discover that you're an arms smuggler. They'll think you were killed in a deal gone bad. That's all."

He stayed quiet and spat more blood. Not at anyone, just out on the ground. "What do you want?"

"I told you. A stranger bought a weapon from you."

"I don't sell to strangers."

"You must've. You're the most prominent arms smuggler within fifty kilometers."

"A hundred," he corrected her, smugly.

"A hundred. You must know who it is."

"I didn't sell to any strangers. But might've been one of my guys."

"You already know who I'm talking about. Don't you?"

Cathery's thin hair was soaked. The rain ran the blood down off his face. "It'll cost you."

She looked back at Lu, who nodded.

"It'll cost me? It'll cost you if you don't tell us."

"Come on, lass. I'm a businessman. I can't give up one of my guys without some form of compensation."

Selling out a colleague isn't an Irish stereotype, but a common criminal one, she thought. "Give me the name, and I'll make it worth your while. Fair enough?"

"Reestablish the payment arrangement I already had in place with your people?"

"That's a done deal. But I tell you what; I'll get them to give you some business."

"They'll buy some weapons from me? China looking to expand into Ireland?"

She chuckled at the thought.

"No, Mr. Cathery. China's not looking to expand into Ireland or the UK or Europe. We're already here."

He said nothing to that, but a look of fear of something

too big for him to understand washed over his face. "One of my guys sold to a Chink...er...sorry, one of you."

She said nothing.

"It must be what you're looking for. It was a big order. Expensive. Unusual.

"When?"

"A long time ago. Maybe a month. Less than two."

"Why so long?"

"I got me ways. But I ain't a miracle worker. And this guy asked for a miracle weapon. It's a specialty item. High profile. I told him it was going to be impossible to get it. I tried to get him to settle for a local piece. We got plenty of varmint poppers out here."

"He had the funds?"

"Oh yeah. He had a stack of green. He paid up. Right then, at the beginning. No half now, half on delivery."

"You said your guy dealt with him?"

He nodded.

"Sounds like you dealt with him."

"No. Not me. Malcolm described the situation to me. Gave me the money already. Of course. He's a good lad. One of my finest."

"Where is this Malcolm now?"

He paused a beat, didn't want to give him up.

"We won't hurt him."

Nothing.

"You know we can find out with or without you."

Cathery nodded and told her where to find him.

"You'd better not warn him when we leave."

"I won't. I don't want him to know you got it from me. Hell, I was gonna go check on him."

"Why?"

"I haven't heard from him."

"How's that?"

He shrugged, said, "The last time I spoke to him was when he picked up the item. Haven't seen him since. Been a week."

She looked at Lu, who stood still, Glock pulled in to his chest.

"What was the gun?"

"It's a sniper rifle called Valkyrie."

"Valkyrie?"

"Yeah. It's an American thing. Really nice. It completely comes apart into several pieces within seconds."

"It disassembles that fast?"

"Yeah. When it came, I thought originally that I had gotten the wrong item. Because it was packed inside a backpack."

"A backpack?"

"It was designed to go in a backpack. The bag had a place for everything. And it changed calibers on the fly."

"On the fly?"

Lu looked at her and said, "He means fast."

She nodded.

"The whole thing is quite impressive. A rifleman could carry it around, and he would look like a normal guy on the street. Could be a college student. Could be full of books."

The woman from Beijing nodded along.

"Of course, I had to press for extra money when I saw it. 'Cause who'd want a weapon like that?"

Assassin was the word that came to her mind. "Did you get the extra?"

"That's why I was going to visit Malcolm today. He's not answering his phone. And he owes me that money."

The woman from Beijing stood up straight. She looked up and down the street. She had no more questions—no more use for Cathery.

"Kill him," she said.

"Wait! What?"

Lu stepped forward and put the Glock to his head. Cathery felt it on the bald spot on his scalp.

"Wait!" he said again.

"Yeah?" she asked.

"Please! I told you what you wanted to know!"

She turned to return to the car. She paused in front of the lights. She turned back, looked down at him, and asked, "Did you see us here today?"

"No. No. I ain't never heard of ya."

She looked at Lu, back down at Cathery.

"You gonna call Malcolm? Try to warn him?"

"No. No. I swear. Besides, he ain't answering. Remember?"

She said something to Lu in Chinese. Then she turned back to the car, closed the umbrella, and got in. She slammed the door and waited.

Lu said, "Close your eyes."

Cathery held his hands up in the air. They shook. He shut his eyes. He repeated the Lord's Prayer. Not on purpose. He was a good ten words into it before he realized it.

He kept his eyes closed and felt the rain beat down on his face.

He waited to die. But the bullet never came. Death

never came. He heard tires on cobblestone. Then he heard another thunderclap.

He waited a long minute. He opened his eyes and saw they were gone.

He finished the prayer anyway.

CHAPTER 18

Fifty miles away, an hour earlier but twenty-one minutes late pulling up to the gate, Widow, Tiller, Rosencrantz, and Guildenstern stepped out of a short hallway leading to the gate and the Cork Airport, which Widow had never been to before and never wanted to come back to again, simply because it was already tainted with hauling around two overpaid bodyguards and one CIA agent he still wanted to blacken an eye on.

Tiller had a carry-on bag on wheels that Widow hadn't noticed before. Rosencrantz and Guildenstern both had messenger bags. All three guys wore black suits—no ties among the three of them.

They must've changed during the flight. He was certain Tiller had. Probably in the bathroom on the plane up in the front in first class.

"Come on," Tiller ordered all three men, including Widow. He noted it.

They walked through the airport, past baggage claim, beyond the ticket counters, past signs for car rentals and shuttle buses and a string of guys holding signs for pickups.

Tiller led them straight out to the arrivals and pickups like he had been there before. He walked like he was at home at this airport. He walked like he was in his element.

Widow noted this, too. He chalked it up to the fact that Tiller wasn't known to anybody here. He probably was in his element because he was a literal stranger. Widow could understand that since he had always been undercover, always leading a double life, once upon a time.

It was thrilling.

That had to be what it was.

Tiller had a grin on his face.

Outside in arrivals, they had to cross a catwalk with moving walkways going both to and away from the airport. Passengers were riding them, standing still. There were half as many walking along the regular concrete parts.

Widow wondered if Tiller had used an app on his phone to get them a ride, like Uber or Lyft. He had seen people do that.

When they got to the other side, they ended up in a parking structure, but Tiller stopped on a pass-through stretch of blacktop.

There were cars parked, waiting to pick up people.

Tiller looked left and looked right. He didn't see what he was looking for. He put his hand up and stepped over to Widow.

He said, "We'll wait. We got a ride coming." He looked at an expensive stainless steel watch on his wrist, just poking out of his jacket sleeve. "Five minutes."

They waited.

Eleven minutes passed, not five. A black, polished, and freshly waxed Range Rover drove up an entrance ramp, pulled around several parked cars and cars going the slow speed limit, and jerked to a stop in front of Widow.

The first thing he saw was police light bars, hidden and embedded under the grille guard at the front and under the front plate, and smaller versions around the inside front wheel wells.

Undercover police vehicle. No question.

The driver's side window was tinted and black and virtually impossible to see into. It rolled down. The front passenger door opened, and a big guy stepped out. He stared at Widow from over the top of the vehicle.

The driver was a woman. She spoke in an Irish accent, not too thick. "Tiller?"

"Yep."

"You're with us. Get in." She buzzed her window back up.

The big guy walked around and offered his hand for everyone to shake. He was maybe an inch shorter than Widow was, but beat him out by twenty or thirty pounds. All solid. All muscles.

The guy had small scars on his face. They were combat wounds. That was obvious. This guy had been in a brawl or two or ten. The scars looked like broken bottle gashes. Nothing hideous enough to scare the common man away in fear, but enough to tell a mugger to think twice before trying him as a target.

His hair was buzzed down to a jarhead fashion. He could pass for a Marine, but he wasn't. He looked more Irish than a shamrock, and tough enough to be as hard as an actual rock.

He introduced himself as Gregor. There was no indication if it was the last name or a first name. There was no "Mc" on the front of it, like Widow would have expected.

Gregor popped the cargo space in the back and helped Tiller stuff his bag back there. Rosencrantz and Guildenstern kept their messenger bags on them. Which made Widow think they might have weapons in there. He shook off that thought. No way did they get firearms past security in the airports.

Probably not.

Widow approached the back door, ready to pick his spot in the Range Rover, but Tiller grabbed him by the arm.

"A quick word," he said. He released Widow's good arm and stepped away from the vehicle and onto the sidewalk, a good fifteen feet out of earshot of the others.

Widow said nothing about the arm grab.

Tiller spoke in nearly a whisper. "Remember, we're not here to help them. They're here to help us."

"You don't want me offering intel to them?"

"Of course not."

"What if they're keeping things from us?"

"You think they are?"

Widow nodded, said, "I would. They want to catch this guy. Four guys sent here from the American government, they're going to know we know more than they do."

"Be helpful without being helpful."

Widow said nothing to that.

Tiller turned and went back to the Range Rover.

Widow got in the back, behind the driver, Tiller next to him. Tiller's guys had to pile in behind them in a third, uncomfortable row. They were crammed back inches from the rear door. Widow was grateful to have gotten in before they had the chance to order him to get in the back.

He couldn't see the driver. What he could see was that she was tiny. She had her seat pulled up, probably on the last bit of track. She was virtually on top of the steering wheel.

Widow saw her eyes in the rearview mirror. They were solid blue and bright, like the afternoon sky.

Her hair was thick, pulled back in a no-nonsense ponytail. She wore a brown leather jacket. Widow couldn't see her pants or shoes. He saw a pair of sunglasses folded and left on the dash in front of her. She stared at him in the rearview mirror.

"Mr. Tiller?"

"That's me," Tiller said.

"I'm Nora-Jane Cassidy from Gardaí Special Investigations. This is Gregor."

The guy named Gregor craned his head and looked back. First at Widow, then Tiller. He nodded hello to both.

Tiller introduced only himself and as a state department attaché, which was a typical label for a CIA agent in a foreign land. Like a signal that said, *Don't ask*, to official members of local government.

Gregor picked up on it right away. Maybe he had run into an American attaché before. He turned right around and lost interest, or he was feigning the loss of interest because, like Widow, CIA agents left a bad taste in his mouth.

Cassidy had no experience with the CIA, nor did she pick up on the alias.

Widow saw her eyes light up. A question furrowed her brow.

Cassidy had said she was Gardaí, which was the national police for Ireland. It stood for *An Garda Síochána*, which meant "Guardians of the Peace." Rough translation. Widow wasn't sure if that was the exact Gaelic meaning. For all, he knew it meant "Guardians of the Galaxy."

It was the Irish version of Scotland Yard, only better, any Irishman would argue. They would prefer a comparison to the FBI, only rolled in with Homeland Security. But they'd still argue that the American FBI and Homeland Security would never compare to the greatness of the Gardaí.

The Irish have always had a "we take care of our own" attitude. And for their neighbors in the United Kingdom, they held a "deal with it yourself" attitude. They didn't like outsiders meddling in homeland affairs. In America, the only thing comparable in Widow's mind was that he was from the South. And the South was like that, in a way.

His mom had been a small-town sheriff in Mississippi. He remembered that her department enjoyed handling things in-house. There was no need to call in the state cops or the FBI, not unless it was clearly a matter of regulation.

Texas was also like that.

The big difference was that the Irish had been like that for thousands of years. During WWII, they remained neutral, even though their neighbors were getting bombed.

Cassidy's cop interest in Tiller was showing, but she remained professional. Sort of. She said, "You must be important, Mr. Tiller. Our bosses told us to cooperate fully with you. He said you might help us with our investigation?"

"Maybe. I need to know what I'm dealing with first."

"As far as we know, we got one dead Brit named James Lenny. We sent you the crime scene photos."

"We need to see everything. Hopefully, we'll catch this guy."

"Where are we going first?" she asked.

Tiller looked at Widow.

Widow leaned forward and said, "I'd like to see the video."

Cassidy finally turned around in her seat. The seat belt wrenched with her, and she stared at Widow. He saw her for the first time. She had pale skin, smooth looking. Her lips stood out against her skin's backdrop. They were pink and not too full. Her cheeks were high, as if powerful bones were carefully placed underneath. She was a good-looking woman, right up there out of all the women that Widow had ever seen in his life, but at the tip-top of all cops he had ever seen. She looked like she had missed her calling to be a movie star instead of an inspector for the Gardaí.

He realized at that moment that she was Gregor's superior because he had a struggling look on his face, like he wanted to argue with her, only he couldn't.

Cassidy said, "What video?"

Tiller looked at Widow with the same question on his face.

"The videos, actually. As in more than one. Two, I figure."

"What video? Mister…?"

"Widow. Jack Widow, ma'am. Nice to meet you."

He offered his right hand up and over the console for her to shake.

She stared at it, hesitated for a long second, and then shook it. "And who are you, Mr. Widow?"

"Me? I'm nobody. Just the poor guy that the CIA dug up to solve this thing."

Tiller looked at him with anger on his face that almost felt as good to Widow as when he had punched him.

"The CIA, huh?"

Tiller stayed quiet.

Widow shrugged and said, "What difference does it make? We're offering to help, in exchange for your help."

Cassidy shrugged and said, "I've been ordered to escort you around."

"You mean you've been ordered to take us for a ride?"

Gregor said, "That's what we're doing."

"I mean, take us for a loop. You know? Give us a brush off? Take us around and show us nothing."

Cassidy smiled. Gregor said nothing. And Tiller looked away.

"What videos do you want to see?" she said.

Widow said, "In the photographs you sent us, there are dents in the dirt. Lenny was trying to recapture his glory days. Trying to hit his old shooting record."

She stared at him.

Those blue eyes, he thought. He couldn't imagine a lot of men telling her no. Just with those eyes alone, she'd get far ahead in her organization because every time she interrogated a suspect, she'd get her way. It didn't matter if she was dealing with a man or a woman. No one could resist her.

"You think he videotaped it?"

"I know he did. He used cameras up on tripods, and they're missing from your photographs."

Cassidy smiled again. She asked, "Who are you again? You're not CIA."

"I'm not. Just these guys. I was a special investigator of sorts."

"FBI?"

"Military, ma'am."

"DIA?"

"Something like that."

"If you're not DIA, then some kind of special unit in the Army police?"

He thought for a moment—no reason not to tell her the truth. "NCIS."

"NSIS?"

"N-C-I-S."

"And what's that?"

"Navy version of the FBI."

Gregor said, "Like on TV?"

Cassidy looked at him.

He shrugged.

She turned back to Widow and asked, "You want to see the videos? Fine. There's not much extra there."

"I want to look anyway."

"You got it."

And that was all that was said.

Cassidy took her foot off the brake, and they left the Cork Airport Business Park, went through security exit checkpoints, and swooped off Avenue 2000 and onto the N27, a national primary road in Ireland. They stayed on it for a straight shot that curved every so often until they arrived on Eglinton Street at the Gardaí's Special Investigations Unit office in Cork.

Cassidy went through the police security gate and

signed in. The guard insisted on taking a peek into Tiller's bag and the messenger bags of Rosencrantz and Guildenstern. He looked through and approved everything.

Cassidy waited for the guard to punch a button near his window to allow a garage door to open. He waved them through, and they drove down a steep ramp into a garage. She parked the Rover in a slot near the front of the motor pool, like reserved parking, and they all climbed out.

Cassidy was short. Only Widow had been mistaken about how short because he saw her boots were lifted a bit by two-inch heels. She walked in them like she was born with the extra lift, natural.

The boots were tucked underneath a pair of blue jeans. They were faded, no holes. Her age was a mystery. She looked twenty-five, tops, but her rank in a male-dominated field told a different story. Widow watched as she passed the police and fellow inspectors. Everyone showed her nothing less than the respect of a four-star general, everything but the saluting.

He figured four years of university, another five to ten on the job, so she must've been thirty-three to thirty-five.

Gregor noticed Widow staring at her a little too long and shot him a glare.

Widow looked away.

Maybe they were a thing? he thought. *Maybe not. Maybe theirs was just a typical partnership, close to each other.*

Gregor was a big guy with plenty of battle-worn features. Widow figured he might've spent his off-hours in the ring instead of lifting weights in a gym. The guy had a jaw of iron. No question. It looked like if someone threw him an uppercut, his jaw would absorb it and return it to the guy with a hearty laugh.

They walked down corridors and up a short flight of stairs and stopped at an elevator. They took it up two floors. Only Rosencrantz and Guildenstern couldn't follow. The lift wasn't wide enough for all of them to fit. Tiller ordered them to wait in the station's lobby, which was fine by Widow.

They got off the lift and followed Cassidy down another hall—all of it covered in a dreary, gray carpet—to a big corner office. It was shared among four agents, at least.

Two other inspectors sat at desks facing the far wall. The office had a huge set of windows overlooking the east part of Cork. The view comprised a fork in a brown river, a pair of bridges, and a major roadway that was not quite a freeway, like the thousands that Widow was used to traversing.

Cassidy sat in a swivel chair at a neat desk pressed up in the corner against a window.

She spun around and pulled an extra chair up to the desk. She said, "Sit down." She was speaking to Widow.

"Me?" He looked at Tiller.

"You're the investigator."

Widow shrugged and dumped himself down on the seat. It sank under his weight. The wheels were hard to maneuver over the carpet.

He managed, and pulled up close to her.

She keyed the keyboard on a laptop. And it came to life. She took another thirty seconds, clicking through notifications and opening her email browser and thumbing through it for an email she had copied to someone else. Maybe Gregor.

She found it, pulled it up, and clicked on a file. "Here. Look. You're not gonna learn much."

She scooted back a bit and gave Widow room. He grabbed the lip of the desktop and pulled himself forward. The wheels struggled over the carpet.

Tiller saw one of the other inspectors get up and leave his desk. He walked over, took the chair, and pulled it up behind Widow so that he could see the laptop screen.

He didn't ask permission. Cassidy said nothing.

Tiller said, "Go on."

Cassidy reached over and clicked the play button on the video player.

The video started out with Lenny in front of the camera. He had just set it up and clicked the record button.

He wore a hunter-green camo Castro hat and camo pants to match, and a black T-shirt under a dark canvas jacket. A pair of sunglasses sat on his face, covering his eyes in a black tint.

He looked into the lens. Then he stepped around the camera, out of the video. Widow heard sounds of clicking and brushing like his jacket scraped the mic.

The camera's view twisted and moved and faced a plot of grass that was flat from having something laid out on it before.

Lenny came back around the front of the camera. He took off his sunglasses, folded them, and put them into a case.

He knelt on one knee and stared into the camera. Widow saw blue hazel eyes. There was a lot of pain in them, like a man who had lost himself. There was a hint of alcoholism there, too.

Widow had seen it before. Bags under the eyes, stress and pain and a battle to hold back tears, all present, all at once.

Lenny spoke to the camera.

His voice was gruff and worn and strained, like someone who had been recovering from years of smoking hard.

He gave a date, a time, and said his name and last held rank. He said he had been a corporal of horse in the cavalry. He had been an elite sniper. He mentioned his kill record. He mentioned how he had held it for ten years until it was wiped out by some "bloody moose lover."

He claimed that the new record had been a fluke, a joke, an insult. He explained it had beaten his because it had been fired from a high elevation. He talked about how because it was from a mountaintop, fired over a hill, plus the curvature of the Earth's surface, all made it an impossible shot. It was so impossible that it had to be a one out of a million, maybe more, maybe one out of a hundred million. He argued that, therefore; it was only made because of sheer blind luck.

Widow looked over at Cassidy. "How long does he go on like this?"

"I don't know. Five more minutes maybe."

"Let's fast-forward."

Cassidy nodded and reached forward. Widow had to sit all the way back in his seat for her to reach across him. He felt her jacket scrape across his forearm.

She clicked the fast-forward icon and had to stay outstretched across him in order to stop the video.

Widow watched the screen. He saw Lenny reverse his hat, leave the camera, return with a rolled-up sniper mat. He watched Lenny flap it out and lay it down flat. He placed the sunglass case on the edge of the mat. Next, he came out with a box of ammunition, opened one end, and set it down on the mat. Lenny went out of frame again, and then he returned with a rifle, an L115A3 sniper rifle, the same rifle from the photographs in the slide back at Andrews.

Lenny set the rifle up on its bipod and got down on the mat. He took cap covers off the scope and got into a prone position.

Several long minutes later, he had set up the sights on the scope. He got up off the ground several times, moving out of frame.

Tiller asked, "What the hell is he doing?"

"Setting up his shot," Cassidy said.

Tiller said, "Why's he leaving the frame?"

Widow said, "He's using a spotter scope. It's behind him."

Tiller asked, "Why would he do that?"

"Snipers are like weathermen, only more accurate. They record everything. Every piece of data. And they love numbers. He's adding up winds and distance and geometry of the range. He's setting his scope up accordingly."

"Can he do that without an actual spotter to help him?"

Widow didn't look at Tiller. He said, "He's doing it."

Finally, Lenny got down prone. This time Widow noticed he had brand-new boots.

"When's he gonna shoot?" Tiller asked.

Cassidy said, "This time."

Widow saw Lenny turn his feet out, arches flat in the dirt.

Lenny looked through the scope, slowed his breathing, his heart rate. Widow looked at the clock on the lower part of Cassidy's laptop screen. He counted the seconds.

Lenny squeezed the trigger.

The gunshot *cracked!* It was so loud the mic rattled, and they heard basically nothing but crashing static. Then they heard it echo across the landscape and die down to nothing.

Lenny moved his head away from the scope, some irritation in his body language. He seemed to curse to himself.

He'd missed his target.

Then he reacted to something he saw. He stared back through the scope at something. He took his head away again and looked over the rifle to something in the distance. He moved his finger away from the trigger and looked back through the scope.

That's when it happened.

Widow watched.

Tiller gasped.

Cassidy did nothing.

Lenny's head exploded.

CHAPTER 19

They watched a red mist mushroom around the mess after Lenny's head and the eyeball side of the scope exploded; then the head fell back against the scope and the mist settled to dust and nothingness.

Tiller was covering his mouth.

Cassidy reached forward to turn off the video.

"Wait," Widow said.

She stopped, said, "There's not much else."

"We don't see the killer?"

"Here. Watch." She let the video play.

It played for a long time. Widow saw a dark figure come into frame. It was someone short, a little below average, but taller than Cassidy.

All he saw was below the shoulders. The killer was dressed in all-black—black canvas pants, shirt, and jacket, a black strap on his shoulder.

He watched as the killer stopped and stood beside the bloody remains of Lenny. Then the killer stepped over the body. A bit of a struggle. He stepped close to the camera lens, and then the video went to black.

"He covered the lens," Tiller said.

Widow looked at the video time. It was an hour later.

He asked, "There's nothing after this?"

"No. Just a black screen."

Widow asked, "What about the other camera?"

Cassidy smiled at him. "Other camera?"

"The other camera."

"How did you know?"

"He's trying to prove that he broke the new record here. He's not just going to have one camera pointed at him shooting and not another one synced to the target."

Cassidy smiled and clicked and tracked on the trackpad until she pulled up another file in the same copied email.

A new video played on the screen.

Widow watched.

This one was pointed at a watermelon staked on a pole.

Widow said, "Fast-forward this one."

Cassidy fast-forwarded it until Widow said stop. He had watched the timestamp on the top of the screen, waited for it to match the part where Lenny was killed.

They heard Lenny's shot. The crack. The echo.

Widow counted the seconds from Lenny's shot to the shot of the killer's bullet. They heard one after the other. The camera angle wasn't set up to see the sniper's shot.

Cassidy leaned in close again.

Tiller said, "That's where he died."

Cassidy said, "We'll get a quick glimpse of the sniper walking by, but there's no face."

"Why did you keep this video from us?" Tiller asked.

"I kept nothing from you."

Widow said to Tiller, "Quiet."

Tiller gave him a look like he was acting disobedient, which he was. Technically. But he'd never agreed to treat Tiller as a superior officer.

Just then, they all saw the killer walk back to the camera in a fast stride. Not running, but racing.

Widow asked, "Can we back up?"

Cassidy said, "You can do it yourself."

"It's your computer. I didn't want to touch it."

She reached over and rewound the video for him.

"Pause it. There."

She paused it.

"Can you back up a couple of frames? Till he's in view."

She backed up the video until the killer was in as good a view as he was going to be in. It was still blurry.

This time, Widow saw the same figure from before. No head visible. Just everything below the shoulder. He studied the image. All black clothing. Jacket. Pants. He assumed boots, but they were off frame in this angle. Maybe the guy wore a hat. He guessed with the sun that high, maybe.

Widow looked hard for a long minute.

Everyone stayed quiet.

He looked at the torso: medium build but probably lean underneath the clothing.

He looked at the waist. Generic black belt. Generic belt buckle. Nothing stuck out.

Then he looked at the guy's hands. Gloved. Black. Empty.

"Can you fast-forward to when he walks back to where he shot from?"

She said, "He never returns. Why would he?"

Twenty seconds later, he leaned forward.

"You see something?" Cassidy asked.

"I do."

"What?

He leaned back in his seat and turned to her, looked at her. "Tell me about the bullet."

"We dug it out of the dirt. The killer took the brass."

Widow nodded. He expected that.

Cassidy said, "It's a C round."

"I'm sure you made a list of all the rifles to fit that caliber?"

"Yes."

Widow moved his chair back. The wheels struggled against the carpet. He looked at her. "Who sold the weapon?"

Cassidy looked past Widow at Gregor. The military experience showed. He was the one with knowledge of firearms.

He came around and said, "We don't know who sold it. Lots of rifles can fire six-point-fives. Nothing particularly special about it."

"Who around here has the power to smuggle a specialty weapon in?"

Gregor said, "There're hundreds of illegal weapons smugglers here. This is Ireland."

"But who could get an illegal weapon? Something very rare?"

Tiller said, "He said there's nothing special about this bullet."

Cassidy said, "It could've been a legally bought weapon. You can get rifles here."

Gregor said, "With a permit."

Cassidy said, "Lenny lived out there in the country."

She pointed north. But Widow was certain that Lenny died to the west. In her office, the west was the wall. So she pointed north, out that side of the window.

Widow followed her and looked north. Probably a lot of backcountry there too.

Widow said, "Got any of these bullets lying around?"

"We got most of the one from Lenny's skull."

He shook his head.

"You must've bought a box of them. For comparison?"

"Of course."

"Can I see them?"

Cassidy looked back at Gregor and nodded.

He said, "I gotta get them. They're in the crime lab. I'll run and fetch them."

"No. I'll come with you. See them for myself."

Gregor looked at Cassidy for permission.

"No problem. We'll all go."

"Bring the laptop," Widow said.

Cassidy closed the computer and scooped it up. She tucked it under her arm, unintentionally pulling up the break line of the jacket. Widow got a quick glimpse at her service weapon. It had been her unintentional move to show it and his instinctual move to look for it.

It was a Walther P99C, a small nine-millimeter handgun for little hands or just for someone who wants easy concealment. Or both. It was compact, with all the standard configurations of the factory design—all the things you need in a concealed weapon and none of the things you don't.

The weapon was in a shoulder rig, light and well-tailored for her torso. The thing he noted above all else was that she was a left-handed draw.

Widow also saw her badge in a black wallet. One side of it was folded behind her belt, the side with the badge was exposed, facing out.

The badge was gold, with four-star points and four circles. It had writing on it, all in Gaelic. And he couldn't read any of it. But he imagined it matched the sign in the lobby near the elevator that showed she worked in the Special Investigations Unit.

Cassidy walked to the door behind Gregor and Tiller. She stopped, turned, and looked at Widow. "You coming?"

He stood up and followed behind. He took slow strides. He wanted to fall back and walk with her, a little out of earshot. "So, do I call you investigator or detective?"

"Does it matter?"

He shrugged. "To some people."

"Just call me Cassidy."

"What's your official title?"

"You couldn't read it on my badge?"

She had to crane her neck to look up at him. She said, "What? I saw you look."

"I don't read Gaelic."

"It's Detective Cassidy."

"Is it Mrs. Detective Cassidy?"

"Just Detective."

They caught up to Tiller and Gregor, who held the elevator door open with one arm extended.

They got on, rode down one floor, and got off.

The floor opened to one large crime lab. The words “Forensic Labs” were scrolled on the glass, separating many cubicles and lab techs and lab equipment, none of which Widow knew the names of, combined with office machines, all of which he knew the names of. The Navy loved paperwork, and the NCIS was even worse. He was grateful to have been in the field and not behind a desk for most of his Naval and investigation career.

There was no physical security in the lab—no armed guards. No standard desk sergeant signing in visitors, which made him realize he hadn't been given a visitor pass or identifying badge to begin with.

Maybe Cassidy just had that kind of pull. Maybe she was the woman in charge of her unit, like Rachel Cameron had been in charge of the unit he worked in once.

"This way," Gregor said. He led them around more glass windows and glass dividers and one long hallway. No glass there.

They ended up in a windowless room that looked more like a student study room in a university library than a lab.

At the center was a good-sized round table surrounded by chairs. At the center of the table was the same symbol he saw on Cassidy's badge. Same four-pointed stars. Same four circles. Same Gaelic.

He stared at the table and suddenly thought of King Arthur and the Knights of the Round Table. He wondered if any of them had been Irish.

"Take a seat."

Widow sat first, with his back to the only closed-off wall.

Tiller next and then Cassidy. She reopened her laptop.

Gregor left the room through a different door than they'd entered. He was gone a good five minutes. He returned with a box of ammunition and a rifle under one arm. The stock was wood. The scope was enormous.

Gregor set the box of ammunition on the table and slid it over to Widow and left his hand clamped down on top for a long second.

"That's the six-point-five."

Widow looked at the box. It was red with an illustration of a white-tailed deer on it. Packaging designed to call out to hunters to say, *This will get the job done.*

Gregor showed the rifle to them. It was a bolt-action hunter rifle. A German thing that Widow had never heard of. "This is an easy rifle to get here. It was bought easily. The previous owner got it with a license."

Tiller asked a needless question. "What did he do?"

Cassidy said, "He climbed up a bell tower in an old church. Shot four people. And then jumped off the roof."

Tiller said nothing to that.

Gregor said, "He saw it in an American movie."

Widow said, "This is a hunting rifle."

"So?"

"So Lenny was shot from two miles away. He wasn't shot with this."

"We don't know who sold the weapon to the killer. Or how the weapon got into the country. Or even if the guy bought it locally."

"You think he snuck it in?" Widow asked.

"No way!"

Cassidy said, "It's possible that he flew it in legally. Plenty of airlines will allow transportation of rifles with proper paperwork. He could've flown it into London."

"Come on. You guys checked all that stuff already."

Cassidy said nothing.

"Did you find a sniper rifle with that kind of range that will fire this bullet?"

"No. Nothing."

Tiller said, "Maybe he stole it locally?"

Widow said, "He bought it here. He must've waited for it for two weeks or maybe even a whole month."

Gregor placed the rifle down, butt on the floor. He sat in a chair next to it. He asked, "How do you know this for sure?"

"Why are you guys so confrontational about it?"

Cassidy looked at Gregor and said, "We just need to know."

Widow reached his hand out, pointed at the laptop. "Pull up the video from the watermelon again."

"It's still up now."

"Can you see the killer?"

"You know I can. Nothing above the neck. It's a black blur."

Widow said, "What's he wearing?"

"All black."

"Look at the frame."

Cassidy looked down at the screen.

"What's he wearing specifically?"

She studied the black, blurry figure again.

"A black jacket. Maybe canvas. Black shirt underneath. Black pants. I guess black boots."

"What else?"

"Nothing."

“Keep looking.”

"No jewelry. Nothing that distinguishes him from anybody else in Ireland. Not based on this video."

"Look carefully. Don't get lost in the exact details. Look for the normal."

She looked again, close.

Gregor scooted his chair over and peered over her shoulder. The rifle moved with him. Tiller scooted back and over around the table. He looked over her other shoulder.

He said, "Just tell us what we're looking for."

Another order, Widow thought. "Keep looking."

"I see nothing, Widow."

Cassidy said, "He's wearing a backpack."

CHAPTER 20

He returned to the Irishman who had sold him the weapon. A hard rifle to get in Ireland, but not impossible. Nothing was impossible to get if you know the right people and you have the right dollar amount.

He wasn't from Ireland. He was a foreigner. He was a foreigner every place he went these days. He wasn't returning to his own country.

That was impossible.

But he should've left the country yesterday, after. Any other criminal would've. But why would he? He had unfinished business.

There was more to do.

More people to kill.

He waited behind the trees at the top of a hill about fifteen yards from the old country road. That's when he saw a beat-up country truck coming down it.

The truck was an import, a white import, he liked to think. He distinguished it as white because it came from a

Western country and not from an Asian country. Not that he had a thing against Western countries. At least not in manufacturing.

A lot of machines with complicated mechanical parts came from Western countries like America. A lot of good stuff came from America.

This truck wasn't one of them. It was a German thing; he figured. It had a good engine sound, smart design, but was beat up. He could hear the springs rocking on the bumpy road from there. He could hear the gears grinding like the guy was switching them between second and third gear or first and second.

The truck was painted blue. It matched the front side of the driver's house. The house that was fifteen yards away from him.

The house was something he had heard described as a rock cottage. It was small and outdated. If he hadn't seen outside lamps posted below the roof, he would've pegged it as a house straight out of *Lord of the Rings,* like a hobbit home.

He didn't know which movie he had seen. He only knew it as *Lord of the Rings*. The copy he had seen was a bootleg. He saw it well over a decade ago in his home country.

The truck slowed, the gears ground, the tires stopped bouncing, and the driver looked around and pulled into the driveway, which was in better condition than the roadway. He pulled the vehicle all the way up, like he was expecting someone else to come home and park behind him.

A girlfriend maybe?

Maybe the guy was expecting a hooker to pay him a visit.

The Foreigner waited, crouched down, stayed out of sight. He took off his backpack, set it down, and unzipped the main compartment. He reached inside, past the disassembled Valkyrie rifle, and grabbed a Heckler & Koch USP. He took it out. It was stuffed in a holster. He drew it and clicked the safety to fire.

He closed the backpack and strapped it on his back.

He waited.

The driver of the blue truck parked the vehicle, killed the ignition, and slid out.

The door squeaked behind him.

He walked to the back of the truck and looked around. He stretched and yawned. He had been up all night, driving back along a six-and-a-half-hour drive from Ballyhillin, a town at the northern tip of Ireland. He had spent the last several days there fishing, drinking, and taking in the scenic terrain. It was one of his favorite spots in Ireland to fish. This time of year it was cold, but not as cold as six weeks earlier.

Mostly, he liked it because there was a little-known brothel there where he could get a lot of bang for his buck. And he had just made a lot of bucks lately off the sale of two high-end rifles from America.

The Foreigner walked down the hill and stopped. He saw a figure approaching up the driveway.

The Irishman saw her, too.

He paused by the tailgate of his truck, where he kept a backup shotgun for unwanted visitors.

The girl walking up the drive was young.

She looked younger than the girls he knew from Ballyhillin's brothel. And she was definitely not like them. They were all Irish, and she was not.

She stood five foot one, maybe. She had a nice walk, like a strut that he had seen before. Probably in the brothel. He saw it as an invitation.

What the hell was a girl like her doing way out here?

He took a street cap off his head, an Irish gentleman's acknowledgment of a lady.

"Can I help you?" he asked, with politeness and sensitivity in his voice and his demeanor, but not in his intent.

She had long black hair, jet black. She had nice eyes. Her clothing was standard Irish country garb. There was a jacket for combating the wind, comfortable black pants, good hiking shoes, and a dark shirt under the jacket. She also had a shadowy wool cap to keep her head warm.

She wore no makeup. But she didn't need it.

She spoke in fluent English, which he hadn't expected.

"Hi."

"Hello."

"Are you Malcolm?"

She knew his name.

He looked around and placed his right hand on the lip of the truck's bed, just above the tire. His shotgun was under a tarp, right there. It was already loaded, if he needed it.

"Who are you?" he asked.

"I'm sorry. My name is Sarah," she lied.

"Sarah?"

He hadn't expected that name. It was probably an alias, or just plain fake. Her real name was probably something too hard for people in Ireland to remember.

She nodded. "And who are you? Are you Malcolm?"

"Why?"

"You look like Malcolm. I was told he was a very handsome man who lived here."

"Who sent you?" Malcolm lowered his right hand, slowly, down into the bed of the truck to the edge of the tarp and the shotgun.

"I was sent by Cathery."

Malcolm stopped going for the gun. He looked at her with a puzzled expression.

"He says you deserve a bonus." She smiled at him in the way the girls at the brothel in Ballyhillin did.

"A bonus?"

"He says you do good job. He says that your big client loved the merchandise and paid him bonus. So he sent me."

"You?"

She stepped closer to him. She opened her coat and reached to the bottom of a black shirt underneath and pulled it up.

He saw her stomach. It was flat and tight, a combination of abs and just being a thin girl. Then he saw the bottom of her bra. It was white and clean.

She said, "Bonus. For you." She smiled a big smile, bigger than the girls in the brothel in Ballyhillin.

"A bonus," he said, and he smiled.

She lowered her shirt and gestured that they go inside.

Malcolm didn't argue.

He led the way. Left his truck unlocked, no reason to

lock it, not way out here, anyway. He left the tarp where it was. He left the shotgun where it was.

They walked into his hobbit house, and he closed the blue door behind them, locking the dead bolt.

Thirteen minutes later, the girl unlocked the dead bolt.

The Foreigner stood near the truck. He looked around in all directions.

He saw no one.

Malcolm's closest neighbor was a mile away.

The Foreigner walked to the door. He didn't wear gloves. No reason to. No one was going to identify him from his fingerprints. He had never been fingerprinted outside of his own country, and they shared nothing with the outside world.

And he had no need for a suppressor on his sidearm, not way out here.

Out here, people shot guns all the time.

He felt the doorknob. It was cold to the touch. He leaned in close to the door, close to the blue-painted wood, and listened.

He heard low voices, low giggling, a female voice, mostly—the girl's voice.

He grabbed the knob and opened the door, and went inside. The blue door closed softly behind him.

Malcolm's house was small and tight. The Foreigner could've ejected a bullet from the USP and probably hit the refrigerator with it from the living room.

The furniture was old and grimy, like hand-me-downs

from his great-great-grandparents who might've been peasant farmers. Not much had changed.

The tiled floor was crisscrossed with white-and-black patterns.

The Foreigner crept through the living room over to an opening that led down a short hallway. He heard the girl giggling louder.

He heard her speak a foreign language, foreign to Ireland. His language.

She called out his name. She said, "Are you here? Now is the time."

The Foreigner took three steps, stepped into the open doorway to a bedroom, where Malcolm sat on the edge of his bed, and the young girl was on her knees.

"Bloody shit! What the hell are you doing 'ere!" Malcolm asked.

The Foreigner raised the USP, pointed the muzzle at him.

"Oh, no! No, man!"

The Foreigner smiled, squeezed the trigger. Once. Twice. Three times.

He'd triple-tapped the Irishman.

Malcolm's chest burst open. Three holes exploded, a triangle pattern where his heart was. Blood exploded and sprayed everywhere like blood-packed squibs. It was the short range.

The girl turned on her knees, like she was begging for her life. She stood up.

The Foreigner could see blood splatter across her face and bare chest.

The Foreigner smiled at her.

Slowly, she smiled back.

CHAPTER 21

"What does a backpack have to do with anything?" Tiller asked.

Widow said, "What does the bullet tell us?"

Cassidy said, "It's common."

Gregor said, "Long-range."

Widow asked, "What else?"

Gregor asked, "Untraceable?"

Widow asked, "What else?"

Gregor shrugged.

Cassidy said, "It had to be fired from a long-range rifle."

Gregor said, "That could be any kind of rifle."

Widow asked, "What does a long-range rifle have to be?"

Cassidy and Gregor looked at each other. No one spoke.

Widow said, "Long."

Cassidy looked at him like she was a kindergarten teacher looking at a student full of smart-ass answers.

Widow said, "This sniper is good. Really, really good. So he knows his rifles. He knows his ammunition."

Cassidy said, "Okay."

"It also means that he's a snob. He's an elitist. An elitist would never use an instrument that was beneath him. He wouldn't use a hunting rifle. No, the weapon we're looking for will be unique. And expensive."

"I'm not following you. What does that have to do with the bullet?"

"Nothing. You guys are focused on the bullet. Why should you look at the rifle?"

Gregor started to say something, but Cassidy put her hand up, pulling rank. She said, "We look at the bullet to match it to the rifle."

Widow said, "That'll never work. Most bullets for sniper rifles can fit multiple guns. You'll never find this kind of weapon that way."

"What do you suggest?"

Widow shrugged and said, "Just look at the rifle."

"How?"

Widow raised his hand, pointed at the laptop screen, at the frozen black figure on the screen.

"There. Look at it. Directly."

They looked at the screen again.

Cassidy said, "Where? There's no rifle."

"Look at his hands."

"I am. They're empty."

"So where's his rifle?"

Tiller said, "He set it down and went back for it."

"No. He didn't. Cassidy already said that he never goes back."

Cassidy's face lit up. She got it. She understood his point. "A snob."

They all looked at her.

"An elitist sniper like him would never leave his rifle behind in the dirt."

Gregor said, "So where is it?"

Widow said, "It's right there. In the frame."

"It's in the backpack," Cassidy said.

Widow nodded.

"He never goes back for it because he already took it apart and set it inside his backpack."

Tiller said, "That backpack is thin. How the hell did he do that?"

Cassidy said, "It looks light. Too light for a rifle."

Widow looked at Gregor.

Gregor said, "It's possible."

"It's not just possible. There's an American company that's already done it."

Cassidy asked, "Would it still fire that far?"

"Sure. It's partially about the caliber, the bullet, and ninety percent the talent behind the rifle."

He had a sudden memory flash. Maybe it was caused by the concussion. Maybe by the man they were after. He went for the pills and the bottle. It was another fumbling with the lid until he swallowed more pills and put it all back into his pocket.

The pills didn't stop the memory flash. Not right then. It came on quickly and left quickly. It was just a flash.

He saw the volcanic eyes again. He saw blood. He saw smoke.

He heard radio chatter in his head. Then it was gone.

He said nothing about it to them.

Cassidy asked, "Who makes this rifle?"

"I don't remember the name of the rifle. But I've seen it before. They were only working on it last I checked. Which was years ago."

"The name of the company?" Gregor asked.

"Nemesis. They probably have a website. Purchase to order. Shipped to your door."

Gregor said, "Only in your America."

"One thing that makes us great."

Cassidy clicked on the trackpad and typed on the keyboard and waited.

"Here," she said and rotated the laptop so that the screen faced Widow.

He looked at it. She had googled the name Nemesis and had gone to their website. This time Widow didn't hesitate. He scrolled his fingers across the trackpad, touching her fingertips briefly. He searched the website for their rifles. It looked as if that was all they made, that and tactical backpacks.

He found the only rifle it could be—their most expensive offer. Just to hold the rifle in his own hands would've cost him five grand.

Gregor let out an exclamation that sounded like "Oh, boy," only it was half in English, and the other half, Widow guessed, was thick Irish.

Cassidy said, "Valkyrie sniper rifle."

The gun had a designation after it, but she didn't read it out loud.

Gregor said, "That's an expensive rifle."

There was a video thumbnail at the center of the page. It led to a YouTube video of the rifle in operation. Widow clicked and played it. The video was short. It showed two guys, American, talking about the rifle. It could change calibers on a dime. It was super lightweight. They claimed all in about ten pounds, with a suppressor.

They showed it assembled, loaded, and fired. Then they repeated the process backward—unloaded and disassembled. They took it apart and set it into a black tactical backpack that could've been the same one the killer carried. It would be unnoticeable in a crowded public square or an airport or a live event or a university campus.

Cassidy said, "This weapon is legal in America?"

"All weapons are legal in America," Gregor said.

Widow stayed quiet.

They weren't wrong.

One commentator on the video said that the Valkyrie took only seconds to put together and to disassemble. Widow counted, and the guy wasn't lying. It wasn't exactly short seconds, but the whole thing could be set up in less than two minutes in the hands of the right operator. Maybe even less than a minute.

Widow stopped the video, went back to the video of Lenny being murdered, and watched it. Then he studied the time stamps. He played the other camera angle from the target, watched the black figure go by again. He studied this time stamp.

He sat back and calculated the timestamps, the time to disassemble the rifle and place it into the backpack and then calculated the yards from the point of the shot to the target, factored in that it took a long time to walk the twenty-seven hundred yards. He used the speed it looked like he was walking and made some rough estimations.

Cassidy said, "What?"

"It took the killer forty-one seconds to take the rifle apart, put it in the bag, and walk across this camera."

CHAPTER 22

"Now, tell us who can get this rifle in-country?" Widow asked. "Who would the killer go to for it?"

Cassidy looked at Gregor. The former military. The unit's gun expert.

Gregor said, "The man to get this in Cork would be Cathery."

"Who's he?" Tiller asked.

"He runs a pub at the end of town."

What end? Widow thought.

Cassidy said, "He's the biggest smuggler within two hundred miles."

Widow asked, "Why is he still operating?"

Gregor said, "We haven't been able to touch him."

Cassidy said, "He's got connections to The Cause."

Tiller asked, "The Cause?"

Widow looked at him.

"The IRA."

Cassidy nodded.

"That'd be the one. He's connected."

Gregor said, "Not highly connected. Just enough to keep his nose clean. As long as he doesn't give us any reasons."

Widow nodded. It was the standard balance found in any ecosystem. Every community on the planet had one. There was crime and there was order. And there was always a balance.

Cassidy said, "If the killer used the Valkyrie, that's the man who would've gotten it for him. Let's go see him."

Tiller stood up and said, "I need to use the bathroom or the toilet or whatever you call it."

Gregor nodded and said, "I'll show him. Meet you downstairs."

They all stood up. Cassidy closed her laptop and tucked it under the same arm as earlier, revealing the same Walther P99C in a shoulder rig.

Widow watched.

Gregor escorted Tiller out of the room, down the hall, and to the men's toilet.

Widow followed Cassidy out of the lab and out past the corridor and the glass and to the elevator.

"Let's take the stairs up."

Widow nodded, and they went up the stairs to her office.

The office was empty. They walked in. Cassidy set the closed laptop on her desk and spun around. Widow stayed in the doorway. She walked toward him, stopped at the center of the room.

"You're not one of them," she said.

"One what?"

"One of them."

Widow stayed quiet.

"Be honest, Widow."

Widow stayed quiet.

"You're not with Tiller and those other two guys."

"I came with them. You picked me up at the airport."

"You know what I mean. You're not with the CIA."

"How d'ya figure?"

"You don't look like a CIA agent."

"What does a CIA agent look like?"

She took a breath and said, "Tiller." She paused. "He looks like a spy. Not you."

"I'll take that as a compliment."

Cassidy said, "It is one. Spies don't look like James Bond, you know. Not in real life. James Bond is handsome, dashing, suave. There's nothing suave about Tiller."

Widow said, "I think that's the point. He's not supposed to be memorable."

Cassidy said, "But he is. He's not repulsive, but he's on the same street in a douchey way."

"Douchey? Is that right?"

Cassidy said, "Yeah, like he dresses to impress, but it's all cheap and inauthentic, like a car salesman. He's slimy. He sticks out because he throws his weight around like he owns the place. And he doesn't really give a shit about helping us catch this killer."

I'm not here to help you either, Widow thought. "He's corporate. That's all."

She nodded. "Yeah, he's corporate. He's just a suit."

Widow nodded, said, "You know Bond wasn't originally supposed to be dashing either."

"How's that?"

"Take his name. James Bond."

She stayed quiet.

"It's a plain, forgettable, common name. James Bond. Could be anybody. That's what Ian Fleming intended. He wanted Bond to be a superspy who was forgettable, unnoticeable. A chameleon. Because that's what you gotta be."

She stepped closer to him, closer to the door. She stopped about a foot from him. "Forgettable name, huh? Like Jack Widow?"

"That's my real name."

"Sure it is."

"It is. Given to me by my own mom."

Cassidy nodded and reached past him, switched off the light. She brushed his chest with her hand, on purpose. "Let's go."

Cassidy led him out of the office, down the hall, and back to the elevator. They rode down to the motor pool, where Tiller and Gregor were waiting, but there was no sign of Rosencrantz and Guildenstern.

Tiller and Gregor waited near the same parked Range Rover that Cassidy had used to pick them up at the airport.

Widow stepped over to Tiller and stood there.

Cassidy said, "Where are your guys?"

Tiller said, "They're going to meet with us later."

She shot him a look.

"We'll catch up to them later."

She shrugged, and they got in the Range Rover and took off out of the motor pool.

CHAPTER 23

The Foreigner and the young girl walked out of Malcolm's hobbit house with his keys and stepped over to his truck.

The Foreigner walked to the bed of the truck, just over the driver's side tire. He reached in and fumbled around, and found a shotgun. He took it out. It was a Mossberg, no stock. He pumped it twice, ejected a shell. Buckshot.

He reloaded the shell and checked the rest. Then he took the gun into the cab of the truck with him. The young girl opened up the other door and climbed in and shoved a tool bag and a bunch of paper out onto the driveway. She sat down and slammed the door.

The Foreigner smiled at her and slid the Mossberg down in the footwell between them.

"Can I listen to the radio?" she asked in a foreign language.

He responded in the same language.

"Of course."

He smiled at her, and she leaned in and fumbled with

the old radio knobs until she found a station that worked. It was Irish music; she guessed. She continued until she found an American country music station. She left it there.

He looked at her.

"I like this music."

He shrugged, started the engine, and backed out of the drive.

"Where to now?"

"We've got another loose end to take care of."

"Does it really matter?"

"Yes. When you're good at something, you have to act professionally."

"But is it professional to kill the guy who sold us the gun we needed?"

He nodded. "It's more professional to protect your identity. We can assume the cops are onto us now. No reason to leave them witnesses."

"Shouldn't we wear gloves then?"

"No need. Our fingerprints won't show up anywhere."

She nodded.

He said, "But in the future, we might have to. On other jobs."

"When we're on the job."

"Yes, when we're on the job. After we get established, then we won't have to kill our allies. Then we can cover our tracks better."

She nodded, like a pupil learning from a master.

"Who's next? Who's the next target?"

"I told you we have to go back to the source and take him out."

"That's the loose end. I mean, who's the next target?"

The Foreigner smiled. "The next target will be fun."

CHAPTER 24

Thirty minutes later, Widow and Cassidy and Tiller and Gregor sat in the Range Rover. The rain had been a thing all morning.

It reminded Widow of Seattle and of DeGorne. *Cork was like a smaller Seattle,* he thought, which made him think of coffee.

They were parked across and down the street from a pub called Cathery's.

Tiller asked, "Why don't we just go in?"

Gregor looked back from the passenger seat and said, "They don't open until noon."

"So?"

"So he may not be there yet."

"He's probably there."

"Yeah. Maybe. But we can't go giving away our presence. Not yet."

Widow asked, "Why not?"

Cassidy said, "Look, this is how we do things in Ireland. Okay? It's called a stakeout."

Cassidy reached up and adjusted the rearview mirror. She said, "Today's Sunday."

Tiller asked, "What's that mean?"

Widow looked into the mirror at Cassidy's eyes. They were beautiful, hard to take his eyes off, hard to recall whom he had just been thinking about.

He said, "This is Ireland."

Tiller said, "What's that got to do with anything?"

"Cathery is Catholic, deep Catholic. It's before noon on a Sabbath. He won't be there yet."

"What? He's at church?"

Widow shrugged and said, "That's where Catholics go on Sunday."

"Why don't we just go pick him up at church?"

Both Gregor and Cassidy looked back at Tiller.

"We respect the house of God around here, Mr. Tiller," Gregor said.

"Are you serious?"

Widow said, "Relax. He'll come around."

"I thought Catholics don't work on Sunday."

Cassidy said, "He's not that Catholic. He sells weapons that kill people, remember?"

Tiller said, "Plus, he owns a bar. Hello? He sells alcohol to the public. Isn't that a no-no in the Bible? Or whatever?"

Cassidy smiled. "Not in Ireland."

Widow smiled.

They were quiet for five long minutes.

Widow asked, "What time is it?"

Cassidy looked at her watch. Gregor looked for a clock face on the radio, but there was only a digital readout of the radio station, which had the volume turned all the way down.

Cassidy said, "It's a quarter after eleven."

Widow asked, "You guys know what we're missing for a stakeout?"

No one answered.

Widow said, "Coffee."

Cassidy said, "There's a café up the block."

Widow said, "Great. Let's go there. I could eat anyway."

Gregor looked at her. "Someone should stay here."

She nodded.

Tiller said, "I'll stay."

Gregor said, "I'll stay too. You need an official cop here."

"You guys want anything?"

They both shook their heads.

"You keep the Rover," Cassidy said.

Gregor nodded, and she twisted in her seat, looked back at Widow.

"There's an umbrella back there. Behind your seat."

Widow nodded and undid his seat belt and wrenched back, searched with one hand, found the umbrella. It was a long thing, black with a cane handle at the base.

He grabbed it and showed it to her. "Let's go." Widow handed her the umbrella first.

She paused and refused it. "You take it. I can't hold it over your head."

He nodded, and they both stepped out into the pouring rain.

The streets were cobblestone. Widow could hear soft music playing in the distance. It echoed over the alleyways. The rain beat down around them like a thumping chorus to the music. Like soft island drums.

He held the umbrella at the lowest height he could and still cover Cassidy because of the height difference between them. He tried to balance it and still be able to see out from underneath it.

It wasn't working out.

Cassidy noticed. She reached her arms around him, taking him off guard for a moment, but he didn't reject her. She held on to his waist like they were on a honeymoon.

She said, "Relax. I'll guide you."

He relaxed.

"You trust me, right?"

"How can I not? You're the police."

"I am. I could arrest you. If I wanted to."

"For what?"

She was quiet. They walked down the sidewalks, and she stopped him and looked both ways, preparing to guide him across the street.

"Jaywalking?" He followed her lead, across the street, over the cobblestone, though the pouring rain. "Do you have jaywalking here?"

"We've got it."

They continued, turning once, twice more, and crossing another street, all downhills until they made it to a long walk that followed alongside a river.

He asked, "What's this side of town called?"

"We're in Popes Quay. That's the River Lee."

He nodded, which moved the umbrella.

"Here we go."

They stopped, and he raised the umbrella. They went into a café that was more like a New York style coffeehouse. And it was called Book Shelf Café Coffeehouse, which was confusing.

Widow guessed they embraced the hybrid combination of both a café and a coffeehouse. And when they entered, he realized it was also a bookstore. They had books shelved on walls and couches spread out near a fireplace and café tables. There was a long countertop with a glass display of bakery foods and roasts of local coffee stocked in bags to choose from. They could be purchased wholesale or opened and brewed for a single cup, according to a sign on the countertop.

There was no waitstaff. It was "order as you go."

They went to the counter and ordered.

Cassidy picked up a large fruit bowl with heated syrup for dipping and a cappuccino, which came out all neat with foam shaped like an Irish shamrock, a touristy thing. Widow picked up an egg-and-bacon muffin, which they heated, and he ordered coffee, black. No cream. No sugar.

They sat near the last window on the street and ate their breakfasts. After he finished, she spoke.

"So, you're in the NSIS?"

"NCIS."

"I know. It's a joke."

He nodded.

"I'm not in the NCIS. Not anymore."

"But you were?"

"Right. Once upon a time."

"Why are you here? You some kind of expert on snipers?"

He stayed quiet, took a pull from his coffee.

"You're not gonna tell me?"

"I was just wondering."

"What?"

"Are you using your looks to interrogate me?"

"How do you mean?"

"You know you're probably the best-looking woman ever to wear a badge here?"

She was quiet. Stared right at him, unfazed.

"You probably say that all the time."

"You think I'm flirting with you to peel off information?"

"The thought crossed my mind."

"Well, I'm not."

"Okay."

She drank some of her cappuccino, ruining the foam shamrock. He watched her, watched her lips, hoped it wasn't obvious. Then he realized he couldn't care less if she was trying to trick him or not.

"Why are you here?"

"Your department didn't tell you anything?"

She shook her head. "You already know what I know."

"You figured Tiller for CIA."

"That's obvious. What about you?"

"What do you think?"

She said, "You're an ex-cop. Got that. Now you're a private investigator? Hired by Tiller because he needs your skills and, no offense, but he needs someone expendable."

"Gee. Thanks."

"I didn't mean it as an insult. That doesn't mean that you are. Just that's what he thinks of you. I imagine he thinks of ninety-nine-point-nine percent of the world's population as expendable."

Widow nodded.

"So, am I right?"

"About what?"

"Are you a private investigator?"

He shook his head.

"No. Not really."

"So, what do you do?"

"Nothing."

"What?"

"I do nothing."

She paused a beat and stared at him. She said, "Everybody does something."

"You know what a nomad is?"

She nodded.

"That's me."

"You're itinerant?"

He shrugged.

"You don't have a job?"

"Not in"—he stopped and looked up at the ceiling and counted on his fingers—"three-plus years."

She said, "You've been unemployed for three years?"

He nodded, said, "When you say it like that, makes it sound like a bad thing."

"Where do you live?"

"I live right here."

"You live in Ireland?"

"Right now, I do."

"You're pulling my leg."

He shook his head.

"You have no job. You don't live anywhere. So what? You're a drifter?"

"More of a nomad, but yeah. I'm a drifter."

"No home?"

He nodded.

"You're homeless."

He shrugged again, looked out the window. People were walking past: umbrellas, raincoats, couples holding hands, families bundled up together. Then he noticed many of them wore nice clothes, like churchgoers.

He looked back at her and joked, "For me, home is where the homeless is."

She stared at him, didn't laugh or smile, which he had hoped she would.

He asked, "So, what else do you want to know?"

"What's your interest in this?"

He was quiet for a moment. He started thinking about the question, started thinking about the answer.

His arm hurt.

His head hurt.

He reached into his pocket and pulled out the bottle of Tylenol, swallowed a pill, and followed it with another pull of his coffee.

He looked into her eyes, stared at them for a long, long second. The concussion dragged his mind back twelve years into the past. He saw the volcanic eyes again.

She had been thirteen years old.

"Widow?"

"I came to help catch this guy. That's all."

"Why that look?"

"What look?"

"The one on your face."

He shrugged. "It's guilt." He stayed quiet.

"You feel guilty about something." She paused a beat. "Or someone."

Widow took a last drink of the coffee, looked out the window again, saw more churchgoers pass. "Looks like church is out."

Cassidy turned and looked out the window, saw the same nicely dressed people. She nodded, and they finished up and left the coffeehouse.

On the walk back to the stakeout, Cassidy stayed close to Widow, closer than before. Closer than she might have to a man who was nothing more than a guy she was supposed to babysit. That was his impression.

He disregarded it because she was out of his league. He made no mistake about that. Or so he thought. But on the walk back to the Range Rover, she said, "Maybe we can get a drink?"

Widow paused a step, which halted their walk back since he held the umbrella again, and she had one free hand on the small of his back.

"We just had a drink."

"That was coffee. I meant like a drink. You know, at a pub."

"Now?"

"At night. After this is all over."

Widow smiled a big smile for the first time in two days, maybe more, because he still wasn't sure about how long he had been in the hospital after the train wreck. He knew today's date. He had seen it on a calendar back in Cassidy's office, but that didn't help because of his lifestyle. He didn't really keep up with dates. The day of the week, sure, but not particular dates. Calendar dates were for people who had kids, bills, jobs, a mortgage, health insurance, spouses.

He said, "I'd love that."

CHAPTER 25

Rosencrantz and Guildenstern, whose real names were Smith and Jahns, had waited in the lobby of the Gardaí Special Unit Headquarters a couple of hours earlier.

They had waited for orders from Tiller. And they got them.

Smith looked at his phone and saw the text messages which Tiller had sent while pretending to need the bathroom upstairs.

Smith told Jahns the messages and the orders, which they had already expected.

They took their messenger bags, which contained a laptop and an external hard drive that contained information. The information would be used as payments for weapons and equipment, including transportation, so that they could drive around Ireland inconspicuously.

They were given a gray panel van with generic markings on the sides. A nonexistent company logo. Some kind of utility company. It sounded real enough. It might even have been real; they had no way of knowing, not without doing some research into the matter. But just like that guy Widow didn't care to know their names, they didn't care to know about the origins of the utility company.

The provider and receiver of their payments was nothing more than a contact that Tiller had provided them. They saw the guy for a whole five minutes in the exchange of the digital information that they had and his giving them a panel van with legal plates and a small bag with illegal sidearms: two Glock 17s and a special handgun loaded with a tranquilizer dart. They had one backup round.

The dart gun was a single-action thing that looked like some kind of modified handgun with a miniature bolt action on it instead of a magazine feed.

They didn't know what was on the laptop or the external hard drives. They figured it must've been something valuable. Probably unrelated to their mission. Presumably some kind of state secrets or other valuable intel that the British government wanted enough to lie about it to the Irish police. Although it wasn't technically lying. It was simply making deals behind their back.

Possibly obstructing justice, but Smith and Jahns couldn't care less about those sentiments. One, they weren't Irish or British. They had no stake in it. And two, they were in the business of breaking laws on foreign soil. They knew they had come there to take the Rainmaker alive. They knew he was too valuable to kill.

They knew what they were dealing with. Tiller had provided intel to them about him. However, the Rainmaker's file was pretty thin. Not much was known about him. Intel out of North Korea had always been scarce.

They knew he was an aging man, probably mid-forties, maybe older. They knew he had survived a rigorous training process since being an orphan, and he had been recruited into it before elementary school.

They knew he was not someone to be trifled with in a long-range firefight.

They weren't sure how he had gotten out of North Korea. No one knew. The file didn't specify if he had escaped or been sent out into the world. It seemed more plausible that he had escaped. And now, he was setting up shop to be a sniper for hire.

That was all fine with the agency. They could just hire him to kill foreign dignitaries that they needed killed. Not a real quandary for the CIA.

That's not what Tiller wanted. He knew that the Rainmaker's knowledge of the top secret North Korean sniper program was far more valuable.

Smith and Jahns parked the panel van around the block at a building that sidelined the street where Cathery's Pub was.

Tiller was certain that the Rainmaker would show up. He would probably take out his loose ends since he had already murdered Lenny.

They waited.

CHAPTER 26

The Foreigner saw the cops for only a moment, staked out on the side street in front of Cathery's Pub. Now, they were parked half in sight, but at a weird angle. The Foreigner could still see the hood of the Range Rover. He saw figures moving behind a small portion of the windshield, but it wasn't enough to see their faces or to shoot them.

Plus, he had no idea how many were in the Rover. He couldn't take the risk of shooting them, not until he had Cathery dead. The cops didn't know who he was. How would they?

Only one target had ever escaped from him before. Only one. He was fairly certain about that.

He watched them for several minutes until he saw a couple coming out of the same alley, holding each other under an umbrella.

Seeing them made him doubt his paranoia, made him doubt their being cops. Why would they park their Range Rover and leave it?

If they were staking out Cathery's Pub, they wouldn't leave their vehicle.

He watched them come out of the alley.

The man was huge. The woman was small. She was struggling to hold on to his waist as they walked off toward the cafés and shops in Popes Quay.

After they came out of the alley, he wasn't sure if the Range Rover had cops after all. He might be paranoid, which was normal for a man trying to branch out on his own as assassin for hire.

The rain hadn't let up for anyone in the city.

Everything was wet. The Range Rover that the couple drove up in. The cobblestone street below. The windowsill of the room he was in.

Only the tip of the suppressor on the rifle was wet. It was wet because he had it assembled and pointed out the window, resting on its bipod on a small, rectangular dining table that came with the room. He was in a small and quaint bed-and-breakfast across the street from Cathery's Pub. It wouldn't be suspicious to Cathery at all because the elderly couple who owned the B&B had been there for forty years before he ever bought the pub down the street.

The Foreigner hadn't rented a room there. That would've been stupid. Renting a room required a face-to-face conversation, a legal passport, a credit card, and a friendly smile. He had none of those things to share with two more witnesses that he would just have to kill. The right way to go about taking out Cathery now was to sneak in through the back in the early morning hours, find an empty room, and wait for the right opportunity.

Of course, when that didn't work, he simply let his

protégé use her skill sets to get them into a room. Cathery had never seen her before. So when she walked into his pub late the night before, dressed as a young girl looking for gentlemanly company, all she had to do was wait for the perfect target.

The street was lined with old B&Bs, tourist shops, and one overpriced hotel. They had thought they might get to Cathery the night before, but no luck. When she found a gentleman staying down the street with fetishes for Asian and teenage-looking girls, it wasn't hard to see he was the next best thing.

The guy she found lay dead in the bathtub, about twelve meters from the Foreigner.

The Foreigner watched the rain through his scope.

The rain reminded him of the ridiculous name that the Supreme Leader had given to the sniper program he was in: the Rainmakers.

The story was that the Rainmaker program originated as a fantasy of the Supreme Leader's late father, some kind of throwback to old American movies from the seventies or sixties about snipers and war and bringing hellfire. He supposed the American war phrase of bringing the rain, which had something to do with shooting massive amounts of bullets, like raining bullets, was where the name had come from. Although, the former Supreme Leader also had a predilection for American Western movies, the kind with cowboys and Indians. And he believed a Rainmaker was a kind of Indian holy man.

All of this was speculation. His knowledge of English was decent. Not as good as his protégé's. She spoke impeccable English, a by-product of going to American language schools in South Korea.

The Rainmaker stared out the scope and watched the two men in the Range Rover.

He breathed normally.

His heart rate was normal, which was slower than most people's. He had been rigorously, torturously trained to keep his heart rate slow and steady at all times under the most horrendous strain and stress. Now it was all automatic.

The Rainmaker lay prone, boots off, on the dining table. He was flat and ready to shoot, ready to kill.

He took another deep breath and saw a panel van drive down the block. It was a utility company, something strange about it. He watched it.

It was strange. He saw the drivers. They were cops. He was almost positive. They looked out of place, like cops. They weren't very good at being inconspicuous.

Taking out Irish police was not preferable. Not when he didn't have to, but here they were. They were giving him the opportunity. In his life, in his experience as a sniper, the best thing to do was always take advantage of the opportunities when they presented themselves, especially if the opportunity was to take out the enemy in silence, with no one else knowing about it.

He studied the van.

He read the name of the company. Then he rested the rifle back and grabbed a burner cell phone out of his inside jacket pocket. He pulled it out, fast-dialed one of the few numbers he had.

He paused and waited. The phone rang.

The girl's voice came on the line. She spoke Korean.

He said her name, and then he said, "What's Cathery's status?"

"He's still in the church."

"How much longer?"

She was quiet for a second, and then she said, "Maybe twenty minutes."

"Plus, he has to walk back here."

She said nothing.

He asked, "What's the name of the local utility company?"

She paused for a moment and then told him.

He read the side of the panel van and asked about the name.

She said, "Hold on. I'll google it."

He smiled. Modern technology. One advantage of having her around. One day she'd make a deadly assassin.

She came back on the line and said, "That company went out of business like a year ago."

"Get back here."

"What about Cathery?"

"He'll come straight back after church. Get back here. I need you for something else."

CHAPTER 27

Smith and Jahns had to park the panel van two blocks south, slightly around a bend and back into a short alleyway because they didn't want to risk being seen by Gregor.

Jahns sat in the passenger seat, the tranquilizer gun on his lap.

Smith looked at him. They didn't speak for five minutes and one second until Smith's phone vibrated in his pocket. He undid his seat belt and leaned back against the seat, and fished the phone out of his pocket.

He looked at the phone.

"Tiller?" Jahns asked.

"Yeah. A text message."

"What is it?"

"He says to stay out of sight. He says that Widow and the woman cop went for breakfast."

"Breakfast?"

"Yeah."

"I could eat."

"He said we gotta wait out of sight."

"He say anything else?"

Smith waited and stared at the phone as another text came in, chased by another vibration.

"Just to be on the lookout for the Korean."

Smith tucked the phone away.

Jahns looked down the street, right and then left.

No one was out in the rain. Not on this street.

Another five minutes passed, and then, suddenly, Jahns perked up.

He stared left, in the direction of Cathery's church. He leaned forward in his seat and craned his head and then followed it with his body, his shoulders facing north. He stared out the passenger side window.

Smith said, "What is it?"

Jahns said nothing.

He stared at a small figure walking in the pouring rain, walking straight toward them.

Smith asked again but got no answer again.

He leaned forward to see what Jahns was staring at.

Then he saw it.

Walking straight toward them down the sidewalk was a girl who could've been a teenager. She had fishnet stockings, a short black skirt, knee-high boots, and a white top. She had no purse, only a black backpack.

Her hair, her arms, her legs, the stockings, the boots, and her white top were all soaking wet.

Smith and Jahns stared at her white top. It transfixed them. They couldn't take their eyes off that region of her body.

As she got closer, her expression turned a little vulnerable and a little seductive, a little like she knew what she was doing to the two men.

Jahns was so mesmerized that he reached over with one hand and almost opened the door. Like a man with a plan, like he was going to hop out and ask her if she needed a ride. He had to consciously make himself let go of the handle.

They both watched her. She walked up towards the panel van, stopped on the street corner, stared at them for a moment, smiled, and then she looked right, looked left, and crossed out in front of the van's nose. She passed them by, not fast, not slow, but a steady walk that could have been a saunter.

They both watched her walk away.

Then Jahns stopped for a second, snapped himself out of it.

He asked, "Hey, was she Asian?"

Before Smith answered, he turned back to look at Jahns' face and contemplate the question. Only he never got past the look because right then, he saw another figure standing on the same street corner the girl had passed by.

The figure was a man, average height, a little thin. He stood perfectly still about five feet from the van's nose. He held something in his hand out in front of him. It looked like a Heckler & Koch USP. It looked like it had a suppressor screwed into the barrel.

It turned out that Smith was right, because right then, he saw a puff of smoke come out of the tip of the silencer. Then he saw an explosion of glass and a hole in the windshield.

Jahns saw Smith's forehead blow open. A small, black hole formed in an unrealistic flash like a bad movie edit.

Blood exploded out the back of Smith's head and onto the headrest.

Jahns turned fast, panicked. He saw a man standing in front of the van. The man paused and stared at him over the barrel of a gun—smoke plumed out of the tip.

First, Jahns saw the same black clothes he had seen only hours before on Cassidy's laptop video. The same jacket. The same pants.

Then he looked at the man's face.

He had a short but deep white scar across one eye. It cut down like a straight lightning strike. The guy's eye was completely white and foggy, like cigar smoke caught inside a fishbowl.

Jahns had just asked his dead friend if the girl was Asian.

The man standing in front of him was Asian.

The man didn't kill him right away. Instead, he stepped closer, circled around to Jahns's door, stayed back five feet.

Jahns thought about the tranquilizer gun in his lap.

His instincts kicked in and forced him to raise his hands near his face. The universal surrender gesture.

Jahns looked at the guy. His lips were moving inadvertently. The man read his lips. The only word he knew was the English word "Rainmaker."

That told the Rainmaker everything he needed to know. These guys were there for him, cops or not.

He shot Jahns in the center of the forehead, like his friend. Only this time, the blood that exploded out the back of Jahns's head sprayed all over the van's cabin.

The Rainmaker looked around the street, looked through the dreary, pouring rain. No one was there except the girl. She walked back toward the van.

She stopped on the driver's side and looked up at him.

"Who are they?"

The Rainmaker stepped forward, his hands covered this time with his lucky shooting gloves.

He grabbed the passenger door handle and popped it open, stepped back, reached in, grabbed a gun off the dead guy's lap. He stepped back out and showed it to his protégé.

She asked, "Cops?"

Then she looked at the gun. It balanced in the Rainmaker's open palm. It was strange-looking.

The Rainmaker holstered his USP and gripped a small bolt action on the strange gun. He ejected the round, which turned out to be a dart, a tranquilizer gun.

He said, "Not cops. Someone else."

"Who?"

"Americans."

CHAPTER 28

The woman from Beijing sat in the passenger seat of a rental Lexus SUV next to Lu. They were stopped on a dirt road just close enough to see the rundown cottage with the blue door, just close enough to see the local police cruiser out front.

They stayed far enough back to not look suspicious to the cop standing in the driveway.

"What do you think? Was it the Rainmaker?" Lu asked her in Chinese.

"Yep. Got here before us."

"How we going to find him now?"

She was quiet for a long beat.

"We gotta assume this guy, Malcolm, must've told them about Cathery."

Lu nodded.

"If he killed Malcolm for seeing his face. It must be because he's worried someone will track him down by following the weapon he used. Then we gotta go back there and sit on Cathery. Eventually, the Rainmaker will show his face there."

Lu took his foot off the brake and backed up to K-turn back the way they came in, but the road was too narrow.

The woman from Beijing said, "Just drive straight. We can turn around down that way."

Lu nodded, and they drove straight past the lone cop standing in the driveway.

His police cruiser was a compact, old white car. He had the blue lights on. He stood up straight with his cell phone in hand. He was calling the station, she figured.

He looked at them for a brief, suspicious moment, and then he watched them pass.

CHAPTER 29

The Rainmaker made it back to the bed-and-breakfast. He walked in - this time with the ball cap that belonged to the dead guy in the room - cap pulled down, chin tucked in, so the owners wouldn't see his face.

One of them, the wife, he supposed, said a cheery good morning to him. She used the dead guy's name. She probably figured he was the dead guy simply by the process of elimination. The bed-and-breakfast only had so many rooms, and she had only so many guests checked in. She knew every one of them. And she had been serving breakfast to each of them in the dining room, right there near the foyer. He had seen them when he entered. Just a quick glance. Then he turned his back to them and went up the stairs.

He heard the "good morning" behind him and waved back to her over his shoulder without saying a word.

Back in the dead guy's room, the Rainmaker had left the Valkyrie sniper rifle on the dining table pulled up to the open window. He had covered it with a sheet off the bed, which seemed stupid up close, but if someone looked into the window, they would see nothing more than a dining table with something covered on it. Maybe it was a model. Someone's hard work. And the watcher would move on.

The Rainmaker saw himself in a small mirror hung up on the wall near the entrance. He saw his familiar foreign face. Only it wasn't what he always thought of when he saw himself in his mind.

In his mind, he still saw the great young Korean sniper that he had been. He had been among the elite of the Supreme Leader's Royal Guard.

After an event that had happened to him twelve years ago, after he was deemed a failure by the Supreme Leader, instead of being executed, he had been imprisoned, sentenced to hard labor. And then one day, the new Supreme Leader let him out. An act of kindness, he was told.

The Rainmaker saw his whited-out eye, saw the gray in his hair from under the bill of the hat. He took off the hat, threw it onto an empty armchair, and returned to the dining room table. He pulled the sheet off the gun with a flourish, like a magician with a tablecloth at a fancy dinner party.

He slipped off his boots, returned to the rifle, to the prone position, and stared out the scope.

He looked back at Cathery's Pub and waited.

CHAPTER 30

Widow and Cassidy returned to the Range Rover. They separated on the way back. Widow gave her the umbrella, said he didn't need it.

She took it and thanked him and walked closer, but couldn't provide him shelter from the pouring rain.

They reached the Range Rover and saw that Tiller had moved to the passenger side front and strapped on his seat belt like he was expecting for them to drive away any moment. Gregor had moved over to the driver's seat.

Without hesitation, Cassidy sat in the back seat. Widow joined her.

"How was your breakfast?" Tiller asked.

Cassidy shot Widow a side glance and said, "It was better than we thought it would be."

Widow nodded.

"Anything happen?" Cassidy asked.

"Not so far."

"Church let out. We should see him any minute."

They sat around, waiting.

After a long minute, Widow noticed Tiller kept looking at his phone. He watched him several times. Tiller kept his phone in hand. He looked down at the home screen, tapped on it, and had an expression of disappointment when he saw nothing there. No notifications. No incoming calls. No voicemails. No unread messages.

"What are you waiting on?" Widow asked.

Tiller looked back at him. "What?"

"You keep looking down at your phone. What are you waiting on?"

"What the hell are you talking about?"

Widow stayed quiet. He looked over at Cassidy. She returned the look, and then she looked straight at Gregor.

Gregor said, "You've looked at that phone several times since they left."

"What? Come on? So what?" Tiller said and shrugged.

Cassidy reached forward and grabbed the seat behind Tiller.

She said, "What's going on?"

Tiller turned flush. He stared down at his phone one more time—instinct.

"You're hiding something," Cassidy said.

Widow said, "Tiller's always hiding something."

"Who you waiting to message you?" Gregor asked.

"No one."

A long moment of silence came over them.

Widow said, "Where are Rosencrantz and Guildenstern?"

"What? Who?"

Cassidy said, "It's from Shakespeare. *Hamlet*." She reached forward and snagged a handful of Tiller's seat belt. Then she ripped it backward, locked him in place. She said, "He's asking where your other guys are."

Widow saw what she was doing, and he reached forward in a fast movement and ripped the phone right out of Tiller's hand while he knew the password was already put in and the phone was unlocked.

"Hey!" Tiller shouted. "What the hell?"

"Shut up!" Gregor said. He reached over and pinned Tiller down from the shoulders.

Tiller struggled and repeated, "What the hell?"

"He told you to shut up," Widow said.

He went through the phone. Skipped the recent calls; that'd be useless. He went straight for the messages.

Widow knew how to use a smartphone. Like every other SEAL, he had to be familiar with modern technology. The world was a technological planet now, and there was no going back.

But he wasn't a fan of cell phones. They were GPS trackers that people carried voluntarily.

He opened the messages and ran through the ones from that day.

"What's it say?" Cassidy asked.

He ignored her and kept reading.

After he was done, he looked up and let the screen on the phone go black.

"What?" Cassidy asked.

"You son of a bitch."

Tiller said, "It's not what you think, Widow."

"What's it say?" Cassidy repeated.

"Widow?" Gregor said.

Widow felt his head pounding again, like a little man

with a hammer lived in his skull. Stress triggered his concussion headaches.

He said, "We didn't come here to help you solve this case."

Cassidy said, "No shit. We knew that."

"It's worse than that. We came here to catch this sniper. And Tiller brought his guys to do just that."

"Isn't that a good thing?" Gregor asked.

"No, I mean they're not with us now because they're out there somewhere waiting to black-bag him."

"Black-bag him?" Cassidy asked.

"Rosencrantz and Guildenstern are out here someplace close by, waiting for the chance to grab him and throw him into a van. They've been ordered to take him alive. They're not turning him over to you. They're taking him out of the country. Probably to a CIA black site, I'd guess."

They were quiet.

Widow said, "What the hell do you want with him?"

Tiller fought back, and Gregor let go of his shoulder. Cassidy released his seat belt.

"It's classified. None of you should know any of this."

Widow said, "That's not good enough. What do you want him for?"

Tiller said nothing.

Widow said, "Why haven't your boys messaged you back? It's been what,"—he looked at the times of the last messages—"twenty-seven minutes? That's a lot of time to pass in the middle of an op with radio silence."

Tiller said nothing.

Gregor said, "Does this mean that our sniper is here?"

Widow nodded, said, "He's here somewhere. Tiller's

using Cathery as bait. The guy probably wants to kill him to cover his tracks about the rifle. Because it's a specialty weapon, he might be afraid that Cathery will talk about it."

Cassidy said, "Why would that matter?"

Gregor said, "Why not kill him after he got it?"

"He probably didn't know the point of origin. There was probably another salesman between the transactions. Plus, the sniper would want to kill his target first. Can't let anyone get wind of him before he strikes. That's how snipers work. He wouldn't tie up loose ends until the last minute."

Just then, Cassidy looked out the windshield, past Tiller. She pointed and spoke.

"Look."

All four of them looked in that direction.

They saw a man underneath a dark green umbrella coming up the street from Popes Quay's direction. He used the same sidewalk that Widow and Cassidy had used.

They saw his face.

Gregor said, "That's him. That's Cathery."

"Let's take him now." Cassidy let go of Tiller and looked at Widow, then at Tiller. "Mr. Tiller, you're the worst part of agencies like your CIA. You no longer have the support of the Gardaí."

"You can't do that. My support comes from way above your pay grade."

"You know what? I can do that. I'm sure that when my director learns about what you were planning to do, you'll be lucky if we don't detain you."

"For what?"

Widow said, "You've violated about a dozen laws, surely."

Cassidy said, "Obstruction of justice and interference with a police matter will be the first things we charge you with."

Tiller said nothing to that.

"Now, both of you stay here."

Widow nodded.

"We'll let you know what he says."

Cassidy got out, followed Gregor in the rain.

Widow stayed behind with Tiller.

Tiller said, "You work for us. Whose side are you on?"

Widow looked ahead, out the windshield, saw Cassidy and Gregor approach Cathery in the rain, saw them show him their badges. They circled around him. Gregor paced around the back of him, ready to leap in and grab him in case he drew a weapon.

Widow watched for a moment; then he looked at Tiller. He said, "Benico?"

Tiller turned and faced Widow, waiting for the rest of the sentence, which never came. At least, it didn't come as words.

Widow plunged his forearm, his elbow, and his fist back, and jackhammered it forward like a bolt gun. He slammed his fist straight into the good cheek, the good eye, the different side of his face from twelve hours earlier. This time, he crushed Tiller's cheek.

Tiller's face flung forward and to the left like a violent, foul ball in Yankee Stadium.

The Range Rover's factory seat belt comes with a five-star rating. It's truly among the industry's best. This seat belt was put to the test.

The belt's slack went forward with Tiller and locked up and jolted him back. Even though it wasn't designed for in-cabin scenarios, it saved his life, maybe.

The seat belt plus the fact that Widow had long arms and couldn't rear his fist back far enough to throw a punch at over fifty-five percent capabilities. Maybe sixty.

If he had asked Tiller to step out of the car, he probably would've killed him. Maybe. He hadn't intended to kill him, but if he had died from a punch from Widow, it wouldn't have broken anyone's heart.

CHAPTER 31

The rain pummeled the surrounding cobblestones. The cracks between the stones filled with running rainwater, pooling together in heavy flowing streams. They ran down the middle of the street about forty yards from Cathery's Pub.

Cathery was walking to his tavern. He was getting closer when he first noticed the Range Rover parked in the alley next to his pub. He wondered who the guys were inside. Then he saw a man and a woman come toward him. He wondered who they were, too.

He wasn't armed. He had been under suspicion in the past, and the last thing he needed was to get arrested with an illegal firearm in his pocket. Plus, it was Sunday. He never carried on Sunday, unwritten Irish Catholic rule.

You don't bring your gun to church. He had never done that before. He knew younger, more naive IRA members who had been caught doing that before. If a chief found out, he made sure that they could never carry a gun into a Catholic church again. Not murder, nothing that dramatic. The standard operating procedure usually called for a simple hand breaking. Break a few fingers and some bones in the gun hand, and you would find that the mentioned IRA members wouldn't make the same mistake twice.

Cathery neared the two people. They were headed to talk to him. The woman had a bad poker face. He could see she intended to speak with him. She didn't have an umbrella. A good Irish lady doesn't get caught in the rain.

As they neared, he figured they were cops.

He was right.

They stopped five feet in front of him. The man circled behind.

The woman said, "John Cathery?"

"Aye. That's me, lass."

The woman reached into an inner pocket of a leather jacket and pulled out a black wallet. *Made for men*, Cathery noted. And she flipped it open to show off a Gardaí badge.

He squinted his eyes to draw it into focus from that distance. "Special Investigations Unit" was what he read. "What do you want?"

"Sir, I'm Nora-Jane Cassidy, and this is my partner, Gregor."

Cathery nodded, didn't care.

Cassidy said, "Questions, Mr. Cathery. We've got questions."

The man circled behind him, staying five feet back. Cathery didn't like that. Usually, if one cop circles behind you, it meant they planned to put you in handcuffs, like they expected him to resist.

"You can come with us on your own volition, or we can talk about the alternative," Cassidy said.

Cathery glanced over his shoulder at Gregor.

"No reason for any violence here. Why the hell would I resist? Where am I gonna go?"

He took his free hand out and shoved it under the pouring rain, out of the dryness of the umbrella, all to illustrate the point.

Cassidy nodded but said, "Still, if it's all the same, we're going to place handcuffs on you."

Cathery said nothing to that.

Gregor stepped forward. He grabbed one of Cathery's arms, the one holding the umbrella, and took out handcuffs, cuffed Cathery's wrist.

Cassidy took possession of the umbrella. Cathery snickered at that. Gregor cuffed the other hand and held them down behind Cathery's back. He pushed him off the sidewalk onto the street and escorted him toward the Range Rover.

Cassidy followed behind them, underneath the umbrella.

CHAPTER 32

The Rainmaker stared through the scope. He saw a woman and a man talking to another man. He couldn't identify one man because the guy was under an umbrella, held down low to cover his face from the rain. The other two had just approached him from the Range Rover.

At first, he thought they were the couple he had seen earlier because one of them was a woman, about the same height as the other one. And she appeared to be wearing a leather jacket like the one from the couple, but the man wasn't the same guy he had seen earlier. This guy was tall, but not as tall as the last guy. This guy was maybe six foot nothing. The other one was much taller.

Then he realized his mistake. His first instincts were right. Earlier, he had thought that the Range Rover's occupants were cops. These were definitely cops. The woman took out a badge and showed it to the man under the umbrella. The other man arrested him.

It had to be Cathery. The Rainmaker could only see the

back of his head because of the angle. Not that seeing his face would matter anyway, because they had never met. Only his protégé had seen Cathery's face.

He took his good eye away from the scope, grabbed his cell phone, and took out a Bluetooth earpiece. He synced it with the phone and dialed the first number on the call log and rang his protégé.

He returned his good eye to the rifle scope.

She answered, and he said her name in Korean, then he asked, "Are you seeing what's going on?"

"I see it. Are we going to kill the cops?"

"No. We only need to take out the Irishman."

"Okay."

"From where you are, can you see his face yet?"

His protégé was quiet for a moment, and then she said, "Yes."

"Is it him?"

"Yes, but…"

The Rainmaker asked, "But what?"

"There's someone else."

"Who?"

"In their truck. There are two other men. And…"

His protégé went quiet.

"And? What?"

"One of them just punched the other one. Hard. And violent. I think he might've killed him."

"What?"

"Wait. The other guy is getting out."

The Rainmaker peered through the riflescope, readjusted, and looked at the part of the Range Rover in his visible range.

He saw the same man whom he'd thought was the

cop's boyfriend earlier. The same walk. The same big stature.

In the back of his mind, he thought he should just kill Cathery and move on. But his curiosity kicked in, and he watched.

His protégé said, "Should we kill them now?"

"No. Let's wait. Stand by."

A hundred forty-five seconds later, the Rainmaker saw the big man's face, recognized him, and wished he had pulled the trigger when he had the chance. He wished he had never seen that man's face again. Because the man he saw in his scope was the only man ever to escape him.

CHAPTER 33

Widow got out of the Range Rover and cut Cassidy and Gregor off at the pass before they saw what he had done to Tiller.

Before he got out, he pulled Tiller's seat belt from behind, tight enough to pull the guy upright; then he laid Tiller's head back on the headrest. He checked Tiller was still breathing. Which he was.

Widow hadn't intended to kill the guy.

Tiller was out cold.

Widow doubted that Tiller would have any memory of the encounter when he woke up. He'd wake up dazed and confused and with a splitting headache, but not much else. His face was already a little swollen from the punch he'd gotten twelve hours earlier.

Maybe he would piece it together eventually, but what could he do about it?

In case Cassidy or Gregor got a little jazzed by it, he thought it best to delay them from seeing Tiller for as long as possible.

After he confirmed Tiller was alive and breathing, he got out of the Range Rover, pocketed Tiller's smartphone just in case, and took the spare umbrella with him.

He approached them under it.

"What are you doing?" Cassidy asked.

Widow thought for a second and said, "I thought it best to talk out here."

"Why?"

"Don't want Tiller to hear what we hear first."

Gregor nodded and said, "I agree. We can't trust that guy."

Cassidy nodded.

Widow handed the extra umbrella over to Gregor, who let go of Cathery's cuffs and took the umbrella, grateful.

"Hey, what about me?" Cathery asked. "I'm getting soaked here."

"You can stand a cleansing," Gregor said.

Cassidy turned to Cathery. Widow stayed where he was, and Gregor moved to one side of Cathery.

Cassidy spoke first.

"Mr. Cathery. We want to know about one of your clients."

"What clients? I run a successful pub."

Gregor said, "We know you're a weapons dealer."

"'Fraid I don't know what you're talking about."

Cassidy stepped closer to him, kept the umbrella just out of reach and out of range to cover him.

Cathery said, "Shouldn't you guys cover me here?"

He started shivering, which could've been an act, Widow figured.

"Isn't it a violation of my human rights or something?"

"Just answer our questions, and you can go about your business," Cassidy said.

Gregor shot her a look like he didn't think they'd be letting Cathery go.

Cathery looked at her like he also didn't believe it. "If I answer your questions, you'll let me go?"

Cassidy said, "Depends."

"On what? If I admit to something illegal?"

She said, "No. Depends on if you help us out."

Cathery said, "What is this? You guys have been busting my balls for five years. Now you say if I answer some questions, you'll let me go."

Cassidy nodded.

"Even if I admit to illegal activities?"

Cassidy stayed quiet.

Gregor shook his head. "We can't do that. If he admits to something illegal, we gotta take him in."

Cassidy nodded.

Widow said, "I can ask him."

All three of them looked at him.

Cathery said, "Who are you?"

"Let me talk with him, just a few seconds. A couple of guys talking. No big deal."

Cassidy nodded and stepped back casually, nodding at Gregor to follow, which he did. They took the umbrellas and stepped several feet away, just out of earshot because of the pounding rain.

"What the hell is this?"

"Mr. Cathery, I'm not the police."

"You're an American."

Widow nodded, even though it wasn't a question. His

cast was getting wet in the rain. He held it close, trying to keep it as dry as he could.

"What do you want?"

"I just want to know about a weapon you sold to someone not from around here."

Cathery stared up at him. The rain pelted one of his eyes. He closed it. Then he looked down at the ground, started shaking his head.

"I knew I should've never sold to that Chinaman."

"Chinaman?"

"Yeah."

"What did you sell?"

Cathery kept staring at the ground.

Finally, he said, "Who did he kill?"

"A former member of the British Army. A war hero."

"Was he Irish?"

"Yes. He was from here," Widow lied.

Cathery shook his head. "I never knew that."

"You knew he wasn't buying an illegal weapon for sports shooting."

Cathery nodded. "I knew he was trouble."

"But he paid you, right?"

"He paid cash. Good money."

"Help me catch him."

"I can't. I can't be implicated in something like this. It'll ruin me. Think anyone will buy from me after? Think the cops here will even let me go if I admit to selling guns?"

"Cathery, I'm not a cop."

Cathery said nothing.

Widow said, "We're not planning to arrest this guy."

Cathery looked at him. "What are you going to do to him?"

"This guy killed someone I knew once. I'm not planning an arrest here."

Cathery looked into Widow's eyes hard. Then he nodded. He said, "I didn't sell him the weapons. So I never actually saw him."

"How did you know he's Chinese?"

"I don't. I know he's Asian is all."

"How?"

"My guy, Malcolm, he dealt with him. I use guys like a sales force. I never deal one-on-one."

"Where's Malcolm now?"

Cathery shrugged and said, "Home. Probably. I haven't seen him for a while."

"You haven't seen him?"

"Or heard from him. He's not answering my calls."

"That unusual?"

Cathery shrugged. "It's not normal. But the Chinaman probably gave him a bonus. He might've taken off. You know, somewhere with a lot of drink and girls."

"You don't seem too upset."

"He'll be back. They always come back. He'll need money."

Widow nodded. "So, you never met the client, but you know the gun?"

Cathery nodded. "Of course. They were tough to get."

Widow looked at him. The rain beat down on Widow's head. The constant pounding on his skull and on the surrounding cobblestones was irritating his concussion. He could feel his head pounding in unison with the rain. Altogether, it sounded like drums in his head.

"You okay?" Cathery asked.

"I'm fine. What do you mean 'they'?"

"What's that?"

"Just now, you said, 'They were tough to get.' Why 'they'?"

Cathery said, "The Asian guy ordered two rifles. Very special. They're called Valkyries."

CHAPTER 34

The woman from Beijing and Lu drove up in the rain to a place that they had already been. They were on the street leading up to Cathery's Pub.

Lu stopped the Lexus and stared ahead. The windshield wipers swiped rain droplets off the glass, creating a monotone rhythm, calming in the conditions in front of them.

"Looks like something's going down."

The woman from Beijing leaned forward and watched. She saw four people: two holding umbrellas, standing off to the side, a man and a woman, and clearly law enforcement. She had been all over the world, and she knew cops when she saw them. "Who are they?"

"Those two are Gardaí."

"Inspectors?"

"That's my guess."

"And the other two guys?" She said and leaned closer, unfastening her seat belt.

"One's Cathery. But..."

"But what?" she asked.

"The other man. I've seen him before." Lu said, "Want me to intervene?"

"No. Let it play out. The Rainmaker is here," she said.

"How come he hasn't killed Cathery yet?"

She didn't answer that. Instead, she said, "Let it play out."

CHAPTER 35

Widow looked to his right. He saw a black Lexus SUV stopped at the end of the street at an intersection watching them. *Passersby, maybe,* he thought.

He looked over at Cassidy, who was also looking.

She mouthed him a question: "The Rainmaker?"

He shook his head. Then he looked back at Cathery.

The Rainmaker would make a move to kill Cathery, they had figured. Would this be the move? Would a lone sniper use a guy in a car? Maybe.

Suddenly, right there, Cathery's head blew apart.

The front of Cathery's face blew out of his head, and skull and flesh and half an eyeball and blood sprayed all over Widow's face and chest.

The dead body flung forward. Widow caught it in his arms—no real choice.

Widow held the body for a split second and dropped it. It flopped over, twitching like a chicken with its head cut off.

Widow looked over at Cassidy, who saw it happen.

He shouted, "Sniper!"

She moved, Gregor moved, taking cover in a doorway.

Widow turned, looked back and up. Then he saw a flicker of something, just a quick sparkle, like diamonds in the night. It shimmered in the darkness of an open window above an old Irish bed-and-breakfast down the street from Cathery's Pub.

Then Widow saw the shimmer again, the Rainmaker's scope, staring right at him.

He was next.

Suddenly, a horn blared, loud like a ship in the fog. It cut through the night, through the rain, and saved Widow's life.

He saw a flash from the Rainmaker's rifle muzzle. Instinctively, he dove right, and rolled on the hard cobblestone, just as a rock exploded from the stones a yard to his right.

He landed on his broken arm. He felt the bones. He felt pain. He pushed it down deep, ignored it.

Not now, he thought.

He came up on the balls of his feet. The Lexus driver had blared the horn, unexpected to everyone, including the Rainmaker. His aim jarred a fraction of an inch and he fired the rifle and missed.

No one outruns or dodges bullets; that was all movie make-believe nonsense. Widow knew the only reason that his face didn't look just like Cathery's was because of the Lexus driver.

He didn't wait to give the Rainmaker another shot. He stayed crouched and ducked and weaved and zagged and rolled again until he was down the alley with the Range

Rover. The Extra Strength Tylenol bottle that had been in his pocket rolled and bounced, and the lid that never wanted to open for him popped off on its own and pills spilled out of the top all over the cobblestones.

Shit, he thought. It reminded him that his head was still pounding and getting worse.

"Widow!" he heard Cassidy shout. "Widow! Are you hit?"

He checked his body with his hands involuntarily. His hands checked to make sure all the vitals were still intact. Everything was still there. "I'm okay. What about you?"

"Yeah. We're not hit."

Widow looked out on the street at the dead body and bloody mess. Blood was bubbling and pooling near the head from the rain. "Cathery won't make any statements." He yelled it and then felt a little guilty after. Bad timing. Bad joke.

Cassidy asked, "Who's in the car?"

Widow edged to the corner, staying out of sight of the Rainmaker. He pushed his back into the wall. "I don't know."

"Is it Tiller's guys?"

No way, he thought. *They wouldn't be helping him.* He took a quick peek at Tiller. He was still out cold and safe out of the sniper's line of sight. "I don't think so."

"Stay put. We're calling in backup," Cassidy shouted.

He stayed quiet and took out Tiller's phone. He thought maybe he could get Rosencrantz and Guildenstern on the line and get them to help. But it was no use. The phone was passcode protected, and Tiller hadn't given him the passcode. The phone must've had a preset to switch off after so many minutes passed without being used. It was useless.

He slipped back and went to the Range Rover. He popped open Tiller's door and tossed the smartphone onto his lap. No point in keeping it.

Then he patted Tiller down, looking for a gun, which he doubted he'd find.

He looked at the ignition switch. No keys.

Gregor was holding them.

He searched the console, the glove box, under the front seats, and the inside door pockets. He found nothing of use.

Then he ran back to the cargo door, opened it, and found one thing that could help.

He scooped up a bulletproof Kevlar vest, which wouldn't stop a Magnum sniper round, but he wasn't sure what the Rainmaker was using. From what he read about the Valkyrie rifle, it had function capabilities for multiple calibers.

Although, he probably was firing the same rounds he'd used with Lenny. Why change them now?

Widow slid off his bomber jacket and suited the vest up and put the jacket back on over it.

Better safe than sorry.

Widow found nothing else of interest.

He closed the cargo door and returned to the end of the alley, stayed out of sight.

Cassidy called out to him. "Widow?"

"Yeah?"

"Backup's coming."

"How long?" he shouted back.

"I don't know."

Which Widow took to mean five minutes or longer.

They'd be dead in five minutes. Or the Rainmaker would get away.

A thought occurred to him.

He called out to Cassidy, "Cathery said something."

"What?"

"He said that there were two Valkyrie rifles."

Two, he thought.

He leaned out as far as he dared. He saw Cassidy and half of Gregor from where they were perched. They were crammed into a doorway like sardines in a can.

"What does that mean?"

Two, he thought again.

Widow shouted, "Cassidy, there's two of them!"

CHAPTER 36

Widow's head pounded. It was getting worse and louder and harder. It pounded like a warning bell shoved into his skull. It pounded like someone was inside his head, shooting cannons off a US destroyer.

He shouted out to Cassidy over the cannon-like pounding in his head, over the rain, over his thoughts. He warned her that there were two.

Just then, he saw the flash of a sniper rifle. It came from a rooftop south of him.

He saw the direction the second sniper was aiming. It was down toward the doorway at Cassidy and Gregor.

Gregor took a bullet to the chest. He flew back like leaves under a leaf blower. His body dumped back into the door, and then he toppled forward, falling completely out of cover.

"Cassidy!" Widow shouted.

The Lexus from earlier began honking the horn again violently.

Widow heard the engine rev up and the tires squeal and the suspension bounce on the cobblestone as the SUV sped forward.

Widow saw the second sniper fire again at Cassidy, and again.

The Lexus tore down the street and barreled right alongside the alley.

A woman kicked open the back door and said, "Get in!"

Widow scrambled in, looking back at Tiller once, having a second thought about abandoning him. But he was out of range and out cold. He'd probably be safe. And if not, Widow wouldn't lose sleep about it.

Widow said, "We gotta get the woman!"

He slammed the door behind them, and the woman who had let him in climbed into the front passenger seat, and he realized that she had been half in it. She had folded back half into the back seat to open the door for him.

Now, he only saw the backs of their heads.

The driver hit the gas, and they sped toward Cassidy.

Widow leaned into his door; face pressed into the window's glass. He could see that Gregor was dead. His eyes were lifeless, his face expressionless, and his body didn't move.

Cassidy was squeezing her body deep into the corner of the doorway. Bullets were firing. Pieces of wood from the door and concrete from the old building exploded around her, creating a heavy, wet dust cloud, which might've been saving her life, blinding the second sniper like a smoke grenade.

Widow shouted, "Step on it!"

The back window behind Widow exploded, then a

bullet shredded through the metal on the roof. The Rainmaker was shooting at the back of the Lexus.

Widow sucked in and hugged the door.

Another bullet tore through the roof and blew through the car radio and touchscreen navigation system. The bullet hole spider-webbed, and the electronics went dark.

The driver swerved to the right and then the left. He knew how to drive under gunfire. Widow could see that.

The driver swerved the Lexus right into the wall of the building and the doorway that Cassidy was hiding in. Steel and concrete sparked in the rain.

Widow shoved the door and kicked it open.

"Get in!" he shouted at her.

Cassidy dove into the back seat with him. He cradled her close.

The second shooter was firing bullets faster than the Rainmaker—sloppier, more amateurish. Widow recognized it immediately.

The second shooter was firing blind.

Bullets came at them from the side. Slow from being shot out of a bolt-action sniper rifle, but fast enough to scare anyone.

He clenched Cassidy with all his strength. He felt her pull into him like a rescued victim pulled out of deep, choppy seas. She was cold and wet and breathing hard.

He held on to her.

The Lexus driver gunned the SUV and within seconds, and several bullets and bullet holes later, they were out of range.

CHAPTER 37

The pounding in Widow's head was becoming unbearable. He felt the skin on his face tightening. He felt his eyeballs swell. They felt like they were as hard as golf balls in their sockets. He felt his breathing getting uncontrollably deep, like he was falling into sedation from anesthesia.

He waited until they were well away from Cathery's Pub, and then he let go of Cassidy and scooped her up so she was seated upright.

He said, "Are you okay?"

She was breathing heavily, nearly hyperventilating. "David. Oh my God, David. We left him."

Widow figured David must've been Gregor's first name. "He's dead," Widow whispered. "Nothing we can do for him now."

"We have to go back. The cops will be there. They're walking into a trap."

Widow shook his head. He whispered to her, "I don't think we're headed back."

"Where? Who are they?" she said back.

Widow squeezed his eyes shut. His left arm hurt. He felt dizzy.

"Widow?"

"I don't know."

Cassidy asked, "Do you think they are friendlies?"

"They saved our lives."

She said, "Ask them."

He stayed quiet. The pain in his arm and the pounding in his head were getting louder and harder.

After several seconds, Cassidy scooted forward and spoke to the strangers.

"Listen, I'm Gardaí. My name is Cassidy. This is Jack Widow. We owe you guys for helping us out."

The strangers in the Lexus said nothing.

Cassidy said, "We need to go back. My cops will be there soon. They can take us."

Nothing.

"The Gardaí will be very grateful to you."

They didn't answer.

"They will pay for your car. I know it."

Nothing.

Cassidy paused a long beat. The Lexus kept driving, turning left, turning right. They ran stop signs and streetlights.

If she didn't know any better, she would've guessed that they were heading to the airport.

She said, "Or you guys can just drop us off on the side of the road."

Widow's vision blurred again.

Cassidy raised her voice. "Listen, I'm Special Investigator Nora-Jane Cassidy, and I demand that you let us out here!"

She reached forward and grabbed the driver's shoulder.

The woman from Beijing twisted in the passenger seat and turned to face them.

Two things struck Widow at that moment.

The first was that she was pointing a Glock 17 at them, mostly at Widow.

The second thing struck him harder than having a gun pointed at him. It struck him harder than the pounding in his head. It struck him harder than a punch to the face. It struck him harder than a bat to the face.

His vision blurred. It got worse and worse. And he thought he must've been hallucinating because he saw a woman staring at him, pointing a gun at him, and she had a familiar face, a face he hadn't seen in twelve years in real life. It was a face that he had seen in his nightmares.

She was the thirteen-year-old Korean girl with the volcanic eyes.

CHAPTER 38

The girl with the volcanic eyes, deep and dark and swirling like brown lava inside a volcano, looked up at him from twelve years in the past.

She pointed at him, giggled, and said, "Chicken."

Widow shook his head and smiled down at her.

He moved his MP5SD and let it hang over his shoulder by the strap. He reached out a gloved hand and presented her with an American high five.

The girl with the volcanic eyes spoke in Korean and high-fived him. The other SEALs chuckled along with her.

Widow glanced past Clery, who now stood closest to him , and at Lyn, who was on his radio, about to call for the evac.

Lyn paused, looked back at Widow, and said, "She said she likes you, Chicken."

Widow nodded. "How far are we from the LZ?"

"Two klicks that way," Lyn said and pointed south, past Clery, who was moving out of the way. Clery focused on the road south, like he was scanning it for any more potential threats.

"Now we got wheels," Widow said, and pointed at the Chinese Police SUV.

Lyn said, "Okay. I'll call in and tell 'em to be on the lookout for us."

Widow nodded and went over to the SUV.

Lyn stopped him, grabbed his arm. "Wait."

Widow said "What?"

"We should clean it first."

Widow looked at the SUV. There was blood misted all over the front bench, and the windshield was cracked and too far gone to be repaired on the fly. He said, "Looks fine to me."

Lyn smiled, "The kids, dude."

Widow nodded, said, "I'll do it."

Lyn glanced back at Reyes and Slabin, who were close together, talking. Then he leaned into Widow and said, "Get Reyes and Slabin to do it. They're the bottom of the totem pole."

Widow glanced at the two SEALs and looked back at Lyn. He said, "I'll clean it myself. I can handle it."

"Are you sure?"

"You question my abilities?"

"No offense, but I've seen your quarters."

Widow said, "My quarters are clean to regulations."

"Are they?"

Widow said, "I've cleaned latrines in less than two minutes flat. I can handle a little blood."

"A little?"

Widow shrugged. "A lot of blood. We're not going that

far. I'll manage. Just get the chopper flying. Get them to meet us ASAP. I want to get the hell outta here."

"You're the boss," Lyn said and stepped away toward Hollander in the north and made his call.

Widow walked to the vehicle and leaned over the driver side window and looked on the front bench, a quick survey of the damage. He saw the keys still in the ignition, which he had expected because the engine was still running and idling.

The front area was pretty bad. He glanced at the back seat. It was really nothing. Then he backed away and went back to the cargo area. He opened it and found what he needed, two gallons of water and some blankets, not towels, but they would work well enough.

Widow took it all and set it down on the road. He unfolded a blanket and tossed it over the mess, then he hopped in the cabin and levered the seat all the way back and got in. He raised his legs as high as he could and used both feet and kicked violently at the glass. After three hard double kicks, he had kicked out the entire glass and framing.

Widow got back out and pulled the rest down and all off the hood. He grabbed the water and pulled out the blanket. He used both gallons and dumped the water all over the front seats, the upholstery, the console, the steering wheel, and the dashboard. Then he wiped all of it, everything as fast as he could. He used the clean side of one blanket to cover up the wet spots and whatever was left.

He stepped back and looked and nodded. Not as fine a job as a Navy latrine, but good enough.

Widow walked back to the Kweon family and the other

SEALs. He led the family away from the SEALs and away from the bank with the dead bodies. The SEALs stayed on the perimeter, scanning and watching out for any threats. Clery kept a watch on Widow. The others scanned the area. Lyn was still on the radio.

Widow helped the Kweon's son pull his mother over to the SUV and place her in the back seat. The son hopped in next to her. Widow signaled for Mr. Kweon to follow suit and have the mom wedged between them.

The girl with the volcanic eyes smiled at him and hopped in the front. She rode in the middle, seated on the console. Not the most comfortable ride, but that's the spot she picked.

Widow leaned in and hauled himself up and sat down behind the steering wheel.

The girl with the volcanic eyes squeezed in close to him. She trembled a little like she was scared, and sitting next to him helped. He stayed quiet about it.

Lyn got off the radio and approached them. He stood five feet from the driver's door and said, "They're coming. We gotta head south."

Widow nodded and stayed quiet.

Lyn said, "Where do you want the rest of us to ride?"

Widow said, "Go around. You ride up front with us. Tell the others to grab on outside where they can."

Lyn nodded and shouted back at the others. He repeated the order. They all acknowledged it and started to the vehicle to find a spot to grab.

Suddenly, Lyn stopped and pointed east into the fog, back toward the dark North Korean side of the frozen river, like he saw something. Widow expected Lyn to go around the hood and get into the SUV so they could be on their way, but that didn't happen.

Widow saw Lyn staring at him one second. And the next second, Lyn's head exploded like a bad special effect from a movie. It was violent and unforgettable and haunting.

Lyn had been standing there with a head; then he was only a body with no head. He looked like a mannequin in a shop somewhere missing its head.

Before anyone could react, a second thunderclap rang out and a quick third. Both gunshots. Both loud and echoing across the landscape.

Widow glanced in the driver side mirror. He could no longer see Reyes and Slabin.

A giant bullet hole had blasted through Reyes's eye sockets. Blood and gore was splattered behind his head and his body had flown back off his feet.

Slabin got it worse than Reyes. He got the same bullet hole in his face, but his body fell and twitched and his arms flapped afterwards, like he was dead only he didn't know it yet.

Clery was the first to react. He shouted at Hollander, only he called him by his first name. Widow saw them in the side mirror. Hollander stood to the north. He was the furthest away. He stood completely still. There was shock stretched across his face as he stared back at his three fallen friends.

Clery repeated his shouts. He shouted, "Glen, let's go!"

Hollander glanced over at Clery, whose back was turned to the gunshots. A bullet ripped through the bottom of Hollander's neck, just above his breastbone.

Blood and flesh and tissue sprayed out the exit wound like water from a fire hose.

Clery was left standing there, staring at his dead friend.

"Clery, get in!" Widow shouted out the window.

Clery spun toward the vehicle and ran around the back. He came up on the side and grabbed the passenger door handle. He popped it open and started to hop in. Just then, Clery's head exploded. His body was in midleap into the truck. It flew back out into the snow. His blood sprayed across the inner window pillar, the window, and the side panel. The door swung out and hit the limit of its hinges and bounced back.

Widow stared at the last of his dead teammates in horror and disbelief.

What kind of sniper could make those shots, and so fast?

The Kweon family screamed and wailed and shouted. All in Korean. Widow didn't know what they were saying or which of them was doing the screaming. He had no rearview mirror to take a quick glance at them in the back seat. Nor did he intend to look. He just ripped the gear into reverse, and hit the gas. The SUV flew backward onto the dimly lit highway in partial mist. He was going north and needed to stop and pop the gear into drive and head south.

He hit the brakes. And heard glass explode behind him, right where his head would've been if he hadn't hit the brakes. The bullet fired had his name on it and it barely missed him. That didn't mean it hadn't hit someone else, because it had.

Widow spun around and gazed into the back seat and saw that the Kweon's son was no longer there—not in a sitting position, where he had been. Now, he lay hunched over across his mother. His head was broken open like a busted coconut, but instead of milk seeping out, there was blood, and a lot of it. It covered Kweon's wife's hands. She screamed in shock.

Widow's eyes widened to their extreme limits. He was also in shock. He'd never heard of a sniper this deadly before. No one had.

The girl with the volcanic eyes grabbed at him from the front bench. She was screaming and crying. She shouted at him in Korean. It was the same words over and over. He didn't know it, but she was shouting for him to drive.

Widow froze. He was paralyzed for the first time in his entire military service—in his life—he froze solid.

Suddenly, the sniper claimed a seventh victim. Kweon's wife's chest blew open right in front of them. She was dead instantly. She'd joined her son.

CHAPTER 39

That red mist plumed and clouded outward. It filled the inside of the SUV and sprayed across their faces. Widow saw it all over the face of the girl with the volcanic eyes. There used to be a young, innocent teenage face there. Now it was covered in blood. Her innocence was gone, stolen from her by a sniper's bullet.

Her father's face was covered in blood.

The father was shouting at Widow in Korean.

Widow's body unfroze, and he popped the gear into drive, hit the gas and sped up to the vehicle's top RPMs, doing the one thing he hated to do—leaving his brothers' dead bodies behind.

The SUV exploded into action, and he raced south, down the long dark highway.

Two klicks that way, Lyn had said, pointing south, just moments before his head was blown off.

What kind of sniper can shoot like that? Widow had no idea. He had no time to contemplate the question.

He hoped that the speed and the white mist would help to keep them safe from the elite sniper.

The two living Kweons were shouting at each other, frantic and in shock. The girl with the volcanic eyes was trying to crawl into the back seat. She was trying to grab on to her father. She was trying to hold on to him, trying to hold onto the only family she had left in the world. But he kept pushing her back like he was protecting her.

By context alone, Widow figured the girl with the volcanic eyes was begging to hold her dad. But he was ordering her to stay away, to stay near Widow, where it was safer. She wasn't the target. Kweon was.

They were both crying and shouting and twisting in their seats like they wanted to escape desperately. But where were they going to go?

Widow took one hand off the wheel and nearly punched the switch for the headlights, thinking they were making it easy for the sniper to track them. But then he realized he couldn't. He couldn't maneuver the foreign, curving highway in the gloom, not without the headlights, not in the thick of the white fog.

He drove on.

One klick.

The speedometer was in kilometers. He watched the dial rise higher and higher. His foot pressed all the way down on the accelerator.

He saw a warning sign for a sharp curve.

He hit the brake and released it. He heard another thunderclap gunshot boom in the distance. He swerved the SUV to the right and back to the left, trying desperately to avoid the super-accurate gunfire.

The girl with the volcanic eyes bucked up into the air

like a bull rider, and the sniper's bullet skimmed the hood of the SUV.

Suddenly realizing that he was holding his breath, Widow breathed out and drove on.

They were coming up on two klicks.

Widow saw an open field coming up off the shoulder. He saw abandoned playground equipment and abandoned buildings, all brick, two of them missing roofs. The whole complex was an abandoned school.

He swung the SUV off the road toward it.

Widow pulled up as close to the buildings as he could. They could use the brick as cover. He heard the father use an English word. He kept speaking the same phrase in Korean over and over, but there was that one English word in his statements.

Kweon said, "Rainmakers." And he said it with sheer terror in his voice.

Widow slammed the brakes, kicking up snow. He grabbed the girl and shoved her head down, out of the line of sight, out of the line of fire. He turned and looked back at Kweon and said, "We go there."

Kweon was shaking. He said, "No. No. Rainmakers."

"Follow us! Now!" Widow shouted. And he busted open the driver's side door and leaped out. He dragged the girl with him. He pulled her into his body, pushing her head down into his chest to make her profile as small as possible. He used his body to shield hers. He was a much bigger target. He just hoped that he could keep her alive, even if it meant that he'd join his dead teammates in Valhalla She didn't fight him. She cried and clenched his vest.

He leaped out onto the snowy ground. He crouched and shoved his back into the front tire of the SUV.

Kweon was out and opposite them, against the rear tire, but the same side.

He was still trembling and repeating the same Korean with the word *Rainmakers* inserted into his phrases.

Widow pointed at the closest structure and held up three fingers. He said, "On three. We run."

They heard another thunderclap, another gunshot, boom in the distance. The sound was a little more distant than before, but it echoed just as loudly. Almost simultaneously, a bullet slammed into the other side of SUV.

How the hell is he shooting that far? Widow asked himself.

Never in his life had he ever heard of a sniper who could do that. Not at this distance and with this much deadly accuracy.

Widow looked at Kweon. He started counting out loud. "One!"

Kweon looked back at him, shaking. He said, "No. No."

Widow said, "Two!"

Kweon quieted and readied himself to run.

"Three!" he shouted and jumped up in a violent explosion of moving mass. He ran toward the abandoned school with the girl with the volcanic eyes tucked into his chest. He kept his arms tight around her to try to shield her from any bullets.

Another thunderclap gunshot exploded on the horizon. Kweon's chest burst open from the side. He went flying off his feet like a barn door blown off its hinges in a violent twister. He was jerked off his feet and slammed into the dirt.

By the time Kweon landed, he was already dead. Widow glanced back over his shoulder to see Kweon behind him about five yards, saw a huge, gaping hole in his right side. Kweon's face registered nothing.

The girl with the volcanic eyes started screaming again. She let go of Widow and pushed off him. He tried to stop her, but couldn't. She ran back to her dead father.

Widow looked in the direction of the sniper shots.

He saw nothing but faint white mist rolling low over the frozen river's surface, like steaming dry ice. He saw the same faint lights that he had seen earlier from the border wall of North Korea. That's where the sniper was, he figured.

Widow turned and scrambled over to the girl. She was crying over her dead father, clawing at him, trying to make him alive again. Widow snatched her up in a powerful effort that would've dislocated her arms if she hadn't let go of her dead father.

Widow took her and dragged her with him toward safety. She didn't fight back. She just cried and screamed. She came up off her feet. He tucked her into his chest again.

He ran with her clinging to him, through the mist and past the SUV's headlights, which was a mistake. They crossed straight through them. They had to. It was on their path to the nearest building.

His primal brain screamed at him over his mistake. The headlamps had lit them up, only for a moment, but it could be enough. It could be a death sentence.

He turned, but he turned the wrong way, like a bad instinct to check where the sniper was. The girl with the volcanic eyes was clamped to his torso, holding on for protection. Widow heard a bullet whiz through the air, through the mist.

It cut straight into the girl's back, below the left shoulder blade and into where her heart should have been.

The force plowed them off the ground. Widow was flung backward onto his back. He heard another thunder-clap gunshot. This one did all the same things. The boom. The echo. But this one missed. They were too close to the ground. Too much in the mist.

The bullet hit the SUV's hood. Metal clanged above him.

There was another boom and a gunshot and echo.

This bullet nailed the passenger side front wheel, and the tire exploded.

Widow held his head up and stared down at the girl. He grabbed her face and pulled her head up. There was blood everywhere. In her hair, on her clothes, on his.

He stared at her eyes to see if she was still alive. He saw nothing, no signs of life.

Twenty-one minutes passed.

Widow tried not to think. He tried to fight the immediate guilt he felt. His training told him she was dead. Lyn was dead. His other guys were dead. The Kweons were dead. They were all dead. No one survived. No one was left, but him. There was no reason for heroics. Nothing he could do now.

The only thing he could do to stay alive was to stay still. Stay hidden. Right now, he was invisible. He knew that for sure because if he hadn’t been, then he’d already be dead.

Every two minutes, the sniper fired another round at Widow's last known position. The sniper, or the sniper team, knew he was alive. They were searching for him frantically.

The bullets kicked up snow all around him—every single shot and every single time. One hit nearby and kicked snow up into his face. That bullet had nearly hit him. It nearly killed him.

He thought the kill shot that killed the girl with the volcanic eyes was meant for him. It must've been.

The girl with the volcanic eyes had saved his life. He tried to be her human shield, but a bad reflex, a terrible mistake, had made her his. That was something he’d have to live with. It was a deep regret that would later haunt him. Right now, he didn’t have time for that. Right now, he had to live, to survive.

Just then, he heard a new sound. It was high above him. It was mechanical.

Then he saw the lights and heard the rotor blades. He heard chatter come on over his earpiece. It was English. It was Americans.

They were calling him. He reached up, slowly, and pressed his throat mic and responded.

The helicopter acknowledged. He heard Tiller's voice. He was on board the chopper. "Widow? What the hell happened?"

Widow said, "They're all dead."

Silence for a long beat.

Tiller asked, "How?"

"A sniper team from the border. Careful, they're still shooting at me."

The helicopter yawed and faced the border.

"Where are you?"

Widow said, "The headlights on the SUV. See them?"

"Yeah."

Widow moved the dead girl and reached down and drew his sidearm. He pointed it at the headlights and shot them out—one after the other.

"I see your gunfire."

"Come get me! Watch for the snipers. They're near the lights on the border wall."

A voice that wasn't Tiller's acknowledged, and the helicopter yawed again and started descending to him.

Widow figured the sniper wouldn't fire on the helicopter because shooting on a US vehicle differed from firing on an unidentified American combatant. The snipers couldn't deny that they knew an American Black Hawk helicopter was American.

The Black Hawk descended, landed twenty feet from the SUV, and waited. It blocked the path of any bullets that might be fired from the border wall.

Widow stood up slowly.

Widow scooped up the dead girl and took her with him. It was automatic. He wasn't thinking it through. He felt the least he could do was see that she had a proper burial, because she had taken a bullet that was meant for him

Two SEALs got out of the helicopter, and Tiller followed. They were all decked out in gear and weapons.

Tiller shouted over the helicopter's loud rotors. He said, "What the hell happened?"

Widow said, "I told you. Snipers."

Tiller's face lit up like it wasn't a surprise. He asked, "From North Korea?"

Widow nodded.

One SEAL saluted him and took the dead girl from him. The other one inspected the bodies and the SUV.

"They're all dead," Widow told him.

Tiller waved him on, and they regrouped at the helicopter.

The SEAL carrying the dead girl put her in the Black Hawk, laid her down, and started looking her over.

Widow climbed into the helicopter's cabin and dumped himself down on a rear bench. He was out of energy.

Tiller got in after him and ordered the SEAL to leave the girl with volcanic eyes behind.

Widow said, "What? No. Take her."

Tiller shouted, "She's dead, Commander. We can't take her."

The SEAL tending to her body looked up, shock on his face. He tried to speak, but Tiller reordered him to dump her.

The SEAL didn't move.

Tiller repeated the order. Right then Naval Command, off the nearest ship, came in over the radio and asked what was holdup was. Tiller explained, and the same order was issued again.

Widow didn't fight back. He had no fight left. He was beaten. He had lost five SEALs and four Korean subjects, including two children. One died in his arms, protecting him. She'd taken a bullet for him. He was done.

Why fight back? What was the purpose?

She was dead. They all were.

The SEALs dumped her out, on Tiller's orders, and the helicopter took off.

Widow remembered learning later that the SEAL who took her in told him something. It was something that he would never forgive himself for. He told Widow she was still breathing before they took off.

CHAPTER 40

Widow heard birds chirping. He thought he smelled grits cooking. He knew he was having a case of déjà vu. He came to. His mind wasn't racing in the way it normally might have. Instead, it was more like jumbling. He had a splitting headache from the concussion.

The sounds of birds faded away as he drifted into consciousness. The grits smell also faded.

The motor hum of twin engines replaced the sounds. He recognized the sound immediately. It was the sound of jet engines. He heard the wind. He felt the soft rattle of a finely made aircraft traveling at top speed.

He opened his eyes and saw a blur. Again. But it didn't last as long as the previous day when he woke up in a hospital.

He knew he was seated, leaned back but seated, and buckled in. The chair was something very comfortable, a captain's chair, like at the helm of a spaceship on a 1960s television show.

He craned his head up and looked down at himself and then the chair. He was still in his bomber jacket. The same blue knit long-sleeve shirt underneath. The same pair of pants. Same boots. And the same white cast; only now it looked weeks old rather than one day old because it had been through the wringer. The rain in Ireland. The rolling around on the cobblestone.

His arm hurt.

He knew he was in the cabin of a plane. He tried to focus on the chair and the surrounding cabin. He saw colors right away. The chair was all white, leather, and very comfortable—the most comfortable chair he had ever ridden in on a plane. Then his eyes came more into focus, and he saw white ceilings. He saw glossy walnut paneling and cabinets and dark-gray carpet, thick and comfortable looking. It made him want to slip off his boots and run his toes through the carpet—an intended design by carpet designers, perhaps.

He recognized the plane. It was a Gulfstream jet, maybe a G650 or something like it. Same class.

He was on another plane.

Sick of planes, he thought.

He moved his right hand up to rub his forehead, to cope with the intense feeling of a hangover. He stopped it halfway, expecting to feel the denial of metal clanging to his chair from handcuffs. But there was none.

He was facing a cabin about eight feet wide. He sat in the tail end. He could see a cluster of blurry people seated from the wing and up. Then he saw a cockpit door and a steward service station. No steward on board that he could see.

No one was serving coffee.

He stayed still. He didn't want to alert the other passengers that he was awake yet. He still wasn't sure who they were. Friend or foe?

After he was sure that his senses had returned, he started moving. He sat up in his chair and looked out the window. It was daylight outside. It looked like early morning hours.

The cluster of people stopped talking and looked back at him.

They all stood up and started moving back to sit around him.

There were three people.

The first that he recognized was Cassidy. She was alive and unharmed.

She made her way through the cabin the fastest and leaned over him and hugged him tightly.

"You're okay?" she said into his ear. Not a whisper, but just as intimate as one. He felt her breath in his ear and on his neck.

"Yeah, why wouldn't I be?"

"You blacked out on us," she said, pushing up off him. She stood in front of him, blocking the view of the two others behind her.

He nodded and said, "I got a concussion."

She said nothing, but a questioning look came over her face.

"Long story," he said.

She remained quiet.

"What's going on? How long was I out?"

"You've been waking up on and off all night."

"All night?"

"Yeah. We've been flying for hours."

"I've been out that long? That's not good."

"It's not from blacking out. They gave you a painkiller. You've been asleep from it."

"Painkiller?"

"You don't remember?"

He shook his head.

"You woke up complaining about your head. You asked for your Tylenol. Something about it spilling back in Cork."

Widow looked at her, dumbfounded.

"Wai Lin offered you a painkiller. You took two. She said you'd be out for a long time."

Widow stayed quiet. He didn't remember any of that.

"How do you feel now?"

"Like a million bucks. If it had been run over by a truck and woke up with no memory of how it got on a plane."

She smiled and said, "You're okay." She hugged him again. She whispered one more thing in his ear. "They took my gun."

Widow nodded.

After that, she moved back and sat in the seat next to him.

The two strangers behind her came into view. They stepped up, and Widow stared at them. It was a man and a woman. Both Asian. The man was armed. Widow could see a Glock in a pancake holster on the guy's pants. He wasn't hiding it.

The man wore a thick brown winter coat, open at the front. He took a window seat in the aisle across from Widow.

The woman stayed standing. She stared at Widow like

she wanted him to recognize her, like she was an old, long-lost friend.

He looked at her. She wore a dark-green pantsuit with a Chinese collar, notched. The jacket had sleeves pushed up over her elbows. She was a very attractive woman. Nicely built. From effort, not genetics, he figured, because she had a muscular frame like a woman who spent a lot of time in the gym. Not bodybuilder status but like an endurance competitor. If he had to guess, he would have figured that she was one of these busy people who woke up at five thirty every morning to go to CrossFit, lifting and pushing blocks and big tires.

Then he had a flash of recognition. It was her eyes. They were eyes he had seen before. They were dark and swirling and volcanic, like something was brewing under the surface.

She smiled at him. She saw he recognized her.

She spoke in a hushed, low voice. Like she too was seeing an old, long-lost friend. She said, "Hello, Chicken."

CHAPTER 41

Widow was on his feet. Involuntarily. Unknowingly. Unintentionally. And he wrapped his arms around the girl with the volcanic eyes, tight.

He felt like he was seeing an old, long-lost friend.

She said, "I'm so glad to see you."

He let her go and backed away. "How? How? Is this possible? I thought you were dead? You were shot in the heart?"

She smiled and stepped back. She looked at Lu with more than a look. It was a look asking permission for something.

Lu said, "Show him."

She said, "My name is Wai Lin now."

Widow stayed quiet.

Lin said, "I was shot. Twelve years ago. You know. You were there."

Widow nodded. It was her. No doubt about it. The eyes, the face that had haunted him for years.

Lu repeated, "Just show them."

Lin nodded again, and she backed away, three steps farther. She reached up and took her jacket off, and then unbuttoned her blouse.

Widow stayed quiet.

She untucked the blouse and finished unbuttoning it and took it off. She let it fall into one hand.

She faced Widow and Cassidy, nothing left but the bra.

Widow saw a gold necklace with a locket on it. The locket fell between two breasts, supported by an expensive-looking white bra. Hard for him to look at because instinctively, he still thought of her as a girl he had let die.

Her skin was fair and smooth.

Lin stayed liked that, on display for them for a long second, like she was waiting for them to see something in particular.

Widow didn't know what he was supposed to be looking at. He could see just about everything. So far, she looked like a normal woman. Maybe she was more beautiful than most. Even so, she was normal. Everything was where it was supposed to be.

Lin turned around slowly and revealed a long back.

She craned her head and looked back over her shoulder at them.

She had grown into a beautiful woman, but there was one major thing that set her apart from other topless women that he had seen in the past.

She had a long, thick scar that spider-webbed just underneath her left shoulder blade. It was thick and old. It looked like a pruned, long-dead ocean starfish suctioned onto her back.

It was a scar from the Rainmaker's bullet.

"How did you survive?" Widow asked. He was begging to know.

She turned back around and put her blouse on, buttoned it, and tucked it into her pants. She put her jacket back on.

"I still don't understand. How is this possible?" Widow asked.

Lin stepped over to her right and plopped down in an empty seat next to Lu.

Widow sat back down. "I saw you shot. Through the heart."

"Have you ever heard of situs inversus?" She looked at both Widow and Cassidy.

They both shook their heads.

Widow asked, "What's that?"

"I was born with it. It's a congenital defect where a person is born with some organs flipped."

"Flipped?"

"My organs are reversed. They're mirrored."

Widow stared at her.

She said, "My heart is on the right side of my body. Not the left."

She reached up and touched over her chest.

She said, "The Rainmaker missed. He thought he shot me through the heart. He didn't."

"Still. I thought you were dead. How did you survive?

"The missing police. The helicopter flying in to pick you up. The gunshots. Someone heard it all. I was taken to a hospital. I survived."

Widow stared at her eyes, never looked away. "I'm so sorry. I didn't know. I didn't choose to leave you behind. Any of you."

She stared, shaking her head. "I know. I know. It's okay. None of it was your fault."

He nodded, slowly, reluctantly.

Widow didn't have a lot of regrets in his life. He didn't believe in them. Doubt and regret are killers to a SEAL. But one of the big ones he did have was that night, leaving her behind and going there in the first place. Maybe her family would still be alive.

He wanted to tell her that. But he stayed quiet.

She could see the hurt on his face.

She got up and walked closer to him. Cassidy knew what she was doing and stood up, hopped over to the next seat across from him. Lin sat next to Widow and took his hand.

She said, "Hey. It's okay, Chicken. You saved my life."

He turned to her. A single tear streamed out of his eye. He said nothing. He couldn't.

"Hey. You saved my life," she repeated.

"How?" he asked.

"You just did. That night I was rescued and nursed back to health. The Chinese had a lot of questions. They kept me alive and gave me a life and a purpose."

"What purpose?"

She looked at Lu. "We're MSS."

She meant *Ministry of Security Services,* which was the Chinese equivalent to the CIA, but with six times the budget like the NSA, the style of MI6, and broad powers like the KGB.

"That explains the sweet ride," Widow joked, trying to get off the subject of his regret.

Lin looked around the cabin. "It's a pretty sweet life all around."

"You've done well for yourself."

"That's because of you."

Widow stayed quiet.

"If you hadn't come, my family would still be dead, and so would I."

"How's that?"

"Why do you think Tiller wanted my father?"

She knew Tiller's name. Widow said, "He was a nuclear scientist? We were told to get him out because he knew things about North Korea's nuclear programs, and back in 2007, we wanted to know what he knew."

She shook her head. "No."

"No?"

"My father wasn't a nuclear scientist. He wouldn't know the first thing about nuclear fission if ten thousand kilos of uranium fell on his head."

"Then what the hell was he?"

"The Rainmakers."

"What about them?"

"He was in charge of the program. The Rainmakers are…were a team of the best-skilled snipers in the world. Back then, the former leader of the North, the father, wanted to create a dark force of elite assassins."

Sounds like a comic book, Widow thought. But then he recalled stories of assassinations traced back to the North, with no proof beyond the borders. He recalled the assassination of an estranged brother of the leader killed by an experimental poison. Someone who had the poison smeared on a piece of fabric they were wearing had brushed it against his skin. That simple touch killed him.

Lin said, "He wanted to do this in secret. He thought

that a group of mysterious super snipers could put real fear into heads of state."

Widow nodded. It did sound scary.

"These guys were selected as children. They were orphans. My father helped to design the program. It was a combination of twenty-plus years of daily, hourly sniper training, yoga, and medications."

"Yoga?" Cassidy asked.

"What kind of medications?" Widow asked.

"Yoga helps snipers a lot. Teaches them how to breathe, how to remain calm. And so on," Lin said. She turned to Widow. "They took all kinds of meds."

"Narcotics?"

She nodded.

"Just different enhancers and things to keep them in a trancelike state. Over the years, they tried everything on them to see what worked to make them better shooters and what didn't."

Widow said, "That's why they were there that night."

She nodded.

"We weren't running from patrolling guards. They're basically incompetent. We ran that night from the Rainmakers."

Widow nodded, felt good about punching Tiller—twice. Felt bad he hadn't done more.

"Tiller wanted my father for what he knew about the program. He probably wanted to recreate it. Or whatever."

Lu looked out the window.

Widow noticed and stared out with him, saw whiteness in the distance.

Lin said, "After my father was killed, the whole

program went to shit. The North Korean leader cancelled the program and jailed the remaining Rainmakers."

"Jailed them?"

She nodded.

Widow felt the jet, felt a short burst of turbulence. "Where are we going?"

Lin said, "Sorry about the jet and surprising you and not speaking up earlier. I didn't know you were you until last night. I swear."

"Where are we going?" he asked again.

Cassidy said, "Let her finish."

"Sorry," he said, "It's my head. It hurts. Making me impatient."

Lin nodded and looked at Lu. "Get him something for that."

Lu nodded and got up and went to the service area in the front.

Lin continued, "He saw them as a failure, and he didn't want them roaming free. They all went to prison. And then several of them got out later."

She paused a beat and said, "We've killed them all… All but one."

"The one we're facing now?"

She nodded.

"The Chinese government is okay with you hunting them down like this?"

"We have an arrangement."

He didn't ask.

Lu came back with two pills in his hand and a bottle of water in the other.

Widow eyeballed them.

"They're good," Lu said.

Widow nodded and took them, swallowed them with the water. He drank nearly the whole bottle, fast. "The one we're after, what's he doing?"

"He was let out of prison after the current leader's father died. The son didn't know who he was or why he was imprisoned. He was let out as some kind of new start. Like a reboot."

Widow nodded and asked, "If he's the last, who was the second shooter?"

"An accomplice. Maybe a trainee."

Widow nodded. "That one wasn't as good as him."

Lin said, "The Rainmaker is old now."

"Was he there that night?"

"Oh yeah. They all were. That's how they got so many shots on us. But I don't know which killed my father.

"I don't have a name for him. Not even sure they gave him one. But now he's out. He escaped North Korea, and he's setting up shop. He made a target list to demonstrate his skill."

"Who's on the list?" Widow asked.

"The top five snipers alive."

Widow drank the rest of the water and crushed the bottle, stuffed it into a cup holder.

"He's already murdered four."

Widow stared at her.

"He has?"

"Yes. He started with the fifth, a Russian, and has been flying around the world, killing the others. Climbing the ladder to the top spot."

"I didn't know that."

Lin shrugged and said, "That's not surprising. Why would you?"

Widow shrugged. "So, where are we going?"

"We're flying to a remote town called Doberman Lake."

"Where is that?"

"It's smack in the middle of Quebec."

"Canada?" Widow asked.

"Yes."

"What for?"

"The Rainmaker will go after the last sniper on his list."

"You know who he is?"

Lin nodded. "We know where he lives. After the Canadian sniper shot the world record, he retired from the Canadian Army."

"I thought he still worked for them?"

She shook her head. "They just say that to have a reason to keep his name anonymous. He lives near the lake, just outside of the city."

"Is it cold there?"

She nodded and said, "Don't worry. We have extra winter coats. You both will get one." She smiled.

Cassidy said, "We should call the Canadian police. We should warn them."

"The Rainmaker is already on his way. We know he's done in Ireland. The police won't help. What can they do?"

"They can go to the last sniper on the list. Warn him. They can give him protection."

She shook her head. "We can't allow that. It'll tip off the Rainmaker. We have to set a trap for him. It's the only way."

Widow nodded, said, "She's right. We gotta catch him. An ambush is the only way."

Lin nodded.

Widow asked, "How do you know he's not already

there?"

"He won't get there faster than us. We have a private jet and funding from the Chinese government. He's pretty much on his own."

"He's got funding. The rifles in Ireland, they're expensive."

Cassidy said, "Plus, the flying around the world. And lodging. And the passports he's using. They gotta be fake, and expensive too?"

"He's self-funded."

"You sure?" Cassidy asked.

"We're pretty sure. He stole the money."

"From where?"

"Here and there."

Silence.

Widow said, "When do you expect he'll show?"

"Probably a couple of days. We have to convince the Canadian to stay put with us. Till he shows."

"How are we going to do that?"

She looked at Lu and said, "We have ways."

Widow nodded. She was the little girl he thought had died. But she grew up to be a spook, not like Tiller but not unlike him either.

They were all quiet for a moment, and Lin asked, "Want coffee?"

He looked at her. "I'd love coffee."

"I knew you would."

"How did you know that?"

She got up, started on her way down the aisle to fetch him a coffee. She stopped and turned and said, "I read it in your file."

And she smiled.

CHAPTER 42

The airport in Doberman had to be one of the smallest, most rinky-dink airports that Widow had ever seen in his life. It was a one-building, one-floor, one-runway thing covered in snow with no visible signs of what most airports call a tower.

They had plowed the runway, so it was the only thing around besides the roads without snow covering it. The good news was it made the runway stick out visibly from the air.

As the Gulfstream jet came in for a landing, Widow saw roads headed away in great, unobstructed distances. The roads were the same plowed dirt.

Along the runway was a long, chain-link fence. Snow hung off it.

He wondered how deep he would have to plunge a leg into the snow before he hit the ground.

The airport was painted blue, also making it unmistakable from the sky.

Widow knew better than to ask about flying with the

Chinese MSS over international airspace and landing in a remote airport in Canada. They had made their arrangements prior to reporting the flight path.

But Cassidy was curious, and she asked Wai Lin, who gave her an answer repeated from earlier. She said, "We have our ways."

They landed the jet and parked it, and the pilots came out and joined them at baggage claim, which was a single carousel.

Lu and the pilots carried the luggage, and Widow and Cassidy followed Lin, who checked in with a guy who looked like part airport manager and part local sheriff, or whatever Canada had in rural areas as their law enforcement. Widow wasn't sure. Was it the Mounties? Or did they have constables?

Walking into the airport, he realized he felt much better than he had when they were in the air. But then he realized he felt a little too good. He wondered what Lin had given him.

Cassidy must've expected his grogginess. She offered to help him stand straight and walk. Truthfully, he wasn't so bad that he needed to be helped to walk, but he didn't tell her. There was no reason to keep a beautiful Irish cop from standing close to him, like the night before, walking in the rain.

He felt her next to him. She was warm, and stronger than she looked.

They walked to the front of the airport and stayed in the arrivals area, which was the same area as departures.

Cassidy finally spoke to him with no one else around. "What do you think?"

"About what?"

"Them? That story she told? Is that true?"

"It's true. I was there."

"What's the rest of it?"

"I'll tell you some other time."

"Seriously? I got to wait?"

"It's not the time. It's a long story. Let's just say it was a mission that went bad. A military op. I watched this sniper and his ilk kill her whole family."

"You actually left her for dead?"

"I didn't know she was alive. And I'm not the one who left her. Tiller ordered it."

Cassidy nodded.

"Anyway, this guy killed my teammates. He's killed your partner. And he killed her family. I say we're due for some payback."

"What about this other sniper in Canada?"

"What about him?"

"He's moved all the way out here. The middle of nowhere. How is he going to feel about Chinese spies and an Irish flatfoot and a homeless man showing up at his door?"

Widow said, "He's a guy like me. He's military. He'll understand. Believe me."

She shrugged.

"Besides, what choice do we have? We're here. Lin seems to know what she's doing."

Lin walked up behind them. She rattled a set of keys in front of them. "We have wheels. Let's go."

They went out to the parking lot and followed Lin to a row of trucks that were identical, just different colors. They were all Ford Explorers, about ten years old but all tough-looking. Weather-tested.

They followed Lin, who hopped in the driver's seat. Lu got in next to her. The rest piled in the back. The pilots sat in the third row of seats. It turned out they weren't just pilots. They were part of Lin's team.

Widow saw them take out Type 05 submachine guns. Chinese military uses them all over the world—their version of MP5s.

They had two of them. They locked and loaded them. Then they pulled out two more and did the same. One magazine each. Each ready for use.

They placed the guns in a black duffle bag.

Widow looked forward over Lin's shoulder.

He said, "You guys got a lot of hardware."

Lu said, "A precaution. We might need it."

"Got any sniper rifles?"

"What for?"

"The Rainmaker and his—whatever, student?—aren't going to be in range of some submachine guns."

Lin said, "If we go up against them with sniper rifles, we'll all be dead in minutes. You know that."

Widow stayed quiet.

Lu said, "It'd be like fighting the Jedi with laser swords. I am not good with a laser sword."

Widow stared at him. The Jedi used lightsabers. At least, that's what he remembered them being called. He didn't correct him.

"Why fight a Jedi on his own terms?" Lu said.

Widow nodded. It made sense.

CHAPTER 43

The house of the Canadian sniper was like Lin had said. It was north of the middle of nowhere. They drove for only about fifteen minutes to get there, but they covered twenty-plus kilometers because the roads were straight and plowed well enough, and the land was flat, and there were no other vehicles in sight. No speed limit signs posted. No police. Nothing.

Lin slowed the Explorer as she approached a solitary home. She spoke to Lu in Chinese. He listened and looked down at his cell phone.

A GPS map, Widow thought.

Lu spoke English.

"This is it."

They drove up a snowy drive, unplowed and uninviting.

Widow knew they could be seen from the house.

The house was less than a hundred yards down a drive and was on a lake. Which would've made for a very serene home for someone, except the lake was completely frozen over. There were signs posted along the track, warning people not to walk on the ice.

Widow looked out over the lake and said, "Thin ice."

Cassidy squeezed his arm, her tiny hand over his good bicep. He realized she had never let go of it. Not since they left the airport.

She leaned in and whispered in his ear—another intimate breath on his neck and skin. "I'm having second thoughts about this."

He looked at her, didn't whisper. "I am too."

They saw no one on the drive.

The house was a brick colonial, painted white. It blended into the snowy terrain. Widow saw plumes of smoke coming out of one of two chimneys. They stood tall and grand, constructed with thick brick.

"Nice house," Lu said, and he made a whistle at the end.

"One day, maybe you'll get one too," Lin said.

"It looks like something out of a novel," Cassidy said.

"Looks like it's owned by a novelist," Lin said back to her.

Widow stayed quiet.

He checked the windows, checking the rooftop, checking the snowy knolls to the sides of the house. He looked at everything that was good sniper cover.

Once they got past fifty yards, he relaxed. If this Canadian sniper wanted to shoot them, he could've done it long ago.

They got to the end of the driveway and parked on the lakeside. No telling what was a driveway and what was yard because everything was snow.

The house had a couple of huge trees in the front yard,

still asleep from winter. No leaves, but there was a tire swing hung from a rope so thick it looked like it came off the anchor of an oil tanker.

No one else seemed to notice it.

There was a truck parked out front. Big, heavy, with big snow tires.

There was a big porch with a swing on it.

They pulled to a stop, and Lin parked and turned off the engine.

She turned to Widow and Cassidy and said, "You guys should go up first."

"Why us?" Cassidy asked.

Lin looked at Widow.

He said, "Because we're white."

Cassidy said nothing.

Widow said, "Four Chinese people who look like government agents—no offense—will cause them some alarm."

"I think they're already alarmed," Cassidy said, and she pointed at the porch.

Widow heard a pair of dogs barking and saw two huge snow dogs running off the porch and to the Explorer. They were huge. Widow didn't know the breed, but they weren't huskies.

Lin said, "Go ahead. Charm them."

Widow smiled.

Then a voice from the porch called out the names of the dogs.

And they went running back.

A man stepped out and let them back into the house. Widow saw someone else shut the door.

The man was about late thirties. He had a good build,

athletic, but not a big guy. He had a full beard, the kind that seemed to be popular with young guys. Widow had seen it a lot, traveling across North America.

The man walked off the porch but stayed far enough back from the Explorer. He held a pump shotgun.

"Hello. Who are you?" he called out in a Canadian accent. Not too heavy, but obvious.

"Widow," Lin said.

He got out and walked around the Explorer to greet the man.

"Hello," he said, his hands offered like he was surrendering.

"Hello," the man said back.

Canadians. Even with gun in hand, they were polite. Widow smiled. "Hello," Widow repeated.

"Are you lost?"

"No. We're looking for someone."

"You are? Who?"

"Well, you actually."

"Me? What for?"

"It's complicated."

"Complicated?"

Widow saw a window on the first floor, close to the front door, slide up and open. A figure stood behind it in the shadows.

"Yeah. It's not a shotgun in-hand, standing-out-here kind of story."

The man pumped the shotgun, the international signal for *Make it short.*

"What kind of story would six strangers drive all the way out here to tell?"

Widow glanced back over his shoulder at Cassidy, then back at the man.

"It's the kind of story that six strangers would fly around the world and drive all the way out here *just* to tell."

The man was silent.

"Look, we're not here to hurt you. We're here to save you."

"Save me?" the man said and looked around, endless blue sky, the limitless blankets of white, and then nothing else in sight.

"Yes."

"From what?"

"A man who wants to kill you."

The man was quiet for a moment. Then he said, "I think it's time for you to leave."

Widow said, "Three thousand eight hundred seventy-one yards."

The man was quiet for a beat. He stared at Widow. "What's that supposed to mean?"

"That's the world record for the longest confirmed sniper kill."

The man said nothing.

Widow said, "That's your record."

The man was completely still, completely silent. Widow saw into his eyes and realized he wouldn't shoot him. He realized this man had killed no one in his life. He felt confused.

Then a woman's voice spoke from behind the window. It was followed by a face that came forward and peered out at him.

The voice said, "Better let them in."

CHAPTER 44

The woman from the window opened the front door and walked out onto the porch and welcomed Widow. "Who are your friends?"

"Well, ma'am, it's kind of long story."

The woman was a little younger than the bearded guy. She had blonde hair pulled back; she wore glasses, and she glowed like a woman who smiled a lot. She wore a big winter coat, blue, and far too big for her. Probably the man's, Widow figured.

She walked with a wide stance, like she was carrying something underneath the coat. "Are you good guys or bad guys?" she asked.

Widow looked back at Cassidy and again at the woman in the oversized coat and said, "Good guys."

"Okay then. This is Lawrence. I'm Lara. Gagnon. He's my husband."

The guy named Lawrence smiled and lowered the shotgun.

"Jack Widow, ma'am."

"So get your friends and come on in."

Widow waved back at the Explorer, and everyone got out, followed by slamming doors. The pilots, who were more than pilots, stepped out with the duffle bag.

They all stepped up onto the porch, following Widow and Cassidy, who went into the house first, after Lara Gagnon.

The enormous dogs sat at attention at the base of a grand staircase.

Widow thought, *Like Dobermans. Like the town's name.*

He asked, "Doberman, is that related to the snow dogs?"

Lara said, "You know, everyone who comes here asks that. I don't know. I like it 'cause it's a quiet lake town. Hardly anyone lives here, and the people mind their own business."

"Do you guys have an actual town?"

"Like a downtown?"

He nodded.

"Sure. It's twenty-five kilometers south."

"All we saw was that little airport."

"They built it way out from the town."

"What for?"

She said, "No clue. Hide the town from visitors, I guess."

He shrugged.

The inside of the house was clean and warm and filled with the smell of baking bread.

Widow saw a living room with high ceilings. There were posts and log paneling and brick around a fireplace, and heavy furniture and wood everywhere, surrounded by white walls. The floor was wood with woven rugs.

The main floor was wide open. Widow could see she was cooking something in the kitchen. The dining room table was set for two.

"I'm sorry if we're disturbing your breakfast," he said.

"Don't worry about it. Getting visitors is the most excitement I've had in months."

Lawrence was the last person to step in. He suggested everyone take off their coats and boots and leave them in the mudroom to the side of the entrance.

Widow stepped back in that direction. "Sorry for dragging dirt in."

"Don't worry about it," Lawrence said.

Widow took off the winter coat Lin had given him, and so did Cassidy. Widow kept his bomber jacket on. He had worn it underneath.

Lin and Lu and the pilots took off their winter coats, and Lawrence found a place to hang most of them.

Lawrence kept the shotgun nearby. The pilots kept the duffle bag near as well.

They all sat around a roaring fire on soft, oversized, too-comfortable sofas and armchairs.

But before they did, Lara took off her coat and revealed that she had been carrying something.

She was pregnant.

CHAPTER 45

"When are you due?" Widow asked.

"Can't you tell?"

He shook his head.

Cassidy pinched his leg and said, "He was raised in a cave. We think."

"It's okay. I'm due soon."

"Not today?"

"No. Week or two."

"Are you having a home birth?"

"Sure."

"No hospital?"

"My husband is a doctor."

Widow looked at Lawrence, who stayed standing. He was near a substantial white island that acted as part of the kitchen and a bar for the rest of the house. He was on the bar side, shotgun resting across the countertop. He was drinking coffee. It steamed out of a white mug. If he had offered any to their visitors, Widow would've had one too.

The pilots sat together. Lin and Lu sat in armchairs. And Widow was on a sofa with Cassidy.

"Lawrence is a doctor?"

Lara nodded.

Cassidy said, "That makes you the sniper."

Lara said, "I was in the Canadian Armed Forces."

"JTF2?" Widow asked.

"Yes."

"Amazing."

"Why? Because a woman can't be a soldier?"

Widow shook his head.

"You a soldier?" she asked.

"SEAL. Once."

She nodded. "You've never seen a woman in uniform before?"

Widow shook his head again. "I've known plenty of women who were in the Navy and the Marines. They make damn good sailors and marines and soldiers, I imagine. Better than a lot of men I knew."

"No women SEALs, though?"

"Not yet."

"So why are you surprised?"

"I just never pictured a world-record-breaking soldier being pregnant."

Lara said nothing to that.

"You might be the first. That might be a new record."

Lara asked, "So you figured out I'm the sniper who holds the world record. Why are you here?"

Lawrence said, "You said something about protection."

Lin spoke up. "I'm Wai Lin of the Chinese MSS. We're all here because we have united interests."

"Which are?" Lara asked.

She didn't ask about the MSS. Widow figured she knew about them. He asked, "Have you ever heard of the Rainmakers?"

Lara looked at Widow. Her eyes were wide. She nodded. "I've heard of them."

"They're real." Widow said, "There's one left. He's coming here."

"Why?"

"He's taken it upon himself to eliminate the best of the best."

Lara said nothing.

Lawrence said nothing.

Widow asked, "You know James Lenny?"

"I know him."

"He's dead. Shot from three thousand–plus yards."

She said nothing.

Lin said, "We're here to stop him."

Lawrence stood up and said, "You're here to ambush him."

Lin said, "We are."

"So, what? You want to use my wife as bait?"

Lin said, "That's right."

Lara said, "Lawrence. It's okay. If he's killed Lenny, then he's gotta be stopped."

Lara looked at the duffle bag. "What's in there?"

Lu said, "Type 05 submachine guns, ma'am."

She nodded and said, "That's not gonna help you very much unless you can get close."

"It's what we have," Lu said.

"No. We have more." She stood up and walked past everyone and stopped and looked at Widow. "You coming?"

He nodded and looked at Lin, who nodded to Lu.

Lu followed.

They moved down a hall, passed a bathroom and a study, and stopped at a door with a padlock on it. Lara took out a set of keys and unlocked it.

The room was about the size of a large walk-in closet or a tight bedroom. It had a table in the center of the room with four expensive sniper rifles. They were standing upright in inserts and unloaded.

Lara said, "We might need these."

Widow nodded.

"How long till they get here?"

Widow shrugged.

Lu said, "We think a day or two."

They returned to the living room, and Lin explained the whole story to the Gagnons. She told them her role, her side—everything. She told them about her family. And her medical condition and how it saved her life.

Lawrence Gagnon was familiar with it. He told her she was lucky she hadn't died. Not because of situs inversus. Life expectancy rates with situs inversus are like everyone else. But the bullet wounds, unsterile environment, and delayed treatment sounded like they should have killed her.

Lin ordered the pilots to secure the perimeter. They took their weapons and coats and headed outside to walk the perimeter of the house and the lake and stand guard.

After Lin's version of the story finished, Lawrence stopped eyeballing the shotgun every minute and offered them coffee. Widow was the first to accept. And Lawrence returned with breakfast on plates for his wife and himself.

He offered to cook breakfast for Widow and company, but no one wanted anything.

The Gagnons ate, and Widow drank his coffee while telling his side of the story. He told them about the train wreck, the concussion, the broken arm, which they could see, and Lenny and Tiller and the op twelve years ago.

By the afternoon, they all knew everything about what had happened so far.

All but Cassidy's dead partner, which Widow didn't want to bring up, and Cassidy didn't want to talk about.

CHAPTER 46

By nightfall, the pilots were sitting on the porch. They had bottles of water and had split up break times, taking turns going back inside to get warm.

One of them took smoke breaks. His cigarette butts were stuffed into an empty soda can on the porch.

Lu went to check on them every hour, and then he returned to the back of the house, facing the lake.

Occasionally, Widow went outside to have a look. And Lin did the same. Cassidy stayed with Lara. By this time, trust had been earned all the way around, and she had been given her sidearm back.

Lawrence had the shotgun. Lara kept one of the sniper rifles with her, loaded. Widow had no idea why. It wouldn't be much good to her as a close-quarter combat weapon unless she planned to climb up to the roof and use it there.

Lu was armed, of course. The only two people who

weren't armed were Widow and Lin, but she had Lu and two other guys for that.

Widow said nothing about it. He knew where the weapons were.

He and Cassidy and Lara and Lin wound up sitting on a deck on the back of the house overlooking the lake.

Just then, they heard a sound in the distance, beyond the lake, echoing over a cluster of snow-covered trees. It sounded like a lawnmower or a Honda Civic that Widow had heard before.

"What's that?" Lin asked.

Lu came running around the side of the house, gun in hand. The noise spooked him.

They saw distant plumes of smoke. And the sound continued.

"Relax," Lara said. "It's a Mosquito."

"A what?" Cassidy asked.

"A Mosquito. It's a one-man helicopter. The neighbors have one."

"You have neighbors?" Lin asked.

"We call them neighbors. They live two kilometers that way."

She pointed across the lake.

"Out here, people have all kinds of hobbies. The Mosquito is Colonel Hardy's hobby."

A second after she said that, Widow saw it. A small black dot on the sky, at first, and then it buzzed the treetops and headed toward them.

Widow felt himself rising to his feet, a precaution. He readied himself to jump over Lara and protect her if he had to.

The black dot grew larger, and he saw a small helicopter, like Lara had said. It flew across the frozen water and buzzed the house.

Widow returned to his seat when he saw the pilot.

He was a short old white man in a wool cap, with goggles over his face. He had a scarf wrapped tightly around his neck.

He took the little chopper close and down to an altitude of maybe forty feet above them, staying clear of one old leafless tree.

He waved down to them.

"I see you got friends," he called out to Lara.

"I do, Colonel," she said and waved back.

The pilots from the front came running through the house to see what was happening. They had their guns out.

The dogs were barking, but not at the Mosquito. They barked at the pilots. They were used to the Mosquito like the old guy flew it over the house every day.

Lin barked orders at the pilots in Chinese, and they quickly hid the Type 05s.

"Well, okay then. Have a good night, Lara," the old guy shouted, and he waved and piloted the tiny helicopter higher and back over the lake.

Lara waved after him.

Widow asked, "Colonel?"

"Yeah. He's retired too."

"Does he know who you are?"

"No. He's just a nice old guy."

Lin asked, "Does he fly that every night?"

"Not every night. Sometimes in the early mornings. He's a widower. Gotta do something out here during the cold months to pass the time."

No one spoke about it after that. The pilots and Lu returned to the front of the house.

A short while later, they were conversing about other things.

Widow said, "I can see why you retired out here."

"Thanks. It's my husband's doing."

"How does he get any work way the hell out here? As a doctor, I mean?"

"He works from the internet."

"How?"

"He started one of those medical diagnostics websites."

Widow stayed quiet.

Cassidy said, "Like WebMD?"

Lara smiled.

"Is it WebMD?"

"I can't say."

"Whoa. Explains the nice house."

Lara smiled. She looked at the sky; the darkness was coming on fast. "Up here, the sun sets so quickly," she said.

Widow said, "Seems like it does that just about everywhere."

The dogs were out running in the backyard through the snow, playing.

Lin said, "Thank you for letting us do this."

Lara said, "Just make sure you get this guy."

Lin nodded.

Widow said, "We don't know how long it'll take him to

make a move. I think we'd better take shifts sleeping for now."

"How long will we be out here waiting?" Cassidy asked.

"Not long. He won't wait long. Trust me," Lin said. "Two, three days, tops."

"I'd better call my unit. They have to be worried about me."

Lara said, "No phones out here, and the internet is out again."

Cassidy frowned.

Lara said, "I know how you feel. Lawrence's business depends on the internet. Good thing a lot of it is automated somewhere else."

Widow shrugged and said, "Better to say you're sorry than ask permission."

No one responded to that.

Widow volunteered to take the first shift sleeping, mostly because his head was hurting again.

Lara showed him to a bedroom on the top floor, and he waited until she left and then hit the bed. He slept over the covers. Bomber jacket still on. Pants still on. Everything still on except his boots, which were in the mudroom.

CHAPTER 47

Widow didn't dream about the dead girl with the volcanic eyes this time. He didn't have to. She was alive.

Instead, he dreamed about Cassidy. A good dream, except he woke up before it got really good.

He woke up to the same buzzing that he had heard earlier, which made him uneasy. Until he remembered Lara had said the old guy was a widower, and he flew the Mosquito in the early morning sometimes.

He opened his eyes and looked around the room. His head wasn't hurting so much anymore.

The buzzing chopper was far away. It grew a little louder, slowly. After a few minutes, it sounded as if it buzzed around the house once.

He listened.

The buzz came and went and was gone suddenly.

Not a big deal if the guy does that a lot, and Lara had said he does. The dogs weren't barking, which was a good sign.

Still, it bothered him. It bothered him because he didn't hear any commotion from whoever was outside guarding, which he assumed were the pilots and Lu.

Best to check it out anyway, he thought.

He sat up in the bed, knew where he was for the first time in two days right off the bat after waking up. He looked over and saw a tray resting on a nightstand. It had a bowl of cereal on it, covered. For him, he guessed.

He left it and got up, tried not to make a sound. He didn't know the time, but it appeared everyone else was asleep.

No dogs were barking. They were used to the buzzing helicopter, though.

His room didn't have a clock. He walked over to a window and looked out.

The nighttime revealed that this place wasn't so empty. He saw the lights from the neighbor's house across the lake, the old colonel's house.

Widow tried to find the Mosquito. No luck. Not in the dark. Even if it had lights turned on, which it may or may not have, it would've looked like a star, depending on how far away it was.

He looked to the south and saw a bit of light in the sky. Must be downtown Doberman.

The sky was full of stars.

He went out to the hallway. He saw no one around.

A door was ajar, two doors down from him.

He peeked in. It was another bedroom, the Gagnons' master. They were asleep in a king-size bed—the dogs on the floor. One of them looked up at him as he peered in the open door. The dog didn't make a sound.

He left the door and checked out the other rooms, and

found Cassidy asleep in one. Her Glock rested within reaching distance on a nightstand. She too slept in her clothes over the covers. Her boots were also in the mudroom.

Next, he found an empty bedroom.

He went downstairs and found Lin asleep on one sofa. The fire was still alive, but glowed less than earlier.

Widow moved to the kitchen and looked around. Nothing of interest, except the coffeepot, which was off. But he looked anyway.

He saw the time on the clock—four in the morning.

A little early for the colonel to be flying that thing, he thought.

He went to the back door and opened it, stepped out onto the deck. The wood was cold under his feet. He went over to the railing and looked around, checked the sky, the cluster of distant trees, the lights from the colonel's house. He saw no sign of the Mosquito.

He also saw no sign of the other MSS men. No Lu. No pilots.

He saw something on the ice. It was on the lake.

He almost stepped off the back deck, but he didn't have his boots on.

He ducked back inside to get them. They were in the front, in the mudroom where he'd left them. He slipped them on and went back through the house, sneaking past Lin.

He realized he'd left the winter coat inside but went outside without it.

The back deck's light was switched off. He left it that way and walked out. He stepped off the deck and into the snow.

Then he saw someone down by the lake. It was one of the pilots. He was smoking a cigarette. As he approached the pilot, he saw the guy trying to see the object on the ice. The pilot took another puff of his cigarette.

Suddenly, his back exploded. A bullet had gone right through his chest.

Widow dove for the snow.

He stayed prone and watched. The pilot's cigarette landed in the snow, burned one last time like it was still being puffed, and it lit up the pilot's face, which had an expression of utter shock on it. His eyes were wide open. But he was lifeless.

Widow felt a sudden pain in his arm. He'd landed on top of it—again.

He stayed still.

He saw a figure coming up off the ice—all black.

His eyes came into better focus. He saw the object on the ice was the old colonel's Mosquito. But the man coming up the ice wasn't the old colonel.

This guy looked old, but he wasn't white. And it looked like he had a scar over one eye.

CHAPTER 48

Widow saw a USP in the guy's hand, silenced. But he wasn't the one who had shot the pilot. That shot had come from the ice or beyond—a sniper.

Widow guessed it was the Rainmaker that he was looking at because the guy fit the bill. The sniper must've been his protégé. The second shooter. The one who killed Gregor.

The Rainmaker approached the dead body slowly and looked it over once; then he started towards the house.

He wasn't planning to kill Lara with a sniper's bullet. He wanted to do this one up close and personal.

Just then, Widow heard footsteps. He turned and saw Lu and the other pilot coming around the side of the house, investigating.

They saw the figure coming toward them but couldn't identify him.

Then Widow thought, *They don't know about the sniper.*

But it was too late.

Widow saw the other pilot's head explode right in front of Lu.

A faint sound echoed across the ice, a suppressed sniper rifle. It sounded like someone hitting a tree with a board, only softer than that.

Lu's chest burst open in two places, almost at the same second.

The Rainmaker had shot him once, with the USP, and the protégé sniper had shot the other pilot.

Widow had been about to call out to them, to warn them. Again, he was too late.

CHAPTER 49

Three men dead right in front of him, four if the old colonel was dead. The Rainmaker and his student had killed them in seconds.

Widow hugged the snow, didn't move.

The Rainmaker walked up to the back deck. He stepped up and entered the house.

It would be seconds before he discovered Lin asleep on the sofa, and everyone else was asleep. Widow had to act, but the student sniper was still out there. Probably on the ice. Maybe they had choppered over together. Or maybe he was on the land, not far beyond the frozen water, near the trees.

If Widow jumped up and ran for the back deck, he would be seen right there. The sniper had nothing else to do—no one else to look at. The house was quiet behind him.

If the second sniper was looking, he'd be seen and killed as soon as he made the first move.

For the first time in twelve years, Widow didn't know what to do.

His head started hurting again.

Not now! He thought.

He closed his eyes, remembered staying still, twelve years ago. Remembered thinking Lin was dead, sprawled out on his chest. He had been stuck then, and he was stuck now—paralyzed.

He had to act.

He couldn't let her die, not again, not twice.

He couldn't let Cassidy die or the Gagnons or the baby on the way.

Widow's life was worth losing if it meant giving them a chance to live.

Seconds passed. He had to act.

Suddenly, Widow got a break, and he was all about taking advantage of the right opportunity. It wouldn't get any better.

Right then, the dogs started barking in the house.

He had to bet that the sniper would watch the upstairs.

He leaped to his feet, stayed crouched, and sprinted as fast as he could, through the snow, up the steps, over the deck, and into the house.

There was no sign of the Rainmaker in the hall or the kitchen.

Then he saw him, standing in the dimming firelight, standing over the girl he'd tried to murder twelve years ago.

The USP in his hand, silenced and held an inch from Lin's head.

Widow exploded into action like he was running in the Olympics, and the starter gun had been fired.

He went through the kitchen, making as much noise as he could. He grabbed the cold coffee pot with his good hand and ran past the bar and into the living room.

The Rainmaker heard him coming and twisted at the waist, ready to shoot the madman running at him with a coffeepot.

Widow was faster and had a longer reach.

He slammed the coffee pot into the Rainmaker's gun hand.

The USP fired as it was knocked free. The bullet slammed into the refrigerator in the kitchen. The gunshot was muted, but the stainless-steel refrigerator door pinged loudly behind him.

The Rainmaker was faster than Widow had thought for an old man. And he was very limber.

He had pulled a K-blade out about as fast as he could draw a gun. He stabbed at Widow with it.

Widow blocked with his left hand. The blade stabbed into his cast, and it got stuck there.

The Rainmaker tried to jerk it out but couldn't. Not before Widow punched him with a fast right hook.

The Rainmaker flew off balance and let go of the knife. The side of his face was red and bloody. Widow had cut his face open somewhere.

Widow went to grab the knife out of his cast, but the Rainmaker scooped up his gun first. He rolled with it and aimed right at Widow's center mass.

He smiled at Widow like he recognized him—the man who got away.

He didn't shoot, not yet.

CHAPTER 50

The dogs barked upstairs, but the Rainmaker didn't seem to care about that. He stared at Widow down the sights of the USP.

Widow should have been dead, but he was still alive.

He spoke first. "Why aren't you shooting me?"

"I no shoot you yet because I know you."

"You know me?"

The Rainmaker nodded. "You the man that night? You escaped me."

Widow nodded, said, "That was you."

"It was me."

"All of them? You were alone?"

The Rainmaker was down on one knee, aiming the gun. It was rock-steady in his hand.

Widow saw that the eye with the scar was completely whited out. He was blind as a bat in it.

"Not alone. But I only one shoot that far. I kill boy. I kill woman. I kill man." He paused a beat and said, "I kill girl."

"What about my team?"

The Rainmaker shook his head.

"Not them. That other sniper. I was reserved for when you got far away."

Widow stayed quiet. He saw Lin moving in the corner of his eye.

"You know what they do when I not kill you?"

Widow said, "Put you in prison?"

The Rainmaker nodded. "You know what that for me was like? It was horror. They kill my wife. They kill my son. They take my eye. Only my daughter left."

Widow nodded.

"She out there. Right now. She getting good. Like me."

His daughter was his student, Widow thought. *A family business.*

Lin moved slowly.

Widow wondered if the Rainmaker couldn't see her because of his eye. He had no peripheral vision on that side of his face.

Widow said, "You're wrong about one thing."

"What?"

"That girl."

The Rainmaker stared at him.

"She lived too."

Lin burst from the sofa, charged at the Rainmaker with a poker from the fireplace. It turned out he saw her moving. He shot her. She went flying back.

Widow shouted, without realizing it.

The dogs were barking loudly now.

Widow attempted to sprint and charge the Rainmaker. But he twisted fast and pointed the USP at Widow again. This time he was going to shoot him. No question.

Talking was over.

This was beyond personal.

Widow jerked the knife all the way out of the cast as he charged. He was ready to die, but the Rainmaker was going to get cut. He wouldn't die without making sure he took that other eye.

A gunshot *boomed!* through the house, and its target exploded.

CHAPTER 51

Widow froze where he was. He had heard a gunshot blasting through the house. It echoed and rang out and quieted down after a long, long second.

The Rainmaker had a silencer on his gun. It wasn't his gun that fired.

And Widow was all in one piece.

The Rainmaker was not so lucky. His head had exploded, like the heads of his victims. A bullet had torn through the back of his head and out his good eye.

Blood was sprayed all over the sofas and across Widow's face and clothes.

Standing at the top of the stairs was a pregnant Lara Gagnon, holding one of her sniper rifles. It was bolt action, and smoke plumed out of the barrel.

It turned out she was pretty good with it at short range, too.

Widow dropped the knife and ran over to Lin.

She was still alive. The Rainmaker had shot her on the left side again, thinking it was her heart. But she was breathing raggedly, and it was still a dangerous wound.

She was conscious. He told her to stay quiet.

Cassidy appeared at the top of the stairs, behind Lara and Lawrence. She had her Glock out.

They all came down the stairs. The dogs too.

The dogs were licking up what was left of the Rainmaker. No one stopped them.

Lawrence took over. Tending to Lin's wounds, he ordered Cassidy to get him water and towels from different rooms.

Widow stood up and grabbed Lara's arm.

"Thank you," he said.

She nodded.

"There's one more thing."

"Yes?"

"You got night vision on that gun?"

She smiled.

They went to the top floor, and she looked out through a window from her bedroom. They left the lights off.

"I see the sniper. It's a girl."

She'd found the protégé, the Rainmaker's daughter. Which he didn't tell her.

"Yeah. How old is she?"

Lara paused and said, "I'd say in her early twenties."

Widow paused.

"Want me to kill her?"

Widow thought for a quick second.

"Hurry, she looks worried. She's shuffling around."

The girl had killed Gregor. She had murdered him in

cold blood. And who knew how many others she had killed.

"Do it," he said.

Lara breathed in, held it, and squeezed the trigger.

CHAPTER 52

Lawrence kept Lin alive long enough for them to get her into a vehicle and drive to town, where there was a small hospital. He told Widow that she would have to be moved to a better one, which was an hour's drive south, but she should make it just fine.

Widow looked for holes in the ice. He thought about having them dump the bodies in the lake, but he had brought enough problems to the Gagnons.

Lara was a by-the-book type. Mostly.

They wanted to get the authorities out there as soon as possible.

Widow convinced them to wait until Lin was safe and stable in the local hospital. He rode with them to bring her, as did Cassidy. Only the dogs stayed behind in the house.

They arrived in downtown Doberman, and Widow helped them get Lin into the emergency room, which was bigger than Widow expected.

He saw her go in; she was talking. She'd be fine, he figured.

He never said goodbye to her.

He took Cassidy by the hand and fell back with her behind the Gagnons and the nurses and doctors.

They returned to the airport.

She mentioned Tiller one time. Asked Widow if he was going to do anything else about him. Widow responded with a shrug and a "life's too short to worry about an insignificant person like him."

That was all they said on the matter.

They held hands, waiting for two different flights. His was first. He said goodbye to her at the gate and took her business card.

They did the "if you're ever in Ireland again" conversation.

Widow kissed her and boarded a plane to JFK.

In the air, he thought maybe he'd call DeGorne when he landed. Then again, maybe not.

A WORD FROM SCOTT

Thank you for reading THE LAST RAINMAKER. You got this far—I'm guessing that you liked Widow.

The story continues in a fast-paced series that takes Widow (and you) all around the world, solving crimes, righting wrongs.

The tenth book that follows is THE DEVIL'S STOP, which refers to all the places in the USA named after the devil like Hellbent, New Hampshire, a small town that time forgot. First day there, Jack Widow meets a beautiful former Air Force MP who's desperately seeking her husband all while being nearly nine months pregnant. Widow being the man he is means that he's got to help. What starts as a simple missing person soon turns deadly when they uncover that the missing husband was involved in a top-secret government nuclear program and the evil team of dishonored mercenaries who are after it.

Book eleven is BLACK DAYLIGHT. Jack Widow walks a lonely, snowy road at night when he witnesses a heinous crime. The only glimpse of the culprit he gets are taillights that fade into the mist. Widow does all he can to help, but when he does the local South Dakota police and the FBI see him as suspect number one.

What are you waiting for? The fun is just starting. Once you start Widow, you won't be able to stop.

THE DEVIL'S STOP: A PREVIEW

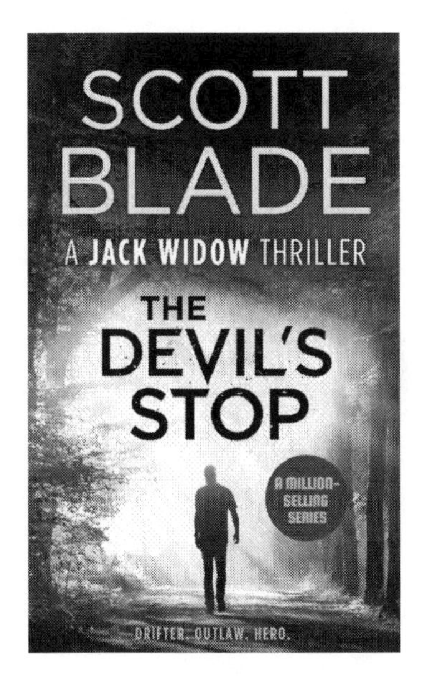

Out Now!

THE DEVIL'S STOP: A BLURB

Not even the devil can stop Widow from doing what's right.

In the remote town of Hellbent, New Hampshire, a woman, eight months pregnant, steps off a train. She is alone, and desperate to find her missing husband—a nuclear missileer. He's gone missing. No one knows where he is. The Pentagon won't acknowledge that he even exists. She believes time is running out, and she fears the worst. Her only hope is a drifter she just met, named Jack Widow. Together, maybe they can find her husband.

What they don't know is that he might already be dead. A gang of Army-rejects has been hunting for him. And they may have already found him. The gang's leader is so evil; he might be in league with the devil.

If you love **Lee Child's Jack Reacher, Vince Flynn's Mitch Rapp,** and **Mark Greaney's Gray Man**, then you will binge the entire Jack Widow Action-Thriller Series once you've read one page.

Readers are saying...

★★★★★ The best author next to Lee Child!

★★★★★ Incredible! This one will take you to the edge!

★★★★★ Full of action! So fast-paced that you cannot put it down!

THE DEVIL'S STOP: AN EXCERPT

CHAPTER 2

At dawn, Jack Widow made a life-threatening decision. Only he didn't know it. It was a wrong choice, the kind of wrong choice that anyone might've made. It was all by chance. But anyone could see that it was the wrong choice afterward, in the post-game analysis.

If there were after-action reports of things to come his way, this would be the decision that turned everything wrong. He would've been blamed for the deadly outcome that would plow straight through his life in the days to come.

At six-foot-four, Widow stood solemn and alone and statuesque and weathered, all like an outmoded old water tower. To the motorists on the highway, he looked like a giant lost on the side of the road.

Widow was unaware of the deadly mistake he was about to make. He was also completely unaware that he stood twenty-five miles away from where a cabin had burned the night before.

Widow turned his head, shifting it due south, stopping southeast, toward a guesstimation of the direction of the state of his birth, Mississippi.

He stared in that direction for a long moment. He let his mind wander back to a different realm, a different life, his first life. If there was a god in the afterlife keeping score, tallying up all the lives a man lived, then technically he was on his third, or maybe it was his fourth. It was hard for him to keep track since he was no longer in the business of lying to protect his cover.

Widow had grown up in a small town in Mississippi, the son of a sheriff mother and a drifter father. His mother raised him on her own, with her own money and with her own capabilities. She had done the best she could with the little she had. He had no complaints, not now.

But back then, he did—just one big one.

She had lied to him his whole childhood. She had lied about who his father had been. He still didn't know the man. Not now. Not ever.

She had told him that his father was some sort of army hero who died in combat. That turned out not to be true. She came clean when he was seventeen. Feeling betrayed, Widow ran away from home, joined the Navy. He stayed quiet for sixteen years, never contacting his mother the whole time. Not once. No phone calls. No postcards. Not one word.

Not until the day some asshole shot her and left her for dead. She was left laid out in a ditch, bleeding and near death, and he wasn't there for her.

Widow came off an undercover assignment to return home—all of that to see her one last time—in a hospital bed, where she died.

Widow's second life had been in the Navy and NCIS after he ran away from home, where he became the best of the best. He worked undercover as a Navy SEAL, which meant that he had to *be* a SEAL. In order to keep his identity believable, he had to train, and go out on black op missions with, the SEAL teams. He followed orders and rose through the ranks like an ordinary SEAL team member. He had killed like a standard SEAL.

It also meant that he had to avoid getting close to people. He had avoided friends. He had avoided love.

No one knew his real job except the NCIS.

No other way around it. It couldn't be faked.

No way could he impersonate a SEAL whenever he was needed to go out on assignment like one of those forty-five-minute TV dramas portrayed undercover cop life.

That kind of thing might've been how spies did it, or undercover FBI agents or DEA or other secret groups.

Maybe those guys had agents who went undercover with a false identity for a limited time until the job was done.

Not Widow. Not his team.

Widow had to be the real deal. He had to be a SEAL. He had to go all the way.

If you counted his childhood, his early Navy life, his SEAL life, and now his life as a drifter, then he was on life number four, he guessed, and not three. But who was really counting?

Mississippi was way too far away to be seen from where he was. From where he stood, he might as well have been looking down from outer space, trying to find the state. The distance was too far away. His childhood was too long ago. He knew that. But even a stray dog thinks of home from time to time.

Yesterday, Widow had stopped in a place called New London, Connecticut, a coastal Navy town. Beautiful place. It felt like home, even though he had never been there before. It felt like home because there was an NCIS installation there. It was on the naval base.

While he was there, the thought of visiting had crossed his mind. And he even came close around lunchtime, when he stopped in an off-base coffee shop, hoping to glimpse sailors coming in on their lunch breaks, in uniform. It was the same hope of someone revisiting his old alma mater.

It felt like home; only it wasn't. It was just a cozy memory that resurged through him because it was homelike.

He visited none of the naval installations. No interest. He'd ended up there the same way that he'd ended up now on the side of the road, deep in the country in northern New Hampshire: life compelled him. That, and he had caught a bus and gotten off there.

Widow took one last look toward Mississippi, toward the past, and then he killed the thought and looked down at the road under his feet, and then at his surroundings.

He was standing at a crossroads, an uneven one. It was uneven because one road was an old highway that headed north into Canada. And the second was a forgotten road to God knows where in both directions.

He looked up in four different directions, like the four points of a broken compass—left, right, back, and front. Left was almost west. Right was practically east. Back was sort of south. And forward was close to straight-on north.

The points of this compass were not perfect, but close enough to be a little suspicious, as if they had been designed that way on purpose.

Some cheap architect right out of college, working for the state, probably did it as a gag or a little secret that only he knew about, the way artists paint themselves into the background of their paintings and never tell a soul.

In all four directions, for Widow, there was a choice to be made, a direction to be taken, a road to take.

Widow stood dead still on a crossroads that he had never heard of, and he wondered, why not? In the world he loved, the Americana world, it could be famous, like Route 66. But it wasn't.

He had never heard of it before.

The crossroads was more of a cross than a traditional X. One road was an old, two-lane highway, reliably maintained but not glorified with new blacktop. It led out of sight in two directions, and the other wasn't quite a dirt track, but not far from it if the state didn't come along and repave it soon.

It looked like it had been created during the days of horse and buggy about two hundred years ago, maybe more, and in the time since, it was blacktopped maybe ten times, with the last time being well over a decade in the past.

The old track led off into two opposite, yet equally forested, equally mountainous, and equally rugged directions.

The highway backtracked a hundred-plus miles back down along the Vermont-New Hampshire border, and eventually became the end of Route 3 and from there led down to Massachusetts, where Widow had spent two days with a girl who had talked with him, slept with him, shared coffee with him, but never told him a thing about her own private life.

This was all after he was in New London, and a lot more memorable.

The girl had a palpable need for privacy, which Widow respected. His life was an open book for anyone to read, but no one ever did. She asked no questions of him, other than the basics. And he asked no questions of her, other than the basics.

After two days fizzled out, he left her and headed north to continue a hollow quest that he had taken upon himself to go on, which entailed visiting all of what he called Devil Stops in the US.

Hell's Kitchen was the last stop he'd made. He'd gotten the idea when he was in Hells Canyon, back in Idaho. From Hells Canyon he moved on to Devil's Lake in Wisconsin. After that, he headed east to Hell, Michigan, and then on to Route 666 in Pennsylvania, and to Hell's Kitchen, where he went a little off course and stopped in New London, out of curiosity.

All this until he was headed north to a place called Omen Bay in Maine. That had been the plan and the last stop on his invented itinerary until he accidentally sat in a bus terminal for ninety minutes before he realized it was decommissioned.

The depot looked in use. The service drive into it was unblocked, and the lights were on, but there were no workers, no other passengers waiting, and no buses came through. Eventually, he figured it out and felt stupid for not seeing it earlier.

It was at this abandoned bus depot, and out of boredom, that he looked over a bulletin board posted with government information packets and an old state map of New Hampshire's roads and highways.

On the map, he saw a town name that interested him.

The town was in the middle of nowhere. It was called Hellbent, New Hampshire.

Hellbent. It fit his current itinerary. It was maybe the best name for a Devil Stop yet. He had to check it out. Besides, he had nothing to lose. He wasn't on any real timeline. No schedule to keep.

He was a man with a regimented past who lived for an uncertain future, full of surprises.

That was the route he'd taken that led him to now. Standing at the crossroads that led in three directions he didn't want to go, and one he did, to Hellbent.

How he got there specifically was on a bus from a different terminal a mile away from the closed one. This bus dropped him off south about twenty miles, where he hitched rides until he caught a ride from two friendly Canadians headed back to their country. Just fifteen minutes earlier, they were happy to drop him off where he now stood.

He had seen no other cars since.

The reason the crossroads were so interesting, other than leading to the town of Hellbent, were the words involved.

The names involved, to be more precise.

The highway that Widow stood on was the Daniel Webster Highway—named after a famous New Hampshire statesman and lawyer. The other road had no posted name that Widow could see, but there was a forgotten sign off to the side that was posted. It read: This way to Hellbent.

Hellbent? Daniel Webster?

A crossroads of Daniel Webster Highway and a road that led to Hellbent?

The Devil and Daniel Webster.

He wondered how this had happened. What were the odds?

After another five minutes passed, Widow looked in all directions again. Still, there were no cars.

He looked at the map in his head and recalled a mountain range that he would like to look at.

He stepped away from the crossroads and stared over the trees, veering down into a grassy valley with treetops as thick as grenade bursts. The sun beamed to the east. Widow cupped his eyes, making a visor out of his hands. He couldn't see the mountains that way. Not surprising. In his mind, he calculated the distance from the crossroads to the particular mountain range he sought to be around eighty-five miles, give or take a mile.

The mountains that he looked for were called the Presidential Range. He was too far north to see them. He had never seen them before. In fact, he had only passed through New Hampshire by interstate or over it by air, never stopping. Never even giving it a second thought, which he realized was shameful.

New Hampshire was a historic American state, one of the original thirteen colonies. Some of the original revolutionaries had lived there.

Widow wasn't a mountaineer, never trained to be a serious one, but he had trained to climb in the Navy. He knew that Army Rangers used to train in the Presidential

Range for mountain warfare. He wasn't sure if they still had a training base there or not. Mountain warfare hasn't been fought in decades. If you don't count Afghanistan, which Widow didn't because Afghan mountains were jagged and deadly, so not much climbing was ever needed. If they needed to blow up a Taliban cave, they'd use missiles or helicopters.

Patrols in the mountains stuck to perimeters around forwarding bases or were kept in the mountains that one could hike through.

Plus, in his experience, it took little to get the Taliban to come out of the mountains to do battle. Just announcing that Americans were nearby was usually enough to get them stirred up.

Another thing that he remembered about the Presidential Range was that it had the most diverse weather systems of any place on Earth. It could be very dangerous, which was why many mountaineers trained there before attempting to climb spectral peaks like K2.

The range has its name because many of the mountains in it are named after presidents and other famous Americans.

Widow moved on and walked northeast; he stuck his thumb out.

He stayed on course to Hellbent, walking along the little shoulder of the track for another thirty minutes, when he heard the slowing of tires, rubber over loose gravel, and the sound of a car with an air conditioner blasting hard inside.

He stopped and looked back to see a vehicle slow, and dust clouds waft from the rear tires. The car stopped five feet from him. The passenger-side tires were over the line on the shoulder, while the driver side tires remained on the track. Not a legal way to come to a stop on a New Hampshire shoulder, but no one was going to say anything to this driver because he was a New Hampshire state trooper in a New Hampshire state patrol car.

The car was a metallic green and tan Dodge Charger that looked more like a park ranger's ride than a trooper's.

The police interceptor package was constructed out of taxpayer money, with every cent accounted for.

Widow could see it all right there.

It was an impressive vehicle.

Homeland Security money combined with federal taxes and state and local, Widow thought. It's got to be spent somewhere.

The trooper inside wore the state uniform: green shirt, khaki pants. All ironed and pressed and creased like any armed service members would do, but it made Widow think of the Corps.

Marines were the military branch that carried that kind of neatness with them into civilian life. Not all former service members who are neat in civilian life were Marines, but odds were that's what this guy once was.

The trooper was a man, a young guy, maybe early thirties, with a baby face like he was playing dress-up, overacting as an officer of the law. But he also had a jarhead haircut, which never sits right on a guy with a baby face. It usually made them look younger than they wanted, like infants out of the womb becoming infantry.

Widow smirked at the thought.

At first, the trooper was on his cell phone, not his radio. He talked for a few extra moments while looking at Widow.

Widow wasn't sure what to do, but was under the distinct impression that he was supposed to wait for the guy to get off the phone, like walking into a gas station and waiting while the attendant spoke to another customer over the store's phone. Even though the standing customer had already pumped his gas, he had to wait for the attendant to get off the phone. No choice. He had to pay for the gas.

Widow thought about just shrugging and turning and walking away. Leave the guy on his phone call. Why not? He had no obligation to stay and wait. He had done nothing wrong. And this was a public road. And the trooper didn't have his lights on. So why stick around?

But of course, Widow stayed where he was. It wasn't out of a sense of civilian duty or obligation to law enforcement from the state of New Hampshire. He stayed where he was because he didn't have the best track record for first impressions and cops.

The trooper hung up the phone. He slipped a pair of Ray-Ban sunglasses down the bridge of his nose and stared at Widow over the rims. He looked at Widow from side to side, as if he were reading the tail number off a plane, and then from bottom to top.

The man's blue eyes probed and stared at Widow. Baby-faced or not, the man had cop instincts and cop training and gave Widow a suspicious cop stare. This guy was experienced enough to be formidable. He was a good cop. No question.

Widow could see him remaining friendly, staying calm, keeping a professional demeanor, but the whole time he was working out what to make of Widow, like a bouncer working the door at a nightclub. The guy was threat-assessing.

Standard department policy with the public was to remain friendly, but also to stay vigilant when threatened, and Widow always seemed threatening. He couldn't help it. Threatening was in his DNA, like having blue eyes. It was harder for him to appear friendly with strangers than not.

Threatening was his default position. No way around it.

Widow aroused suspicion in nearly everyone he encountered daily, especially law enforcement.

The trooper's nameplate gave his name as Wagner. He buzzed his window down, driver's side. It was automatic. He flicked a switch and waited and leaned his arm out.

Wagner didn't roll down the passenger side. Widow realized the trooper must've wanted him to walk around to the driver's side. So he did.

The trooper waited until Widow was standing in full view, three feet from his door, and then he spoke.

"Sir, you okay?"

"I'm good. How's your morning going, Trooper?"

Wagner ignored the question and asked, "Sir, are you broken down out here?"

"Nope."

"What you doing out here, then?"

Widow paused a beat. Because this would cause him a problem. If he told the truth, a red alert would go off in the man's brain. It was just human nature. Typically, people didn't understand why a perfectly able-bodied man would choose a life of wandering around aimlessly. And standing out in the middle of nowhere at a crossroads made him look like a drifter wandering aimlessly.

But what else was he going to say? If he claimed he was going to Hellbent, he'd still look like a hitchhiker, not a real difference between a hitchhiker and a drifter. A hitchhiker was just a drifter with a destination in mind.

So, he kept it simple.

"Walking."

"What's your name, sir?"

"Widow."

He didn't bother giving his first name.

"Are you from Hellbent?"

"No. But I saw Hellbent on a map. And then again on a sign back at the crossroads."

Wagner stayed quiet.

Widow said, "So, what is Hellbent? A town?"

"No. Not really. It's not officially a town. It's more of a place."

Widow stared at him, confusion on his face.

"It's not recognized as a town. There's no mayor or nothing. It's just a community. Technically, it's a part of the county, but the nearest sheriffs are sixty-plus miles north. So, it's my jurisdiction, basically. We consider it a state matter. Somebody's got to look after it."

Widow stayed quiet.

"It's about ten miles north and east. Down this road. In fact, it's the only thing down this road. Unless you're looking to get lost in the wilderness," Wagner said and pointed down the cracked, winding road.

Widow said, "It can't be the only thing?"

"Until Canada, it is."

"Is that so? Can you get to Canada this way?"

Wagner shrugged.

"You can if you're so inclined. It's a treacherous track, though."

"How so?"

"This road only goes to town. There are other roads leading out of town on the other side, but they all lead out into the wilderness, eventually. And out there a man can die. If he doesn't know where the hell he's going."

"Is that a fact?"

"That's a fact."

"You implying I could die out there?"

"You seem not to know where you're going. Not exactly. Could be you."

Widow stayed quiet.

"Are you going to Hellbent?"

Widow shrugged.

"Looks that way."

"So, were you going there intentionally?"

"I go nowhere intentionally. If I can help it."

Wagner frowned at that and asked, "Where do you live?"

Widow paused a beat. This question caused him another problem. It always had, when asked by law enforcement. Soon as he told them he didn't live anywhere, he often ended up in a conflict situation. Cops don't like guys without a permanent address: partly because ordinary people couldn't understand it, and partly because most guys without addresses were criminals evading current warrants calling for their arrest.

Widow wasn't much on telling lies, but he wasn't against it either. Telling lies used to be part of his job description.

"That's where I'm headed."

"Hellbent?"

Widow nodded.

"A second ago, you seemed like you didn't know what I was talking about."

Widow shrugged and gave no answer.

Wagner said, "Well, get in. I'll give you a lift."

Widow paused a beat, stared at the road ahead. Still, no cars were coming. He didn't want to ride with a trooper into town or anywhere else. He preferred to avoid cops and cop cars. They come with handcuffs.

"Come on," Wagner said.

Widow shrugged and stepped around the nose of the car and tried the passenger door handle. It popped back. It was locked.

Widow heard the trooper's voice, muffled by the glass.

"Get in the back. It's department policy. Civilians ride in the back."

That was what Widow was afraid of.

He stepped to the rear door, opened it, and dumped himself down on the back seat. A bulletproof glass divider separated him from the front, from Wagner. Several pea-sized holes were spread out in the center of the glass in a circular pattern, like a straight on shotgun blast had created them.

The seat was warm, as if it had just been emptied of prisoners. But then Widow realized it was because the air conditioner vents in the back weren't blowing anything. Maybe that was why Wagner had it blasting in the front?

Widow sat and didn't buckle his seatbelt. He stared forward. And felt the car accelerate, slow at first and then hard. It moved forward and a little north and east.

They drove on for about ten more minutes, yet it felt like an eternity because of the dynamics.

Widow was in the back of a cop car, uncomfortable because he hated being under arrest. Even though he wasn't, it all felt the same to him.

A SPECIAL OFFER

Get your copy of Night Swim: a Jack Widow Novella.
Available only at ScottBlade.com

NIGHT SWIM: A BLURB

Under the cover of night, Widow swims through dangerous waters to rescue an FBI agent from a death sentence.

A blown cover for an FBI agent means a death sentence, unless Widow can stop it.

Under cover of darkness along the Malibu coast, Widow takes a night swim. It's meant to be soothing and stress-relieving.

Instead, Widow's night swim turns deadly with the echo of gunshots over open water. A covert FBI operation is blown apart, leaving only blood in the water and a lone undercover agent exposed to a den of lethal international criminals. From the quiet night swim to a high-stakes criminal party at a mega millionaire's beach house, Widow faces grave danger to warn her.

Widow, the drifter who stands for justice, emerges from the waves. With literally nothing but his resolve, he faces unbelievable odds. Time is running out, the enemy is within reach, and for Widow, stealth and cunning are his only weapons.

In this pulse-pounding Widow novella, the line between the hunter and the hunted blurs in a deadly game of espionage and survival.

THE SCOTT BLADE BOOK CLUB

Fostering a connection with my readers is the highlight of my writing journey. Rest assured, I'm not one to crowd your inbox. You'll only hear from me when there's exciting news to share—like a fresh release hitting the shelves or a can't-miss promotion.

If you're just stepping into the world of Jack Widow, consider this your official invite to the Scott Blade Book Club. As a welcome gift, you'll receive the Night Swim: A Widow Novella in the starter kit.

By joining, you'll gain access to a trove of exclusive content, including free stories, special deals, bonus material, and the latest updates on upcoming Widow thrillers.

Ready to dive in? Visit ScottBlade.com to sign up and begin your immersion into the Widow universe.

THE NOMADVELIST

NOMAD + NOVELIST = NOMADVELIST

Scott Blade is a Nomadvelist, a drifter and author of the breakout Jack Widow series. Scott travels the world, hitch-hiking, drinking coffee, and writing.

Jack Widow has sold over a million copies.

Visit @: ScottBlade.com

Contact @: scott@scottblade.com

Follow @:

Facebook.com / ScottBladeAuthor

Bookbub.com / profile / scott-blade

Amazon.com / Scott-Blade / e / B00AU7ZRS8

ALSO BY SCOTT BLADE

The Jack Widow Series

Gone Forever

Winter Territory

A Reason to Kill

Without Measure

Once Quiet

Name Not Given

The Midnight Caller

Fire Watch

The Last Rainmaker

The Devil's Stop

Black Daylight

The Standoff

Foreign and Domestic

Patriot Lies

The Double Man

Nothing Left

The Protector

Kill Promise

The Shadow Club

The Ghost Line

Jack Widow Shorts

Night Swim

Manufactured by Amazon.ca
Bolton, ON

38388536R00210